PRAISE

"Daniel Coleman has a brilliant take on Lewis Carroll's poem. This story is filled with magical creatures, bravery, danger, love and betrayal. Kids and adults alike will fall in love with this story."

—M.R. Ferguson, *ThePraefortis*

"Truly irresistible. This is definitely an author to watch!"

—Grace from MotherLode Review Blog

"Those greatly endeared with Lewis Carroll's whimsical tales would do well to pick up Jabberwocky by Daniel Coleman—a straightforward tale with a manxome twist."

—Amber Argyle, *Witch Song* Trilogy

"Daniel Coleman takes Lewis Carroll's poem and gives it a life of its own while remaining true to the initial writings. This novel kept me entertained from the first page to the last."

—E.A. Younker, *Future of Lies*

"The world that Coleman created was extremely fleshed out and felt like a real place. The characters were relatable and the writing was excellent. One of those hidden gems that should get more attention. I totally recommend this."

—Michelle from In Libras Veritas

"Coleman has a captivating way with words. His characterization of the Jabberwocky is beautifully rendered. Readers young and old, those familiar with Carroll's Wonderland and those who have yet to discover it, will be enthralled. Coleman has made splendid sense of Carroll's spectacular nonsense, and I loved every moment of it. Jabberwocky is a MUST read!"

—Aeicha from Word Spelunking

A NOVEL BY

DANIEL COLEMAN
WITH ILLUSTRATIONS BY E. K. STEWART-COOK

Based on the poem by Lewis Carroll that appears in the book
Through the Looking Glass, and What Alice Found There

Jabberwocky: a novel

Copyright © 2014 by Daniel Coleman
www.dcolemanbooks.com

Published by Vorpal Words, Wellsville, UT 84339
vorpalwords@gmail.com

First edition

ISBN: 978-0-9881969-1-9

Illustrations © E.K. Stewart-Cook
estewartcook@gmail.com

Cover Art by Antonio José Manzanedo Luis
dibuja2@gmail.com

Cover Design by Jodie Coleman
jodiecolemanphotography@gmail.com

Cover Design © 2014 by Daniel Coleman

Interior Design by KristiRae Alldredge of Computers & More Design Services

All rights reserved. No part of this book may be reproduced or transmitted in any form or by any means without written permission of the author.

To Jodie
who may not believe in Jabberwocks
but believes in me

'Twas brillig, and the slithy toves
Did gyre and gimble in the wabe:
All mimsy were the borogoves,
And the mome raths outgrabe.

"Beware the Jabberwock, my son!
The jaws that bite, the claws that catch!
Beware the Jubjub bird, and shun
The frumious Bandersnatch!"

He took his vorpal sword in hand:
Long time the manxome foe he sought—
So rested he by the Tumtum tree,
And stood awhile in thought.

And, as in uffish thought he stood,
The Jabberwock, with eyes of flame,
Came whiffling through the tulgey wood,
And burbled as it came!

One, two! One, two! And through and through
The vorpal blade went snicker-snack!
He left it dead, and with its head
He went galumphing back.

"And, hast thou slain the Jabberwock?
Come to my arms, my beamish boy!
O frabjous day! Callooh! Callay!"
He chortled in his joy.

'Twas brillig, and the slithy toves
Did gyre and gimble in the wabe;
All mimsy were the borogoves,
And the mome raths outgrabe.

—Lewis Carroll
Through the Looking Glass, and What Alice Found There

*See the Glossary at the end of the book for unfamiliar terms.

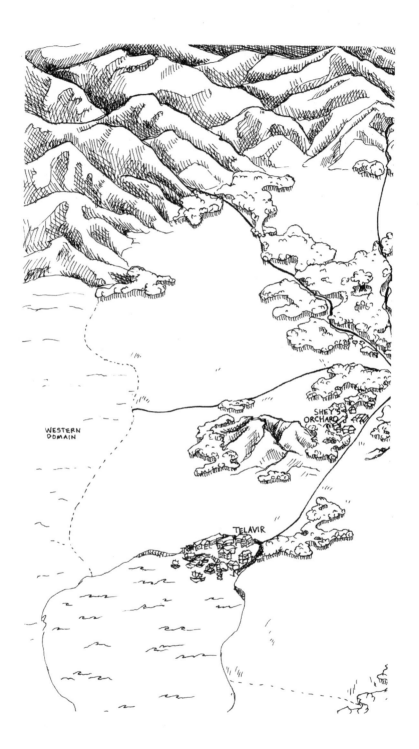

PART I

'Twas brillig, and the slithy toves
Did gyre and gimble in the wabe:
All mimsy were the borogoves,
And the mome raths outgrabe.

'Twas brillig[1].

The time when Misha typically helped her mother chop vegetables or prepare coals to broil dinner. But it was not a typical day.

It was the perfect day.

Misha stood on the outskirts of the wabe[2], the grassy area that surrounded the sundial at the center of the village. Her best friend Teia stood next to her. Each held a new red ribbon with golden tips. Misha knew everyone there, and everyone she knew was there. Nearly two hundred people had come to witness the Sixteenery in which ribbons would be tied in each girl's hair until their wedding days. It was one of the few occasions that took people away from their fields and flocks and their tending and trading.

---

[1] **brillig**: Around four o'clock in the afternoon. The time to begin broiling things for dinner.

[2] **wabe**: The grass plot around a sundial. So called because it goes on a long way before it, a long way behind it, and a long way beyond it on each side.

Not many years ago, Misha was just like the eleventeen[1]-year-old girls clustered nearby, staring with wide eyes, and wondering if her day would ever come. The young men, including Garrick, fidgeted and wiped their palms on thick trousers. The silly girls with whom they'd grown up would be gone soon, replaced by eligible young ladies. She winked at Garrick and smiled when he blushed.

Next, Misha looked over at her parents. Predictably, her mother was dabbing her eyes. Even after attending the Sixteenery of five daughters she still cried.

Borogoves[2] flying overhead cast mop-shaped shadows as Mayor Arad stepped forward. Misha glanced at her friend and they shared a smile. Misha was already promised to Garrick; she had been counting down the days for a year. There were plenty of boys in Dehva interested in Teia, but no promises had been made.

One of the shadows began to grow, larger than any borogove could cast. An odor like a putrefied wound filled the wabe and brought with it the taste of rotten meat. Covering her nose, Misha looked up. A twisted animal was falling out of the sky. The monster was a tangled mass of limbs, teeth, wings, and tail all in the wrong proportions and angles.

"Jabberwock!"

People screamed, scattered, and stumbled all around her, but Misha couldn't move. The Jabberwock, something she thought was just a thing of nightmares, was shattering her perfect day.

The Jabberwock clunked onto the stone sundial, which crumbled under the impact. Its simmering eyes were heavy-lidded, making it look dim-witted. However, its irises burned

---

[1] **eleventeen**: Between the ages of ten and thirteen.
[2] **borogove**: A thin, shabby bird with feathers sticking out all around.

a fiery red that waxed in intensity as it bellowed. The eyes displayed both fury and stupidity—a terrifying combination.

Mayor Arad had the misfortune of standing within reach of the Jabberwock. With serpentine speed, the monster lashed out and clamped the mayor's chest in its jaws, leaving the mayor's body twitching in the mayhem.

The Jabberwock lumbered forward and scooped up Cobbler Poll. Bones snapped under the power of the creature's teeth. It opened its mouth, releasing the body, and the cobbler's bones crunched again as the broken corpse hit the ground.

Misha clung to her best friend's arm and Teia clung to hers. The Jabberwock scanned the crowd and settled on the two girls standing alone in a small opening. They began to back away. In four slinkish strides the Jabberwock closed the gap, catching Misha in one scaly, clawed hand and Teia in the other. It lifted them into the air and roared at the crowd.

Garrick and some other boys stepped across the threshold into manhood by rushing to rescue the girls, even though none of them had a weapon bigger than a belt knife. A swipe from the creature's tail sent them all sprawling limp as cloth dolls.

One of Misha's arms was free, but the other was pinned against her body. She realized she was screaming. With her free hand, the one that gripped the ribbon, she tried prying and punching but the Jabberwock didn't even notice.

A muffled silence fell as Misha was lifted from the wabe. People still shouted and shrieked but they were falling quickly behind. A small herd of raths filled the air with wheezy bellows from their pen next to the wabe.

Men returned to the wabe and waved swords and bows, but it was too late. As the Jabberwock flapped its massive wings, Misha rose higher into the air. Cold wind threatened to rip the ribbon from her hand.

She held on tight. The stories said no one ever survived

after being snatched away. But if they ever found Misha—or her body—they would know she always held out hope of rescue.

Tjaden loved water. It was dependable. Consistent. He watched a trickle escape a small pooling at the front of the irrigation and set off on its own, finding a new path. If there was somewhere to go, water went there, always in a predictable direction.

He had heard about the open ocean that tossed large ships like twigs, the mighty waves on beaches that knocked men down and dragged them under. The worst he'd seen were violent monsoons, which came in with fury and left quiet destruction behind.

The irrigation was running smoothly. He had indulged himself long enough. There was work to be done. He walked back to the uncleared land where his friend and foster brother Ollie waited.

Ollie acted surprised as if he hadn't expected him and said, "Oh. Just Tjaden, jauntily joining the job."

"Oh joy," replied Tjaden, reaching for his axe.

Ollie picked up his axe and picked up the conversation where they'd left it. "I don't even think the Jabberwock's real." He swung at the base of a tree.

"How can it not be real?" asked Tjaden, chopping at his own scrubby mesquite.

Ollie leaned on his axe and asked, "Have you ever seen it? Do you know anyone who has seen it? Has anyone within a hundred miles spied so much as one of its filthy claws?"

Between breaths Tjaden answered, "Go talk to people who've been attacked. Ask the families of the girls it's carried off."

"Introduce me to one of them, and I will," Ollie replied.

Still swinging, Tjaden said, "The silk merchant's guard said it killed a dozen people and snatched two girls from their own Sixteenery in a town called Dehva last month."

"Dehva? Really?" Ollie nodded with mock interest then gave a dismissive wave. "That's what I'm talking about. It's always a village on the other side of the kingdom that no one's ever heard of."

"You go look for the Jabberwock if you want. I'll stay here and clear this land."

Ollie cursed as he half-heartedly chipped away at his tree again. "Fantastic fables for feeble folk. The Jabberwock's a myth invented by peddlers and minstrels. The King's Elite encourage it so they can take credit for keeping us safe from things that don't even exist."

Tjaden's next swing barely caught the edge of the tree, and his face flushed. "So all soldiers are greedy liars?"

"I'm sorry, Jay," Ollie said. His voice took on a bit of a whine. "But bandersnatches? Barbantulas? The Jabberwock? Some of it's just too fantastical."

A stubborn saltbush took the brunt of Tjaden's frustration before he answered his friend. "Personally, I'm glad we don't have any of those around here. But as far as barbantulas, my father's seen one, so cross those off the list of creatures you choose not to believe in."

It wasn't a hot day, but the sun was intense. Sweat rolled down Tjaden's face and off his jaw to the ground. He paused to watch a few drops fall as water always had and always would.

Ollie stopped swinging again and watched Tjaden take a small mesquite tree down in five strokes. "I don't care much as long as old Jabberjaw doesn't come around here picking up maidens and hauling them off to who-knows-where."

"He'd just be doing you a favor, Ollie, saving you from all that rejection," Tjaden said, trying to hide a smile.

"This from someone who can't say more than two words to a certain girl without tripping on his tongue."

Tjaden's eyes darted to the narrow road that led up to Twinnig Falls. Once every few weeks he caught a faraway glimpse of Elora and her sister walking up or down it.

"See? You spend all day watching for her, but you're like this stump when I try to get you to ask her for a dance."

Tjaden had no answer, so he picked up a fallen branch and playfully took a swipe at his smaller friend. Ollie dodged and grabbed a stick to defend himself. After a minute of sparring, Tjaden traded his stick for a saw and started on a scraggly creosote bush.

"The Swap and Spar's in ten days," said Ollie as he reached for his axe. "You gonna dance with her at the bonfire?"

"Probably." He knew how many days away it was because he'd been counting down the time until he saw Elora again.

"I'm not letting you off that easy. Promise you'll ask for at least one dance."

"Fine," said Tjaden. "How come it's so easy for you? There isn't a girl in town you haven't danced with."

With a smile, Ollie said, "Some of us were born with uncommon bravery."

Tjaden chuckled and took a second to wipe sweat from his brow. "What are they doing at Soaper Falon's shop today?"

"Gathering tallow," Ollie replied, making a retching noise. He was hitting the butt of his axe against one of the stumps but not accomplishing anything. "Working here we have good days and bad days, but there it's one filthy mess after another. How can making soap be so dirty?"

"Sounds like the schedule worked in your favor this week."

Ever since his parents died, Ollie had rotated between two families every week. They assumed it would make him well-rounded. In reality, he grew up without any stability or prospects, and there was very little he took seriously. Every month he picked up a new hobby or interest, but he never put enough effort into any of them to be successful.

For as long as he could remember, Tjaden wanted to be a soldier. He spent most of his free time practicing with a staff. The Swap and Spar would be his chance to impress the army's recruiter.

Ollie continued grumbling about making soap as they worked toward the line of string Tjaden's father had placed to mark their work for the day. "Everything is 'Measure this exactly,' 'Pay attention to that,' 'Don't let that boil.' It's always messy and hot . . ." he trailed on.

The remaining minutes in the day were no match for Ollie's words. Within an hour the sun fell behind the long cotton fields that lined the horizon. With just enough light remaining to gather their tools, Tjaden's father appeared and examined the progress.

Nodding, he said, "I wasn't sure if I'd given you too much for one day."

That was as close as his father came to praise. It made the day of hard work worth it.

"I had to keep a grueling pace" said Ollie. "Your son did his best to keep up."

His father switched his bow to the other shoulder and picked up a saw. "Maybe I'll start marking separate sections for each of you so you don't have to keep picking up his slack." With a small grin on his face he gave Tjaden a knowing look.

"I don't mind," said Ollie. "It's worth having someone to talk to."

Instead of taking the road, they cut through the familiar orange groves. After placing the tools in the shed behind the house, Tjaden pulled up well water while his father removed the string from his bow then carefully wrapped and stored it in a pouch.

Rich aromas pulled all three of them toward the house.

After filling two large bins with tangerines the next morning, Tjaden and Ollie ate lunch as they led a pair of horses toward the main part Shey's Orchard. At the narrow section of road just past Flatpurse Farm, they heard laughing coming from a copse of scrubby trees. Tjaden continued leading the horses, but Ollie rushed to investigate. He returned a short time later, motioning for Tjaden to follow him.

After setting the wagon brake, Tjaden ducked into the brush after Ollie. In a small clearing he saw three people about his size crouched around a struggling form.

"I say we take off its beak and find out what it sounds like."

Tjaden recognized the voice. It was Brune, a boy who always tried to prove his toughness by intimidating people smaller than himself. Ollie, a year younger than Brune and shorter than most boys his age, was a frequent target.

If that's Brune, then the other two are Buck and Ablon, thought Tjaden.

One of them said, "No, I say we cut the legs and wings off and use it as a shaggy kickaround."

Brune shifted, and Tjaden saw that their captive was a terrified borogove. Most borogoves looked like scraggly mops with perpetually bored faces. This one was as nervous as a bird in a cat's mouth. It was tied up with a rope, and a small cord held its beak shut. It tried to honk, but it couldn't open its beak.

The third voice said, "I say we light it on fire and fling it. It'll be a screaming, flying fireball."

Tjaden pushed past Ollie into the clearing. "I say you untie it and let it fly away."

Spinning in surprise, the three moved quickly toward Tjaden and surrounded him.

"I say you stay out of this," said Brune, standing so close his bulbous nose nearly touched Tjaden's. His face was wide and he had a prominent underbite like a bulldog's. "That tweedle[1], Ollie, isn't even here to back you up."

"He's no tweedle," said Tjaden, showing no emotion, "but you are if you think I'll let you torture that bird."

Brune stepped even closer. "What did you call me?"

Tjaden stared back. They had never fought, but Brune had never had such good odds.

---

[1] **tweedle**: An imbecile, simpleton.

Emboldened by the advantage in numbers, Brune shoved Tjaden, but he still refused to react. Brune's breathing grew heavier, and muscles in his face started to twitch.

"It's not going to work, Brune," said Tjaden flatly. Although he wanted to punch Brune, punch all three of them, Tjaden maintained control. "Let the bird go and I'll leave."

"Why should we? You're too scared to do anything about it." Brune bumped Tjaden with his chest.

Tjaden stood his ground.

After a few more huffs, Brune said, "Let it go yourself." He pushed uffishly[1] past Tjaden and added, "You're lucky you're young enough for the boys group at the Swap and Spar, or else you'd *have* to fight me."

Once they were gone, Ollie emerged from his hiding place in the underbrush. "Why didn't you fight them? Even without my help, you could . . . thoroughly thrash those three thugs."

"A soldier's first opponent is himself," Tjaden quoted. "If he can master himself he cannot be defeated." His oldest brother was a soldier and this was one of his lines that Tjaden tried to live by.

He bent to untie the bird.

"I want to be a soldier just as bad as you do," Ollie said.

Tjaden looked up from the frightened borogove, wondering when Ollie had decided that. "Not just a soldier, Ollie. An Elite." One more knot and the skinny bird burst out of Tjaden's hands, honking as it escaped through the thin canopy.

"The point is, the more you fight now, the better you'll be," Ollie insisted. "Persistent practice produces proficient prowess."

---

[1] **uffish**: A state of mind when the voice is gruffish, the manner roughish, and the temper huffish.

JABBERWOCKY

"Nice one," Tjaden said insincerely. "How about this one: Start with self-mastery. Swordplay second."

"No." Ollie cringed. "Horrible." They scrambled through the trees to the wagon. "You stick to fighting and leave the talking to me."

"Is that what you were doing in the bushes? Trying to come up with something clever to say?"

"I could have come out so Brune could call me a tweedle and a thirteen[1]." Ollie scowled and kicked a pebble down the road. Thirteen had nothing to do with age; Ollie was fifteen like Tjaden. It meant *worthless runt*, and Ollie had heard it his whole life from Brune and his cronies.

"Besides," added Ollie, "I was preparing an ambush. If a fight broke out, I could've taken them by surprise. I know you always want to charge ahead, sword a-swingin', but I prefer to use my brain in a fight."

"That's great," said Tjaden. "When we're Elite and Fellow, I'll feel safe knowing that you're always thinking. Might not be fighting, but at least you'll be thinking."

Ollie opened his mouth, but a piping voice called, "Tjaden!"

Tjaden turned to look up the dirt road and saw a small figure running toward them. It was Lily, Elora's sister, and she was moving fast. They were only a year apart in age and as inseparable as twins.

"What's the matter?" he yelled, jogging toward her. "Where's Elora?"

"By the falls!" She pulled her blonde hair back out of her face.

Tjaden picked up his pace and quickly reached the out-of-breath girl. "Is she all right?" he asked.

---

[1] **thirteen**: A worthless person or animal. A runt.

"No! She slipped. She's stuck on a ledge," Lily said between breaths.

Tjaden started moving uproad, a sick feeling stinging his stomach. "Is she hurt?"

"I don't know," Lily blurted. "I ran for help as soon as she fell."

Over his shoulder, Tjaden shouted, "Ollie, get some rope. Lily, keep running into town and find your father." He had no idea what he'd do when he got there but the thought of Elora trapped and alone scared him enough to be able to sprint the half mile to Twinnig Falls.

Out of breath, he called for Elora, but there was no reply. His stomach sank even further. He rushed to the edge of the road and peered down toward the river.

Elora stood below him on a large ledge that protruded over the fast moving water. She should have seen and heard him, but she didn't look up or answer. Something at the edge of the cliff upstream from them held her gaze. Her face was as pale as the rapids, and her large eyes were even bigger than usual.

Tjaden followed her gaze and didn't see anything at first. Concentrating, he noticed something unnatural in the foliage—a slight discoloration. A figure moved on two legs along the edge of the scrub oak. It was shaped somewhat like a man, but it had the legs and hooves of a goat, which gave it a forward-leaning, sprythe[1] appearance. Though he'd never seen one, he recognized the bandersnatch.

Tjaden looked around for a weapon and saw a four-foot stick. It wasn't straight, and it was a little too thick, but his choices were limited. Reaching for the weapon, he examined the creature. The bandersnatch was the size of a large man. It was dried-alfalfa green and overly muscled. It had claws like

---

[1] **sprythe:** Spry and sharp like a scythe.

a bear, and thick spikes lay flat down the center of its spine. Sharp plates of armor like giant insect shells covered the joints of its arms and legs.

The stories always made them sound terrible and ferocious. This one just looked curious. In the stories, however, bandersnatches were always treading the frumious[1] line between fuming and furious.

---

[1] **frumious**: Fuming and furious.

The beast watched Elora as it glided to the lip of the cliff upstream from where Tjaden stood. He was relieved that a steep incline separated it from the lower ledge where Elora watched, petrified. But the creature paid no attention to the slope. It loped down the sheer cliff as easily as a cat climbs a tree, not taking its eyes off Elora.

Tjaden didn't hesitate. He swung his legs over the edge and slid down the incline, landing sprawled on the ledge between Elora and the bandersnatch. The creature paused. It rose sharply and cocked its head like a bird. The bandersnatch made a clicking purr as it studied Tjaden.

The beast tensed, and in an instant it lunged forward so fast Tjaden barely had time to jut his makeshift staff in front of him like a lance. The bandersnatch covered the distance in an instant, colliding full force with the outstretched staff. The impact knocked Tjaden backward, bringing him close enough to Elora for her to steady him. If not for the strength from daily work with tools, Tjaden would have lost his grip on the weapon.

Elora screamed sharply and the bandersnatch wailed, but Tjaden was too stunned by the speed of the beast to make a sound. The bandersnatch clutched its wounded chest, and its breathing got faster. The creature seemed to swell in size. A sinister red color spread through its skin, from trunk to limbs, accenting the creature's natural green. The dull eyes flared the color of fresh blood, and the elongated spines on its back protruded menacingly.

So this is what they mean by frumious, Tjaden thought.

He didn't wait for the monster's frenzy to mount further. He lunged forward, swinging his club. In one motion the frumious bandersnatch crouched and sprung into the air. It passed over Tjaden like a child hopping a stone. Spinning, Tjaden reflexively raised his staff to defend himself as the monster's claws swept toward him. The sturdy wood deflected them, but they left gouges in his staff.

    Tjaden used the momentum of the blow to spin around and swing his weapon like an axe. The bandersnatch was caught off guard, and the blow struck it on the shoulder. It howled and Tjaden took the offensive. The beast continued to swell with rage as it deflected and dodged blow after blow. The malevolent purr was interspersed with threatening snarls.

    "Run, Elora!" Tjaden shouted as he continued to swing his club.

    The bandersnatch dodged the staff and dove at Tjaden's legs. The creature connected, and they both sprawled toward the lip of the ledge. The club skidded away from Tjaden as his back slammed into the rocky ground. The monster landed on top of him, and he instinctively grabbed its leathery head. As Tjaden tried to wrench the head from its shoulders, the creature slashed his arms with razor claws.

    The combination of blood and pain made Tjaden's stomach lurch. His arms began to lose strength, and his grip weakened in the slick blood. He was about to lose it entirely when he saw Elora looming behind the bandersnatch, the club raised above her head.

    With a spark of fire in her dark brown eyes that matched the glow in the bandersnatch's, she swung the club at the monster's back. The impact sounded like pottery shattering.

    The bandersnatch's red eyes flared and it reared back, freeing its head from Tjaden's grasp. It continued to slash at Tjaden's arms.

    Better me than Elora.

    But Elora wasn't done. She swung again, this time connecting with the creature's head exactly where a human's ear would be. Blood gushed from the wound. The bandersnatch howled and sprang to its feet, turning to face Elora. Tjaden kicked at the bandersnatch's legs, but it was too strong to care.

Elora held the staff, but if it hadn't worked for Tjaden, what chance did Elora have?

Tjaden pushed himself up to a crouch and shouted, "Hey!" as he shot forward to tackle the bandersnatch. Without turning, it mule-kicked him in the chest hard enough to send him sliding backward. Fear for Elora pushed the pain aside, but he was going to be too late.

He'd only made it up to a kneel when the bandersnatch brought an arm down across Elora's face. If she hadn't tried to duck, it would have sliced her neck.

Nothing in Tjaden's life had ever been more important, but his body responded like it was full of sand. The bandersnatch raised its claws again, and Tjaden heard a low whistle followed by a *phwap*. An arrow protruded from the creature's shoulder.

Everyone froze and stared as another arrow phwapped into its gut. Covered in red rage, the frumious bandersnatch bellowed and retreated. It sprinted up the same steep slope it had come down and disappeared into the trees.

Tjaden took one plodding step after it before realizing that only a tweedle would give chase. He turned toward Elora, and suddenly she was there in his arms.

"Elora, I'm so sorry." He could only see the top of her head, not her injured face. Above them on the ridge, his father and Ollie looked ready to fight.

They had saved him—saved Elora because he wasn't able to. He had a chance to do it, but he let her get cut. He had failed.

But her arms were around him. It made it hard to worry about anything.

He'd never held a girl so closely, much less this particular girl. Though almost too weak to stand, he let her tremble in his arms for a while.

"How bad are you hurt?" he asked.

She looked up at him. "Not as bad as you."

Tjaden didn't know if that was true. The left side of her face was flayed open in two gashes. One went from under her ear almost to the corner of her mouth. The other wrapped in a half circle under her left eye. Blood seeped from both wounds.

"We have to get you to Doc Methos," said Tjaden.

"Both of us, I'd say." She pulled his arms straight, palms down. There seemed to be more open flesh than closed, and blood still oozed from many of the gashes. Queasiness and a hot flush made Tjaden's knees buckle. Elora was close enough to steady him and help him to the ground. The sensation passed as soon as he looked away from his injuries and back to Elora.

Her wounds were his fault, but her face would always make him smile.

She knelt in front of him and asked, "Are you all right?"

"Yeah. Sorry."

As she examined his wounds, she said, "The blood's flowing, not spurting. You're lucky."

"Any day I get to see you is a lucky one."

A tiny grin made Elora grimace in pain. Tjaden wished he could take the words back. It wasn't the time to flirt, despite what Ollie would say. Tjaden glanced up and saw his father standing with an arrow at the ready while Ollie began letting a rope down.

"I've got something for that bleeding," Elora said.

Elora always wore a leather sash across her chest with pockets and loops that held various-sized vials of herbs. Tjaden expected her to pull something from it, but instead she left him to retrieve a linen-wrapped bundle from the ground. In the excitement, Tjaden hadn't noticed it earlier. It contained a stack of flat plants, rectangular and cactus-like, with thick thorns along both edges. She peeled one open to reveal a clear goopy substance, like jelly made without any juice. She coated his arms with it and applied it carefully to her own face.

Gritting his teeth, Tjaden helped Elora tear linen into

strips. He wrapped her face then held out one arm at a time for her. He doubted the thin linen would stop so much blood. The blood already on his arms would probably saturate them, but he didn't argue.

"Let's see how that works," she said, tying the final knot.

Not only did the blood stop flowing, the sting dulled slightly. Her face had stopped bleeding as well.

Beautiful, brave, *and* clever. More than ever, Tjaden was smitten.

Tjaden took the rope that Ollie had lowered and tied it around Elora's hips. Miraculously, the movement didn't cause his wounds to bleed through the bandage. She was raised, then him. Before giving him a chance to untie himself, his father took him into a strong embrace. Tjaden felt his father's heart racing.

"What are you doing here, Father?"

"I passed Lily on the road. She told me Elora was in trouble, so I ran." Tjaden had never been so grateful for his father's habit of always carrying his bow. "Can you walk down to the wagon?"

"Yeah," said Tjaden. He offered an arm to Elora. She smiled at him and gently wrapped her arm in his. His father walked behind them, with an arrow nocked. Ollie led the way.

Before long, Tjaden began to falter. Elora must have sensed it because she slid under his arm and helped support him as they walked.

"Thanks," said Tjaden. "Sorry."

Before reaching the wagon, they saw Lily, who was trailed by Elora's parents, Adella and Aker. Adella's hands flew to her mouth when she saw the bandages and blood. If not for Aker's hand on her shoulder, she might have fallen. Lily ran to hug Elora.

"Bandersnatch," said Tjaden's father. "She has two cuts. Both missed her eyes and mouth but she needs the doc."

Elora wouldn't allow her mother to remove the bandages. "The stypcia's working," she said excitedly. "Stopped the bleeding right up."

Her parents smothered her in a dual embrace. Finally, tears began to flow from Elora, but they were brief and silent. Lily linked arms with Elora as they began to walk.

Aker put his hand on Tjaden's shoulder. "Thank you, Tjaden." His jaw and lips clenched as if he wanted to say more, but he settled for a nod.

Tjaden couldn't bring himself to tell him he wasn't the true hero.

Doc Methos had finished stitching one arm, and was dozens of stitches into the second arm. The next stitch was as painful as the first. Tjaden bit down on the thick leather strap, surprised he hadn't chewed through it already. Around the fortieth stitch he had lost count.

While Doc Methos took a while to thread more string through the needle, Tjaden pulled the leather out from between his teeth and asked for the tenth time, "Are you sure Elora will be fine?"

Elora had gone home with her parents as soon as Doc Methos had finished with her stitches, though it had taken some convincing to get her to go. She'd wanted to stay and assist Methos in treating Tjaden.

Doc Methos nodded. "Girl like Elora? Strong as you and three of your friends combined. She'll be fine as feathers." He took the leather strap and stuck it back in Tjaden's mouth.

"You should probably be more worried about Ollie," said his father. "He's outside telling stories."

The leather muffled Tjaden's groan.

"Girls lining up outside to see the hero, yet?" asked the doc.

"It wouldn't surprise me," said his father.

The blush on Tjaden's cheeks made the men chuckle. He bit the leather harder and stared at the screen blocking the view of his arms. By the time Doc Methos finished stitching, Tjaden's jaw hurt nearly as badly as his arms. The doc wrapped them, not nearly as gently as Elora had.

While Tjaden stretched his jaw and fingers, his father dug into his purse for coins.

"No, no," said Methos. "Elora's like an apprentice to me. I'm in your debt for saving her. Now, if you have any of those sweet oranges next week at the Swap and Spar . . ."

Tjaden's father smiled. "I'll have Ollie bring some in the morning. Thank you."

Outside, Ollie had gathered a small crowd. He was in his element in front of them describing the frumious bandersnatch. ". . . as tall as Mayor Tellef and more muscular than Drover Titus's boys."

The group lost interest in Ollie when they spotted Tjaden.

"Was it as swift as Ollie says?"

"Were you scared, lad?"

"I guess you showed the beast what was what."

Tjaden wanted to escape. Before he had a chance to tell them who had saved them, his father waved everyone away with both arms. "He's been through enough, hasn't he? Go home and let him do the same."

He and Tjaden walked away and there was nothing the crowd could do about it. Ollie fell in with them, and Tjaden gave him a look that kept him from saying a word the whole way home.

The morning after the attack, Tjaden's father earned his own stern look from his mother when he asked if Tjaden was up to working.

"I can manage," said Tjaden. The bruise on his chest from being kicked hurt as much as the sting in his arms, but he'd go crazy sitting around worrying about Elora and thinking about what he could have done differently.

With Tjaden injured, Soaper Falon agreed to let Ollie spend extra days with Tjaden and his father. The three of them started the morning hauling away the trees and brush Tjaden and Ollie had cut down. Tjaden didn't have enough strength in his hands to drag anything heavier than a tumbleweed, so his father rigged up a harness with a chain and turned him into a mule.

A figure appeared on the road leading to their farm.

Elora! thought Tjaden.

He squinted and realized immediately it wasn't Elora. The wiry figure turned out to be Thatcher Sami who tracked them down. After returning the awl he had borrowed a year earlier, he said, "So, a bandersnatch?"

Tjaden nodded as he fastened the chain around his waist.

"I'm surprised you survived? Did it hurt you?"

"It tore up my arms," said Tjaden, showing his bandaged forearms.

"And Aker's girl? How bad's she hurt?"

Tjaden had purposefully not mentioned her and didn't want to think about and especially not talk about how bad he'd let her get hurt.

"I don't know," he said. "I should get back to work." He started walking and the harness cinched as the chain went taut.

With time for Elora's injuries to sink in, Tjaden stopped wondering why she hadn't come by the farm. She probably didn't even want to see him.

Thatcher Sami called out, "It's too bad you can't fight this year. After last year's victory we all had high hopes."

Thanks for bringing up another painful topic, thought Tjaden.

Ollie caught up with him, dragging a scrubby bush with each arm.

"I'm still going to fight," muttered Tjaden. "If I can hold a staff by then."

"On the bright side, you're young enough to fight in the boys' group," said Ollie.

"I wanted to fight in the men's," said Tjaden.

"On the other side," continued Ollie, "I'm young enough too." He knocked Tjaden off balance with his shoulder and took off running.

Tjaden stumbled for a few steps, hoping he wouldn't have to break his fall with his arms, then raced to catch Ollie.

Not much later a pair of people much too sturdy to be Elora came down the lane. Coles and Hettie, the bakers, a day early to get the lemons Tjaden or Ollie usually delivered. They had even more questions than the thatcher. Tjaden found an excuse to escape and as he walked away, he heard his father being as untalkative as usual.

After lunch the three moved on to clearing weeds from irrigation ditches. When the next person appeared on their road, Tjaden didn't even allow himself to hope that Elora might come. It's not like they saw each other very often before, and after what had happened she probably wanted to see him even less.

It turned out to be Galla the gossip and she didn't even have an excuse for coming. She just wanted to hear the story.

Tjaden's father saved him from the embarrassment of telling how he'd failed by saying that they had work to do. After persisting but failing to glean much information, Galla went away highly disappointed.

Four more townspeople came to the farm. None of them was Elora, which would have surprised Tjaden even more than if he'd seen another bandersnatch. He almost let her get killed. Even if Doc Methos could keep her wounds from getting infected, her face would never be the same again. Because he wasn't good enough to protect her.

All Tjaden could do was work away the time until the Swap and Spar and hope to fight skillfully enough to be invited to the Academy. Avoiding as many nosy townsfolk as possible would be a plus. It wasn't like anyone in town could gab him one step closer to the Academy.

Just before sunset, Tjaden took another glance up the road.

"You've been staring up the road all day," said Ollie. "But everyone who comes up it gets brushed off like crumbs from a table."

Tjaden didn't reply. He resisted the urge to look again.

"Why don't *you* just go see *her*?" asked Ollie.

"What?" How did Ollie know what he was thinking? Or who he was thinking about. "She probably hates me, or at least blames me for not being able to stop the bandersnatch."

"That's crazy," said Ollie. "If you hadn't been there, she'd be a lot worse off."

"If I would have protected her better, she'd be fine as feathers."

Tjaden's father said, "I was going to ask you to stop at Mirrorer Aker's and order a mirror for your mother while you make deliveries tomorrow, but if you don't want to see her—"

"No, I'll go," said Tjaden quickly. No matter what she thought of him, just the idea of seeing her made him smile. He tried to hide it so Ollie wouldn't say anything.

Tjaden hurried through chores in the morning. His arms hurt just as bad as the day before, but they were a little stronger. As he and Ollie gathered the items for delivery, Tjaden realized more questions would be waiting at every stop they made. There would be enough fuss over him to last a lifetime. But if he didn't go, he wouldn't see Elora.

It was an easy decision.

Ollie didn't complain when Tjaden changed their usual route to stop at the mirror maker's shop first. The charred scent of molten metal coming from the shop gave Tjaden hope that Elora would be inside. If Mirrorer Aker was crafting, he'd probably have someone with him to help tend shop.

When Tjaden opened the door of the shop, he saw Aker and Adella talking to a woman. She turned to see who had come in and Tjaden groaned. Galla the gossip. Her face brightened when she saw him.

"Good morning, Tjaden," said Aker.

"Hi," said Tjaden. He quickly scanned the shop for more people, but it was empty.

"Elora's just in the house," said Adella. "Want me to get her?"

For a moment, Tjaden was frozen. He wanted to see her, but if he made a big deal about it, Galla would start a hundred new rumors by midday. He also couldn't say anything in front of Galla about the mirror or word would get back to his mother.

"I'm just here to . . . My father sent me to . . ." Tjaden backed out and closed the door.

"You're about as smooth as a porcupine's tail," said Ollie.

Tjaden felt his face turn red and had to laugh at himself. "Galla was in there. I panicked."

"Try again after our deliveries?" asked Ollie.

"Yeah. Can't go worse than that, can it?"

As they made their rounds, Tjaden kept his mouth shut, but Ollie was happy to tell anyone who asked about the bandersnatch. It got bigger and meaner every time he told the story. The only thing that made the torture bearable was the thought that at the end of it he could see Elora. He even had something to talk to her about.

When they returned to the mirror maker's shop, Tjaden peeked inside. If Galla was still there he didn't want to make a fool of himself. She wasn't there, but neither was Elora. Mirrorer Aker didn't know exactly where she was, only that she wasn't home.

Tjaden regretted not taking Elora's mother up on the offer to get her from the house earlier. Who cared what Galla or anyone else said?

He had a week to regret and replay the mistake. And to convince himself that she really must not want to see him. It shouldn't be a surprise. A girl as beautiful and talented as her.

The evening before the festival, Tjaden went with his father into town to sign up for the staff fighting. He still hadn't seen Elora, even when he went to Doc Methos to have his wounds looked at. The stitches were still in his arm, but he felt as strong as ever. Ready to fight.

The dayroom of the Dusty Tunic was full to overflowing with visitors from out of town. Only a fraction of the people who came for the swapping could fit in the inn and it was enough to stretch it to its limits.

As Tjaden and his father waited in a line to add Tjaden's name, Innkeep Tellef, who was also the mayor, approached them. In his younger days, as Tjaden often heard, he was a frequent sparring champion. Now middle aged and big bellied, the only reason he entered the battle circle was to referee.

"Mikel." The innkeep rested a hand on his shoulder. "Are you going to step into the ring and show the young men how to fight?"

"No," Tjaden's father said with a chuckle. He was close to Tellef's age and hadn't entered the tournament for years. "The men's group is safe from my family for one more year."

"I expect one of Titus's boys will win again," said Tellef.

"Not if I can help it," said Tjaden. "I'm fighting in the men's group."

His father looked at him and raised an eyebrow but Tellef spoke first. "Have you reached sixteen years already, lad?"

Tjaden was resolute. "The older group is open to anyone, and I choose to compete against men."

His father said, "You can beat any of the younger boys in town with a staff."

"I know," said Tjaden.

"Even with the injury you have a chance at winning that age group again."

Tjaden nodded.

His father continued. "You've worked hard with the staff, son, but there's more than one man that can give you as much as you can handle."

"I'll be sixteen soon enough. Besides, the King's Legate is going to be here. He won't be impressed by someone who beats kids."

"If you don't win, what does it matter?"

"I can do this, Father."

"And the stitches? It's barely been a week."

"Eight days. My arms are practically healed." Tjaden slapped his forearms for emphasis. It stung, as if punishing him for the lie, but Tjaden tried to keep the wince from his face.

They stared at each other. Tjaden wasn't surprised by his father's doubt after the bandersnatch incident—everyone would doubt him after he nearly let Elora die—but he knew he could compete with anyone in Shey's Orchard. Not only did he have a chance to impress the Legate, but also redeem himself for failing Elora.

His father shrugged. "It appears I misspoke, Tellef. The men's competition is definitely not safe from my family this year."

The first day of the Swap and Spar started with vending and trading. Merchants came from many parts of Maravilla to buy and sell alongside residents of Shey's Orchard. Tjaden hadn't seen many towns, but he had heard that the wabe in Shey's Orchard was one of the largest in the kingdom. Traders, tents, and the auction scaffolding filled the entire area. On one side of Tjaden and his parents' booth was Tonin, a merchant from the Provinces who sold household goods and manufacturing supplies. On the other side were the local bakers, Coles and Hettie.

Tjaden tended shop most of the day with his parents. A steady stream of curious customers kept them from doing any browsing or shopping of their own. At first Tjaden tried to deflect their questions or find another task, but people with coins to spend weren't easily dissuaded. He learned that the easiest way to get rid of them was to answer their questions, and by the end of the day he had a few short, rehearsed responses that seemed to satisfy. As the day went on, more of the customers were people he didn't know or even recognize.

When the oranges sold out, Tjaden's mother hurried off to shop before the sellers began closing their booths.

"Getting tired of repeating the story yet?" asked Tjaden's father after he sold the last of their honey to an old musician from somewhere Tjaden had never heard of.

"I was tired of it before the sun came up. If I knew anything about making soap, I would have traded places with Ollie, and we'd both be happier."

"You mind watching the shop?" asked his father. "I need to pick up the mirror from Aker before your mother comes back."

"I could get it for you," volunteered Tjaden. His father looked at him sideways, and Tjaden blushed. His father grinned. "Just to get a break from all these questions," Tjaden added.

"Ah, of course. The questions," said his father. He gave Tjaden four silver pennies. "If a certain girl happens to be tending the booth, mind you don't forget the mirror."

Tjaden was about to rush off when his father grabbed the shoulder of his tunic and held out another stack of coins—five thripennies[1].

---

[1] **thripenny**: A coin equal to three silver pennies.

"What else do you need?" asked Tjaden, scooping them up.

"We've never sold like this at the Swap and Spar. The fruit's the same as always, so people are paying money for something else."

"Is this mine?" asked Tjaden.

His father nodded. "Take a look around."

"You sure you don't need help?"

"Unless people want tangerines, I'm just taking orders. We already have enough to fill the next three weeks."

"Thanks!"

Fifteen pennies! With that much money he could buy almost anything he wanted—a sword, a horse, or even a fancy cloak. Not that there was much use for it in a warm place like Shey's Orchard, but he wasn't staying forever. If he waited for Ollie to finish at the workshop, he could buy something for both of them. People greeted him as he walked through the crowds toward Mirrorer Aker's shop, but Tjaden didn't slow down enough to get stuck talking.

One vendor had nothing but sweets and candy, some in colors Tjaden had never seen. If Ollie wasn't hooked on some passing hobby, he'd probably try to convince Tjaden to stock up. The money in Tjaden's pocket was enough to set them up with candy for months.

Boots. More than one booth offered dozens of options, and he could afford a pair for him and Ollie with some leftover to save. Telescope. Throwing knives or axes. Maybe he should just save it.

He was no closer to deciding when he approached the mirror-maker's booth. It was lined on three sides by frames and stands that held mirrors. In the morning, a full stock of mirrors would have formed a booth with three walls. This late in the day, large gaps where mirrors had sold let him see Master Aker in the booth. No Elora.

He still hadn't seen her; no one had as far as he knew.

Maybe she had decided to skip the festivities. He could spend the coins on her. Buy a fancy veil or scarf? Some makeup to hide her wounds? They seemed to be the reason she had disappeared and if he could do anything to get her out again he wouldn't hesitate.

Turning his head to face the other side of the walkway, Tjaden kept moving with the crowd. If Mirrorer Aker saw him, he'd have to pick up the mirror and wouldn't have an excuse to come back.

In the next aisle he slowed enough for a wiry man to say, "Hey there, boy," and toss him a ball. A kickaround, but lighter than anything he'd ever used.

"What's it made out of?" asked Tjaden. The balls they played with in Shey's Orchard were wrapped cloth or wool. He was reluctant to stop and chat, but the man had called him "boy," so he was probably safe from interrogation.

"Calf bladder and leather. Strong kid like you, I bet you could kick it from here to the Telavir Spoke."

Tjaden looked around and saw a variety of balls, sticks, hoops, and clubs. The week before, Ollie would have given anything for juggling pins. Tjaden wasn't sure what his new interest was.

"Looking for something else? I have everything you need for hurling, ninepins, cammag, bandy, shinty, and marbles. And kickaround, of course. Even got shoes 'specially meant for running and kicking." The man reached down and lifted a shoe with a flat front and no ankle support.

He must be from Palassiren, thought Tjaden. Only city boys would wear shoes while playing kickaround.

"I might come back with a friend." Tjaden tossed the ball back and started walking away.

"Not so quick," said the man. "I've got end-of-the-day bargains."

"Maybe in a while." Tjaden kept walking.

Nothing else on that aisle caught his eye, but he did pass Master Falon's booth. His wife, Ingri, told Tjaden she expected Ollie at any time. She promised to point him in Tjaden's direction.

The first merchant on the next aisle put an arm around Tjaden's shoulder and began leading him before Tjaden knew what he was browsing. The man had the bushiest mustache Tjaden had ever seen and eyebrows to match.

"I'm not a girl," said Tjaden as soon as he realized the man was selling jewelry.

"No, but there is a certain girl, now, isn't there?" His jowls quavered when he spoke, and a slow smile made Tjaden wonder if he actually knew something.

"How do you—" Tjaden didn't finish the sentence. "How much does this stuff cost?"

"How much do you have to spend?" asked the man. "I have as many varieties as there are young ladies."

"What kind of jewels do girls around here like?"

"A young woman? Seventeen? Eighteen?"

"Fifteen," said Tjaden. "Almost sixteen." He peeked around and was surprised that no one had stopped to stare or laugh at him.

"Gold and rubies," said the man quickly. "A girl of that age is on one near side of her Sixteenery or the other, and the only thing that matters to them is the red and gold of the ribbon."

"That narrows it down a little."

"What's your name, young man?"

"Tjaden."

"They call me Walrus," said the jeweler. "Now, what does your dearest wear? Brooches? Bracelets? Rings in the ear? The nose? Around the neck?"

"She's not my—the nose?" asked Tjaden.

"Mostly a style of the barbarians in the Western Domain, but not unseen in some high circles of Maravilla."

"Definitely not a ring around the nose," said Tjaden, unsure how that would even stay on.

The merchant suppressed a smile and said, "Not around the nose, my boy." He picked up a loop of gold and held it next to his face. "Through the nose."

"Oh. Yes, she definitely doesn't wear those." He couldn't think of any jewelry he'd seen Elora wear. Just the leather herbal belt. It was probably a bad idea. "I don't think she wears jewelry."

"Something simple, then," said Walrus before Tjaden

could get away. "A pin? A ring?" He motioned to a table with a small wire tree that had rings hanging from the tips of its branches. A chubby finger and thumb picked out a band with a small ruby.

"Wouldn't that get caught on things and scratched up?"

"A lady does not wear her fine things for daily life. They are for moments when she wants to remember how special she is to you long after the words are spoken."

No words ever sounded better to Tjaden, but the ruby didn't seem right. "How much does that ring cost?"

"Duodec[1] and a half."

Thirty pennies? That much for a scrap of metal and a tiny stone? The merchant picked up on Tjaden's look. "Perhaps a silver ring? Black steel?"

"Do the other gold rings cost as much?"

"There is a range, but remember that the value of the metal represents the value of the lady in your eyes."

"If I buy jewelry, it has to be gold," said Tjaden. He examined the rings, some inset with some stone or another, some plain. Toward the bottom of the tree hung a large ring fashioned out of leaves overlapping each other in a circle. Leaves might work, but not so clunky.

"Do you have anything else like this?"

"With leaves, you mean?"

Tjaden nodded.

"How would you describe your inamorata? Slender? Healthy? Extra healthy?"

"She's not my . . . whatever you just said." He didn't think she was, anyway. "Um, I think you'd say she's petite." He glanced around again. Still no one watching or eavesdropping.

"Let me see." The man produced a key from inside his coat and bent over a small chest. He muttered as he searched.

---

[1] **duodec**: A small gold coin worth 20 silver pennies.

JABBERWOCKY

"Petite . . . leaves . . . gold." He glanced over his shoulder and asked, "Flowers?" Tjaden couldn't even see the man's mouth move behind the facial hair.

"Yeah."

"In that case," he straightened and held a ring up into the light and examined it as if he hadn't seen it in a very long time. With a nod he said, "If your lady does not love this ring, I will wear it through my nose."

Tjaden chuckled and held out his pinky. Walrus slid it down to his second joint, where it stopped. That size had to fit one of Elora's fingers. Unlike so many of the plain rings, there was no flat gold anywhere on it. Delicate leaves and strong vines wrapped around each other. Two small flowers that appeared to be gold with green and pink tints seemed to grow from the vines.

"How much?" asked Tjaden. "It doesn't have any gems." It seemed a stupid thing to say, but Tjaden had seen his father make obvious statements when he negotiated.

"No gems, but the scrollwork on the leaves is exceedingly fine, and the flowers . . ." Walrus raised his eyebrows and whistled. "So delicate and made from gold so rare it cannot be found anywhere in Maravilla. I'd wager you've never seen pink gold."

He'd never even *heard* of pink gold before. "How much?"

"A duodec plus one."

Tjaden pulled out his coins and held open his palm. "I have fifteen."

The man peered into Tjaden's eyes suspiciously. "That's a stretch."

"Then a stretch is everything I own."

Walrus's mustache moved as his mouth worked underneath it. He checked Tjaden's belt for a purse. He had none.

Tjaden said, "You've had that ring tucked away for a long time. People are packing up. You might as well make one more sale."

They stared at each other.

"An end-of-the-day bargain," said Tjaden.

Walrus made a low grumble in the back of his throat. "I suppose I can sell it for that, even though I'm losing money." He shook a thick finger at Tjaden. "For that price you'll get no pretty box or even a ribbon."

"I don't need those," said Tjaden. "Just polish it."

"You drive a bargain like a peddler drives a mule, but I'll take it." He scooped up the coins and opened a short flask with clear liquid for Tjaden to drop the ring in. A minute later he removed it with tiny wooden tongs and rubbed it briskly with a soft cloth. When he pinched it in the tongs and held it out, the ring gleamed like the sun itself.

Tjaden reached for it but pulled up short. His fingers would just grub it up if he touched it. He couldn't ask Walrus for anything, and he couldn't just shove it into a pocket.

From very near Tjaden's ear, a voice said, "A ring? When you decide to act, you go all out." Ollie snickered and stepped up next to him with his arms folded.

"Don't say anything to anyone," said Tjaden.

"Me? Would I do that?"

Tjaden didn't give Ollie the satisfaction of a groan. "Do you have a scrap of cloth?"

"I can do better than that," said Ollie. From the sack he was carrying he pulled a tiny pouch. "You owe me."

"Where did you get this?"

"Might as well ask a snake where he gets his scales." Ollie shook his head and raised his eyebrows. "A ring. Never would have given you credit for so much guts. I have to get these to Ingri." He held up the sack and walked off.

"Meet me at our booth," called Tjaden.

Ollie waved and disappeared around the corner. The merchant dropped the ring into the pouch. Tjaden carefully cinched the drawstring, thanked him, and stepped away.

"One moment," said Walrus, tipping his head to listen to something. He patted Tjaden's hip and the coins for the mirror jingled. "All you have in the world, eh?"

"Those coins are for a mirror my father had made for my mother."

"Well done, young man." Walrus shook his head as he stepped back. "I thought I could read people better than a scribe reads a book, but you've bested me." He tipped his funny hat.

"I'm serious," said Tjaden, but there was no point in wasting more time. The mirror booth would be taken down soon. Hopefully Elora would be there so he could give her the ring.

A ring? Tjaden slapped his forehead as the implication settled. Ollie was right. It wasn't like he wanted to marry her. Well, he did. Someday. He decided to find out if she was even there. If so, a lot depended on who was with her. As he approached the mirror-maker's booth, he pinched the ring in his pocket.

Through the gaps he saw Elora's long brown hair. She was polishing a large square mirror and singing to herself. There was no sign of her parents but Lily was in the back corner. When Tjaden reached the front of the booth, he heard Elora singing quietly and saw her face from every angle. The mirrors were plain, but her face in so many of them made them exquisite. There was no sign of the pale stitches Doc Methos had used. Livid red lines marked the injuries.

As always, the sight of her made him feel ten feet tall.

When he realized she'd stopped singing, Tjaden scanned the mirrors and found her watching him watch her through one of the angles.

As soon as their eyes met, his fell quickly to the ground. He lifted them and found her turning shyly toward him. The lower scar prevented the left side of her mouth from moving, but the other side turned upward.

As beautiful as ever. If he could just see that smile every day, he'd be as happy as a tove[1] under a sundial.

Elora turned her face so he could only see her right side. When he looked from her smile to her eyes, all thought fled. He was as speechless as stone.

"Hi, Tjaden."

Oh, yeah.

"Hi."

"How are your arms?"

"Fine as feathers," Tjaden said, flushing. "Your face looks, um, fine."

Elora's head dipped farther away from him, and Lily stepped up and held her free hand.

It was the wrong thing to say. Beautiful, stunning, hypnotizing. Anything was better than *fine*. He had to say something else. "Hi, Lily."

"Hello," said Lily. Her manner was like a mother or an older sister.

"Can you give us a little while?" asked Elora.

Lily considered, looked at both of their faces. "Sure." She kissed the back of Elora's hand, gave her an encouraging nod and disappeared into the crowd.

Elora draped her rag over a nearby mirror and reached for one of Tjaden's arms. He'd stopped bandaging them, but wore long sleeves to avoid attention. Judging by the stares he'd received all day, covering his arms only added to the intrigue.

Elora pulled up his cotton sleeve and softly traced the rows of pinched skin. Eleven of them on that arm. He hoped she wouldn't turn his hand face up and see the moisture on his palm. The tingle her finger sent up his arms and down his spine made Tjaden's face burn. He reminded himself that

---

[1] **tove**: An animal resembling a badger, a lizard and a corkscrew.

she was used to touching patients and examining wounds. The touch was nothing more than professional curiosity.

"Looks like we're both healing up well." She looked up into his close face, blushed, and took a step back.

She's treating you like a patient, he told himself. It wasn't the time for rings or romance. "Uh, Doc Methos said it was because of the stypcia you put on before he sewed me up."

Elora smiled and from her comfortable distance, said, "They look ready for the thread to be pulled."

"After the sparring tomorrow."

"You're going to fight?"

"I have to." Tjaden looked down at his arms to avoid her concerned face. If she said or implied that she thought it was a bad idea, he didn't know what he'd do. He pulled his sleeve down. "The Legate will be there. I don't want to have to wait two more years."

"Even with the injury, those boys don't stand a chance."

He blushed all over again and cleared his throat. "So, uh, is that mirror ready?"

"Oh, of course," she replied.

From the back of the makeshift shop she produced a rectangular tin-backed mirror. It wasn't the fanciest type of mirror her father made, but it was a step up from the bronze ones. His reflection was clear enough to make him self-conscious.

Tjaden took the mirror so he could turn it away. Every time he was forced to look at himself, he replayed his actions with the bandersnatch. There were so many things he could have done to protect her.

"Oh, here," he reached into his pocket. His hand brushed the small pouch, but he grabbed the coins. After handing her the pennies he looked around at the dozen Eloras.

The ring would never do for someone so beautiful. How could he ever have thought metal could match her beauty?

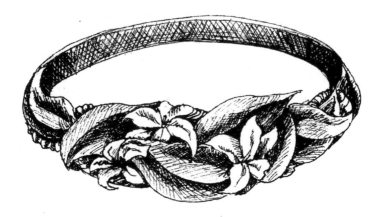

Even on the chance that she did feel the same for him, the ring had been a bad idea from the start.

Maybe Walrus will buy it back.

"Anything else?" she asked.

He was staring again. "Um, no. I don't think—oh! Are you going to the bonfire tonight?"

Elora's hand came up to touch her cheek. "I don't know. I think it's too soon."

"Yeah, you're right. I mean, I might not go either. Too soon." He didn't know exactly what that meant and instantly regretted saying it.

Elora's cheeks reddened and she said, "I hope your mother enjoys the mirror."

"Thanks. I'm sure she will." Tjaden stole one more glance and walked away with the new glass and a smile he knew wouldn't leave his face for the rest of the day.

There was no sign of his mother at their booth, so Tjaden handed off the mirror to his father and hurried back to Walrus. It took some pleading, but he agreed to buy it back, minus a thrip[1]. Still, twelve pennies was better than a ring he couldn't give a girl who probably didn't even want it.

---

[1] **thrip**: Common name for a thripenny.

By the time he found Ollie, the merchants and vendors were closing their shops.

"So what did she say?" asked Ollie.

"Who?"

"What do you mean, 'who'?" Ollie rolled his eyes.

Tjaden didn't want to tell him he had chickened out.

"Elora. The ring."

"Don't talk so loud," said Tjaden.

"You think that's loud?"

"There is no ring," said Tjaden. "I sold it back."

"What?" Ollie stopped and spread his hands. "Why would you do that?"

Tjaden turned to stare at him. "You said it was a horrible idea."

"I said it was about time you admitted how you felt about her."

"No, you said . . ." It was boggled in his head. He just wanted his friend to go away. "Let's just drop it."

Ollie laughed. "You found the perfect gift and you lost your nerve. The boy who isn't scared of anything."

"The ring was a stupid idea." Tjaden started walking.

"Only if you don't want her to know that no one in Shey's Orchard, no one in Maravilla, cares as much about her as you do."

Tjaden stepped closer so they could talk without being overheard by the people walking toward the auction.

"She doesn't even have a ribbon in her hair."

"A temporary dilemma," said Ollie. "It's never too early to plant the idea. You did save her life, remember?"

"Have you seen her face, Ollie?"

"Don't ever let her hear you say that." Ollie's expression was as stern as Tjaden had ever seen. "Besides, you said you didn't care about the scars."

"What? That's not what I mean!" Tjaden lowered his voice. "If you hadn't showed up with my father, she'd be dead."

"Oh, do we have to go through this again?" Ollie let his hands fall to his sides.

"Fine," said Tjaden. "I'll stop, but the ring was thoughtless. It would only remind her of me and of that day."

"Jay, I know you know nothing about girls, but can you really know *so much* nothing?"

"Huh?"

"She'll remember that day every time she smiles, or meets a stranger, or sees herself in a mirror. And you do realize who her father is, right?"

"I'm not stupid," said Tjaden.

"No, but you act like it sometimes. That ring said more than you could ever say with words. Especially since you won't say any words to her. A ring like that would say more than a boy who actually had a tongue could say."

"How so?"

"I can't believe I have to explain this to you." Ollie considered for a moment, then said, "When you give gold to a girl, it means you could not possibly think more highly of her. When you put some thought into it, and show that you know anything about her interests, she knows you care not just about impressing her, but you care about *her*. When you find something that speaks to who she is deep down, that's when you find her soul. You showed that you know her more deeply than any boy who can't say five words to her should possibly know."

"That ring does all that?" Tjaden didn't know what to think anymore.

"If you're half as crazy about her as I think, selling the ring back was the stupidest thing either of us has ever done."

Tjaden looked back to the market. Only one in five booths still had merchandise out.

"Where do you learn all this?" asked Tjaden.

"Where don't you learn all this? It's like you've never even seen a girl."

"I have to find that merchant." He started jogging upstream into the crowd. Over five thousand people crammed into Shey's Orchard for the first day of the Swap and Spar. Many caravans would be leaving before dark, which was less than an hour away.

"Slow down," said Ollie, grabbing him from behind. "Let me help."

"Come on, then."

"We need to split up," said Ollie. "Give me half of the money."

"What for? If this is a trick to get half of my coins . . ." he left the threat hanging.

"If it is a ploy, I deserve half for being so convincing."

Tjaden rolled his eyes and started running again.

"Jay," said Ollie, grabbing his tunic again. "If I find him I have to show him I'm serious."

That made sense. Tjaden gave him two thripennies.

"What's his name?" asked Ollie.

"Walrus."

"Fat? Giant mustache? Weird hat?"

Tjaden nodded.

"Got it. I'll start on the south end, you go to the north," said Ollie. "If you find him, head toward Falon's stall. That's pretty central."

"Falon's. I got it." He started running against the crowd again.

Before he reached the booths, he heard his mother calling his name. He had to backtrack to find her.

"What's the rush?" She was carrying a sack full of her spoils for the day.

"I have to, uh, find a, a merchant before he leaves."

"Who is it?"

Even if he had time, Tjaden didn't want to tell her. "I can't explain right now, but is there any way I can borrow a thrip? I'll pay you back as soon as I have a chance to earn it."

She raised an eyebrow. "This has to do with a girl, doesn't it?"

"Yeah, but I'm not doing anything stupid. Ollie and I talked it through."

"I'm not exactly reassured."

"I have to hurry."

His mother considered for precious seconds. "Is it Elora?"

Tjaden nodded. It felt like his whole body nodded.

"Why didn't you just tell me?" She reached into her coin purse and pulled out a thripenny.

"Thanks. Sorry I can't help you carry that."

"I'm fine. Now go do whatever brilliant thing you're planning." She gave him a little push to get him on his way.

Up and down the aisles he ran, dodging merchants and mules. No browsers remained, only people trying to close up shop. No luck on the first two aisles. Halfway through the third aisle he saw Ollie sitting on a barrel, whittling at his fingernails. Behind him stood Walrus. Even better, Soapers Falon and Ingri were nowhere to be seen.

"You did it, Ollie." Tjaden slapped his back.

"Ollie often obtains honorable objectives."

"Nice." Without pausing to catch his breath Tjaden asked, "Do you still have the ring?"

"You're in luck." Walrus held the ring up to gleam in the light of the setting sun.

Tjaden finally felt like he could breathe. "I'll pay you full price."

Ollie shook his head emphatically, but the merchant said, "Deal. But what happened to 'This is every cuppy[1] I own'?"

---

[1] **cuppy**: Common name for a copper piece, the smallest coin in Maravilla.

"I borrowed some on the way here, just to make sure."

"The deal is done, my boy. No sense in ruses now." They traded coins for ring. "What craft are you in, son?"

"My father and I grow citrus," said Tjaden. "Oranges, lemons, orangeberries. But I'm going to be an Elite."

"Here's a free lesson you'll need when the Elites don't work out for you: you've got a good face for lying; don't throw everything out on the table right up front."

"I wasn't lying."

"How long does it take you to earn a thrip?"

Tjaden shrugged. "I don't get paid."

"A grown man earns this much in six days if he's a good worker with a generous master. You just worked for me for a week. For free."

Ollie shook his head and said, "I tell him all the time to slow down and think."

The merchant held up a thripenny. "This coin should be in your pocket. My chips were on the table. You know how much I would have taken for the ring. You know I was willing to come here out of my way to make one more sale today. You should know that I'd never let you walk away with a fair offer on the table."

"I know how much I care for her. Is the rest of it really that important?"

With a clink of the disappearing coins he said, "You'll be able to care for her this much more if you get smart. Good day." He walked away whistling, his mustache puffing out in front of him.

Ollie put his arm around Tjaden's shoulder and led him away. "The auction would have been a lot more fun if we had a thrip to spend."

"It'll be a lot more fun now that I have the ring. Let's go find her."

"Too late, Jay," said Ollie. "They've already cleared out."

He should have given it to her when he had the chance. "At least I get more time to figure out how to give it to her."

"While you're dancing with her tonight."

"She probably won't go."

"That's probably fair since you probably won't have the guts anyway."

They followed the bulk of the crowd to the auction. The first item up was Zelena's turtle pie, which led to a heated bidding war between two brothers, Rox and Talex. Talex paid a staggering five pennies for the pie. The brothers probably wouldn't speak to each other again at least until the next Swap and Spar.

A few items later, while a cask of aged whiskey was up for sale, the auctioneer took a bad step and tumbled off the stage. Someone in the crowd shouted, "That must be some good swill!" The crowd roared with laughter, and the bid doubled immediately.

Toward the end of the auction, a yew longbow from Palassiren was offered for sale. Tjaden was surprised to see his father bid on it since his bow was still in decent shape. Besides, this one looked too small for his large frame. It was a fine bow, maybe the finest in Shey's Orchard, but Tjaden couldn't figure out why his father would want it. A dozen silver pennies won the auction for him.

Ollie leaned over and said, "Looks like you're getting a new bow."

"Are you kidding?" Tjaden shook his head. "That bow cost more than a horse. If I'm lucky, I'll get his old one."

"What would you want with that old nag?" Ollie asked with a wink.

"The bow, not the horse," Tjaden said.

"Mark my words—you'll be holding that bow come your birthday."

Music started as soon as the auction ended and the crowd spread out around the giant bonfire. More than half of the people were completely unfamiliar to Tjaden, visiting from other towns. Ollie stayed busy dancing with any girl who didn't have a partner and stuffing himself at the traditional bird buffet, which had quail, dove, borogove, duck, turkey, ostrich, and even Jubjub.

Tjaden circled the outskirts watching for Elora. Betany, Jayla, Arvin, Molner, and the rest of the group she'd normally be with were all there, but no sign of Elora. Even Lily, who was always the most popular girl at any social event, was absent. If anything was proof of her loyalty to her sister, that was.

Tjaden hoped it wasn't something he said that made her decide to stay home. He ate moderately at the buffet, wanting to be fresh in the morning for his first match, and left early. The music and laughing from the festival faded behind him. Thoughts about the reasons Elora would miss it taunted him. He forced his thoughts to the sparring contest. In a matter of hours he would have a chance to earn a spot at the Academy. *If* he fought his best and his arms held up and he was able to focus on fighting instead of the stupid things he said to Elora.

By the time he made it home, he was too excited to even think about sleeping. Alone in the moonlight behind his house, Tjaden went through all the forms he knew. He and his staff incapacitated hundreds of imaginary opponents and worked up enough exhaustion to finally sleep.

At the wabe the next morning, the auction scaffolding had been removed. In its place, rows of elevated seating for spectators had been erected. The contest took place in a circle ten paces across. Each combatant's staff was wrapped with wool to soften the blows. The goal was to land five blows or force the opponent out of the bounds of the circle. Strikes to the head were illegal and resulted in the loss of one point or disqualification if the struck fighter was unable to continue.

Everyone in Shey's Orchard, over two thousand townspeople, lined the tiered benches around the circle. Hundreds of outsiders, including the king's representative, swelled the number. The Legate was one of ten who traveled across Maravilla as a recruiter for the King's Elite. Many towns and few Legates meant representatives of the Elites only attended every two or three years.

The Legate watched both the boys' and the men's competitions to determine if the winners would be offered an invitation to the Academy. Runners-up and other contestants were not eligible. The ranks of the Elites were comprised of champions only.

The boys' tournament took place first. Thirty-seven boys between the ages of eleven and fifteen fought for the title Tjaden had won the year before. Ollie had never mastered staff fighting, but if Tjaden knew him, he'd provide some entertaining trick moves for the crowd. He started his first match by advancing and parrying a few times. Then he stepped back out of range and dropped one end of his staff, holding it like a walking stick. In the instance his confused opponent dropped his guard, Ollie used his foot to kick the planted end of his staff up. It struck Tidris's staff and knocked it out of his grasp. Ollie easily finished off his unarmed opponent.

Before the next match, Elora appeared at Tjaden's side where he waited in the shade.

"It would mean a good deal to me," she said in a reserved voice, "if you could beat Brune."

"I don't know if we'll be matched up," said Tjaden. "If we are then I have to beat him. I have to beat everyone to make it into the Academy."

"I mean *beat* him. Like a goodwife beats a carpet in the spring." Her face held no hint of the smile she almost always wore.

"Why?" asked Tjaden. "What did he do?"

"It's something personal. Will you do it? For me?"

"Sure, yeah. Of course."

She was gone as quickly as she had appeared. He didn't even have a chance to ask if there was something else she wanted him to do to Brune. The rest of that round of fighting dragged. Now that Tjaden had become Elora's champion he was even more anxious to start fighting.

Ollie's second match was against Zee Thomson. He came close to winning by planting his staff and launching himself forward, leading with both legs. He caught Zee by surprise and sent him sprawling backwards toward the edge of the ring. Ollie turned and started doing a victory dance, thinking his opponent had fallen out of the bounds. "I am the best! I . . ."

An unexpected leg sweep brought him down flat on his back, and he blacked out.

". . . am the best ever," he mumbled when he came around.

Zee won his next four matches to become the Youth Champion. He received the trophy, but the Elite Legate was not impressed enough to extend an invitation to the Academy.

After a short break for lunch, Tjaden lined up with the other twenty-eight entrants, waiting to find out who would face whom in the first round. The names for the first round were drawn at random. The winners would advance to the next round; the losers would be eliminated.

The men ranged in age from Carter Larse, who had seen more than four decades, to Tjaden and Brune, who were on different sides of their sixteenth birthdays. Brune already had a black eye; must have tried pushing someone who pushed back.

As they lined up in the morning sun, most men stretched and attempted to shake their jitters down their arms and legs and out their fingers and toes. The anxiety was lost on Tjaden. None of these opponents could be half as daunting as the bandersnatch, and no prize could be as precious as Elora's life. Even as an Elite, the only stakes would be his life and the lives of his fellow soldiers. As long as Elora was safe, how could he ever worry about a battle?

As for the stitches, they'd either be a problem or they wouldn't. There was nothing he could do about it. His muscles pulled the stitches tight as he gripped his staff. Five matches would test the limits of Doc Methos's work, but Tjaden had confidence in his fighting abilities. The line of fidgeting men only boosted it.

Mayor Tellef drew out the first names. "Grower Whit versus Grower Bren," he announced.

"Steffen versus Pratt."

Steffen, just a year older than Tjaden, was the defending champion. The previous nine champions came from Steffen's family. They were a rough crew who raised cattle in the hills. Their father, Titus, had died years before in a stampede, leaving his ten sons to wrestle the cattle. Their livelihood gave them the brawn to be dominant in any physical competition, and the older brothers ensured that each succeeding boy was tougher than the previous. They were a cruel bunch of brawlers, and Steffen had learned from all of them.

People speculated that none of them had been invited to the Academy because of their ugly fighting style. It was all brute and no finesse. Two trophies in a row might just be enough for Steffen to do what none of his brothers could.

"Cooper Thom versus Willam." Tellef's booming voice filled the air. "Talex versus Grower Burt.

"Thom Thomson versus Elis."

"Tjaden versus Brune."

Tjaden grinned in satisfaction. Not only would Brune be a good warm-up, but Tjaden could be Elora's champion after all. And get even with him for the borogrove incident and a hundred other things over the years. Brune himself paled and it just made his black eye stand out more. He didn't meet Tjaden's eyes.

Tjaden was lucky to not have to face Steffen until the final round, assuming they both made it that far. There was the possibility of facing two of Steffen's brothers before that, but Steffen was the biggest threat. Focused on Brune and Steffen, Tjaden didn't hear the announcement of the other match ups.

Tjaden waited anxiously for the first five matches of the men's competition to end. Steffen easily beat Pratt without getting touched. He was strong and aggressive, not much different than the bandersnatch. By the time Tellef got between them to stop the fight, Steffen had scored seven or eight touches.

The next four matches seemed to take hours, but finally, it was Tjaden's turn.

Tjaden stepped confidently into the circle, stealing a quick glance into the audience at Elora. There was the smile he loved to see. Even from a distance he saw a glimmer in her eyes.

Ten feet tall.

Brune walked into the circle, scowling like a bulldog. He took a defensive stance before the fight began, like a mutt waiting for a beating. Tjaden scored four points as fast as Mayor Tellef could count them. He hesitated before the fifth and stepped back. Brune lunged forward and swung his staff with two hands. It was easy to block, but there was no doubt Brune was going for a head strike.

Stepping side to side, Tjaden feinted, feinted, and feinted again. Brune tripped over his own feet onto his backside. A sharp jab to the gut ended the match.

The crowd cheered as Brune rose and stormed across the wabe. Elora was not the most enthusiastic in the crowd. She was clapping and nodding, but her face was serious. She wiped at her eyes a couple times. Maybe Ollie would know what it was all about.

As the sun grew in intensity, so did the competition. Tjaden's second match lasted longer than the first, but not much. He struck five blows without taking any. The hours and years he'd spent training with the staff paid off.

In the third round, Tjaden's aggressive fighting style was countered by Thresher Langon's excellent defense, and the match turned into one of the longest battles of the day. Tjaden's tirelessness won the match for him. The final score was five to one, but Tjaden had expended much more energy than he'd wanted to.

Ten days had passed since the encounter with the bandersnatch. The wounds on his forearms were holding up well. Only two spots bled through the stitches.

Four fighters remained. Steffen facing Cooper Thom and Tjaden battling Algus, Steffen's brother. The anticipation of the crowd reached a new height as Steffen and Cooper Thom stepped into the ring. The crowd overwhelmingly rooted for Steffen, hoping a victory two years in a row would be sufficient to impress the Legate and earn him an invitation to the Academy—the first from Shey's Orchard in nearly twenty years.

A town which was unaccepting of the family of rubes would happily take credit for raising an Elite.

As expected, Steffen handled Cooper Thom. He still had a sour look on his face as he walked over to Algus after the fight. With the anxious crowd calling for the next fight, the brothers conversed quietly. While Tjaden couldn't tell for sure what was being said, he knew it went beyond brotherly well-wishes and congratulations. Titus's sons were not known for their fair play.

Tellef called Algus's name, and Algus joined Tjaden in the circle. Tjaden concentrated on his task; the roaring crowd was merely background noise. Only the two brothers separated him from victory and, possibly, the Academy.

The only mode of fighting Tjaden knew or had ever considered was all-out attack. In staves, the goal was to strike your opponent, and he did it with a passion that was unmatched in Shey's Orchard. He knew he was fighting at his best when he felt like a mighty waterfall, relentlessly buffeting his opponents.

It had been such a day.

The instant the fight began, Tjaden advanced on Algus like a cat on a mouse. Surprisingly, Algus didn't attempt to defend himself or take the offensive. Instead, he turned his body full in to Tjaden's attack. A solid blow landed on Algus's upper arm. He gave up the point, but as Tjaden's blow bruised him, he swung a vicious, tight strike at Tjaden's exposed forearm.

Pain erupted in one arm and Tjaden faltered on the brink of unconsciousness. A collective gasp from the crowd sucked the air from the arena. It had been a purposeful attack on Tjaden's injured arms—not even worth a point. It meant an almost automatic disqualification. But the chance for Steffen to attend the Academy had tainted the fair play of the tournament. In the clarity of battle Tjaden realized what Steffen and Algus had been plotting before the match.

Mayor Tellef began to call the disqualification, but rage and instinct took over Tjaden. He whirled on his off-balance opponent and landed a strike on the small of his back. Algus had obviously been expecting the disqualification to end the bout; he wasn't prepared to respond. Tjaden struck again, this time a heavy blow to the stomach. Algus doubled over, and Tjaden landed two more blows on his opponent's back before Mayor Tellef caught Tjaden's staff in mid-air.

Tjaden let go and sank to his knees. Blood soaked his sleeve, and Doc Methos was rushing in to inspect it, Elora close behind him. Whether her concern was personal or professional, Tjaden couldn't tell, but the sight of her helped ease some of the pain.

Methos lifted the arm, and Tjaden involuntarily flinched. The pain was deeper than the bandersnatch's reopened cuts. It hurt to move his fingers. A dozen stitches had been torn open.

After inspecting the arm, Methos said, "It might be broken."

Tjaden thought the possibility was much stronger than a might, but he said, "I doubt it."

His father said, "I don't think you should continue."

"One more fight," said Tjaden. "I won't have this chance again for two years."

"If it is broken you could do permanent damage," said Doc Methos.

"It's probably just bruised or sprained." He flexed his fingers despite the wave of pain that momentarily took his vision away.

Both men continued their attempts to convince him to give up, but they had a better chance of convincing water to run uphill.

Methos turned to Tjaden's father and said, "We can tie the arm to keep him from using it. That's the only way I'll clear him to fight."

"Do whatever you have to do," said Tjaden. "I will not forfeit."

Tjaden bit leather once again as the doctor added dozens of stitches twice as wide as the original ones. A splint, bandages, and a swathe were placed to bind the arm to his chest and keep him from using it. He chose a shorter staff that could be hefted with one hand like a sword.

As Tjaden stepped back into the circle, the crowd exploded with applause, but as far as Tjaden was concerned, only three people were present—himself, Steffen, and a dark-haired girl with a light in her eyes that he could see half a wabe away.

Tellf wasted more breath trying to talk Tjaden out of fighting. He eventually gave up and backed out of the circle. Tjaden swung his stubby weapon on each side of his body and stared at Steffen. He had more scars on his face than the rest of the town combined, his brothers excluded. There

weren't many young men in Shey's Orchard as burly as Tjaden, but Steffen was one of them. What he gave up in height, he doubled in brawn.

As soon as Tellef announced the start of the fight they rushed each other, both trying to gain the offensive. They each earned a point with their initial blows, but as Steffen regrouped, Tjaden was already making another thrust. Tjaden's one-armed awkwardness gave Steffen a chance to block, but

Steffen had lost the offensive, and Tjaden didn't give him a chance to recover.

He continued the assault. Thrust. Strike. Reverse swing. Tjaden managed to gain two more points, but the battle was at a stalemate with Tjaden working much harder in his off-balanced attack than Steffen was at defending against it. Steffen caught on to Tjaden's right-sided attacks and timed strikes on Tjaden's left to earn a couple more points of his own.

Three points each. If Tjaden was going to the Academy, it wouldn't be on his current path. Against his custom, he forced himself to take a defensive stance, catching Steffen by surprise with the reprieve. They circled once before Steffen stepped in. Tjaden instinctively struck instead of defending. They both connected.

Four points each.

In the split second it took for them to regain their stance, Tjaden thought, *One point*. Surely his youth, his injury, and competing against men would give him the prestige in the Legate's eyes to earn the invitation.

One point.

He couldn't do it by conventional means.

Staying on the defensive, he allowed Steffen to drive him back little by little. When Tjaden was less than a foot away from the line, he thrust, purposely missing Steffen and inviting a counter-thrust. The counter came, and Tjaden was ready for it. Dropping his own staff, he grasped Steffen's and pulled him toward the circle's edge.

Everything seemed to happen in slow motion. Steffen's eyes grew wide as he realized the ruse. His momentum carried him forward, unable to stop. He spun, wrenching his staff from Tjaden's hand and thrust it forward. Tjaden arched away from the tip of the staff as he watched it approach his chest.

He could see the grain in the wood, smell the dust in the air, and taste sweat at the corners of his mouth. His dreams hung in the air as he watched the staff make contact with his shirt and lightly tap his chest, releasing time. Steffen sprawled out of the ring. Tellef signaled one point for Steffen.

The tip of the staff had touched Tjaden a fraction of a second before Steffen crossed the line. Tjaden had lost.

PART II

"Beware the Jabberwock, my son!
The jaws that bite, the claws that catch!
Beware the Jubjub bird, and shun
The frumious Bandersnatch!"

*D*_{ay}.

Day.
Despair.
The sunlight on his skin only fed the fury that had grown for months.

Gnawing.
Swelling.
Not much longer. He had been alone too long, and the rage would soon be uncontrollable. He closed his eyes and drew in a cavernous breath. As he exhaled, trees in the vicinity swayed and lost leaves.

A borogove griped nearby. Before its pitiful cry was through, he swung his tail and flattened the creature.

Anger.
Hate.
He lashed out an arm, severing a small copse of trees at their trunks. He closed his eyes again and allowed in images of the past, of days that were different. Days when he was not alone. When fury did not rule him. Days when hate was foreign to him. Days that were no longer days but mere memories.

The images persisted, but he was incapable of experiencing the former feelings.

Alone no longer, he growled.

With a bellow, the Jabberwock sent a flock of small birds tumbling into flight. On wings stoked by hate, he rose into the air. His rage had reached a frenzy and the Jabberwock would not rest until its rage was sated. As he flew in search of human prey—for only human prisoners would slake his wrath—the image of one human filled his mind with one thought:

Revenge.

Tjaden was in shock. The spectators heaped praise on him as he left the arena, but all their compliments and consolation stung like canvas clothing rubbing against a wound. Like Elora's scars, their words reminded him of his failure.

Without victory, the Legate's hands would be tied. Two more years as a farmer. Tjaden had nothing against farming, but would never feel fulfilled until he reached his goal.

The stream of well-wishers seemed to last forever; Tjaden just wanted to get away. Each face that presented itself just caused his own to redden, and he found it hard to meet people's eyes.

On top of everything else, his wrist throbbed. Where was Doc Methos?

As the crowds thinned, the Legate approached. Tjaden forced himself to meet the man's gaze.

"I was impressed by your aggressive fighting style," said the Legate.

"Thank you, Sir." He resisted the urge to excuse his loss because of the injury.

As if reading Tjaden's mind, the Legate said, "If not for the injury . . . well, that's irrelevant. More importantly, it's plain your mettle is as strong as metal."

"Thank you, Sir. I *will* see you at the Academy in two years." He forced himself to say it, but for the first time he wondered if it would actually happen.

"I believe you will, Tjaden."

Elora was among the last to approach. Looking down at the arm in the sling she said, "It might not be a bad thing to have you closer to home for a couple years." She seemed intent on not meeting his eyes, and he didn't know how to take the comment.

As usual, he had no reply.

With a quick hug she whispered, "Thanks for beating him," then walked off without looking at him. Lily followed closely behind.

Doc Methos was the last one waiting to approach him. "If you're done basking in congratulations, let's get a better look at that arm."

As they walked toward Methos's shop, Tjaden said, "Trust me. I didn't want any of their congratulations. I definitely didn't earn them."

"Don't be so hard on yourself. It was the most excitement we've seen at a Swap and Spar in years. The only way it could have ended better was if you had edged Steffen instead of the other way around."

The following morning Tjaden was awakened by a pair of borogoves outside his window. He climbed out of bed, peered through the wooden slats and decided he had been wrong—they actually did look more pathetic than they sounded.

But they still don't look half as pitiful as I feel.

Breakfast was bread and slabs of rath[1] meat with fresh juice. The brightness of the green meat and orange juice annoyed him. He forced down mouthfuls of food.

His mother told him for the hundredth time that she was

---

[1] **rath**: a sort of green pig.

extremely proud of him. "Besides, you're only fifteen. You have time."

"I don't want time," he said as gruffly as he could manage. "I want training. I'm ready now."

"There's no reason to be uffish with your mother, Tjaden," his father said. "Maybe you are ready now, but that's not the point. The life of a soldier is one of discipline and following rules. Well, this is your first test. How will you face it?"

Tjaden set his jaw. "I'll pass any test they give me. Including this one."

He went to work in the groves with his whole heart and body, minus the use of one arm. Lacking it frustrated him. He wanted to forget everything in the work, if only for a few days. As he cut weeds, dug irrigation ditches, and picked fruit, the agony began to fade—but it was still a bruise in the back of his mind that refused to heal.

One week after the Swap and Spar, Tjaden and his father finished their work early. Tjaden grabbed his staff and loped to Falon's workshop to see if Ollie was free. When he arrived, they were pouring a thick sludge into a mixing vat. It smelled like a wet borogove. Tjaden waited outside until Ollie was done.

The two liberated boys made their way to the wabe, planning their day and a half of freedom. Knowing Tjaden wouldn't be content until they did some sparring, they decided to start with staves. Each wabe, so named because it extended way beyond and way behind, featured a large sundial in the center. As certain as the sundial in the center of every wabe were the toves that built their nests underneath.

After shooing a few of the slithy[1] animals from the area, the boys prepared to duel. Tjaden's left arm was still bandaged, and he wore a swathe to hold it against his chest. Ollie's excitement at fighting a disadvantaged Tjaden showed as he

---

[1] **slithy**: slimy and lithe

fidgeted with his staff before they began. Tjaden was usually a larger pup toying with the runt of the litter, but now that he was injured, Ollie acted like the big brother.

Ollie scored much more than usual, and it was obvious by the way he spoke. "Give up now, and I'll stop hurting you. You fight like an injured borogove. I let you have that one 'cause I didn't want to hurt a cripple."

In the middle of a long exchange, Ollie looked over Tjaden's shoulder and asked, "Who's that coming up the road?"

"Yeah, like I'm going to fall for that," Tjaden replied, jabbing at Ollie's midsection.

"No, I'm serious," Ollie said, blocking. "There's a dust trail."

Tjaden took three steps back before looking away from Ollie and was surprised to see that his friend was telling the truth—a line of horses was approaching from the South.

There were no wagons in the group, so they couldn't be peddlers or traders. All the outlying farms to the south put together didn't have enough horses or men to make up a company that size. As the riders got closer, it was easy to see the strict formation and dark blue uniforms—the men were soldiers.

By the time the two columns arrived in the center of town, a crowd of a hundred had gathered. The men on the horses rode with perfect posture and a dignified air that exuded discipline. Emblazoned on their uniforms and on their horses' barding were the Circle and the Sword, signifying the highest level in the king's service. These were not mere soldiers. They were Elites.

Each Elite was accompanied on the left by his Fellow. They wore the same uniforms, but the Fellows' lacked the Circle and the Sword. Instead of the swords and battle axes of the Elites, the Fellows' weapons were more varied—mostly bows and crossbows. One Fellow carried a spear and an assortment of throwing daggers.

Tjaden took personal pride in the appearance of the unit. One day he would ride alongside them. If he ever made it to the Academy.

The man at the head of the column commanded Tjaden's attention. Any Elite Squadron leader would have been worthy of the utmost respect, but this was the First Knight, Captain of the Elites, General of the king's armies, and the most respected man in the kingdom—Captain Darieus. Each man in the squadron wore a patch that matched one of the medals on Captain Darieus's chest, a solitary blue '1' against a field of white, signifying First Squadron.

Captain Darieus hadn't visited Shey's Orchard since Tjaden was seven years old, but there was no mistaking him. He was roughly the same age as Tjaden's father, but his face was lined with experience and his back was as straight as decades of leadership. Rows of rectangular medals covered the left side of his chest. He sat in his saddle proudly and confidently.

This is a man worth following into battle.

Captain Darieus reigned up the tallest horse Tjaden had ever seen in front of the assembled crowd. After a quick inspection, his eyes settled on Tjaden.

"I intended to ask for directions to Tjaden Mikelson's residence. But either my deductive skills have gotten as rusty as a sword left out in winter, or he's standing in front me."

"Yes, Sir. I'm Tjaden."

The captain looked him over with an appraising eye. "We need to talk."

Half an hour later, five people sat around the table in the kitchen of Tjaden's modest home—Tjaden, his parents, Ollie, and Captain Darieus.

Tjaden's father said, "I never expected to have the First Knight, or any Knight, in my home, Captain."

"Thank you, Mikel. I'm sure you are aware I'm here regarding your son. As I was traveling to Palassiren, we encountered Legate Whitroe. In his report of promising recruits, he was overflowing in his praise of Tjaden. Did Tjaden truly battle a bandersnatch single handedly?"

Tjaden cringed. *Why did he have to bring that up? He'll find out for sure I had to be rescued.*

"Yes, he did," his father said. "I saw it with my own eyes."

Looking at Tjaden, Captain Darieus said, "Why did you not attempt to flee? The bandersnatch is a particularly ferocious fighter but rarely pursues a foe. Until, of course, it reaches a frumious state."

"A friend of his, a young lady," Tjaden's father glanced at him, "was cornered on a ledge. The creature was advancing on her. I don't think Tjaden even thought about it."

Tjaden decided to admit his failure before someone else did. "To be fair, Sir, I wouldn't have survived if Elora hadn't distracted it and my dad hadn't shown up. The bandersnatch was aggressive, sure, but it didn't feel like sticking around to get filled up with arrows. And Elora didn't escape without injury."

"I've seen a bandersnatch dispatch a half dozen men armed with proper weapons." Looking directly at Tjaden, Captain Darieus continued, "The gallantry displayed in that encounter is the precise attribute we desire in recruits. Not to mention your determined fighting despite injuries. Skill and discipline we can teach if a young man has a shred of talent, but heart, I believe, is an innate characteristic."

Tjaden's face flushed, but his back straightened. This was not the empty praise of townspeople. Captain Darieus's approval meant something. It meant everything.

"Tjaden, based on your outstanding performance despite debilitating injury and your unparalleled courage defending a vulnerable individual, I formally invite you to attend the Elite Training Academy."

Tjaden wanted to jump out of his chair and holler. He maintained his composure and managed to say, "But I didn't win the competition."

Captain Darieus smiled at the objection. "I am the First Knight. I founded the Elites. We have routines to find qualified soldiers, but they are not foolproof. Do you trust my judgment, Tjaden?"

"Of course, Sir."

"Then will you accept this invitation?"

Tjaden couldn't believe it was happening. There was only one answer. "Yes, Sir. Thank you, Sir. You won't be disappointed."

"You have remarkable potential, but training is exceedingly difficult. And being one of our most promising recruits will make it more difficult, not easier."

They struck hands firmly. Tjaden's mother embraced him, and her tears wetted his face. His father shook his hand and said, "I'm proud of you, son."

As Captain Darieus walked toward the door, he added, "Training starts in six weeks. Give some serious thought to whom you will choose for your Fellow. A contingent of soldiers will escort you and your father to Palassiren when the time arrives."

It seemed half the town was waiting outside. Tjaden thrust a clenched fist into the air and shouted, "I'm going to the Academy!" The crowd cheered and swept him away. Captain Darieus was saying something to Tjaden's father, but the tapping and clapping of the crowd was too loud for him to hear.

Although Tjaden knew the next six weeks would feel like six years, he was caught in a swift current from crowd to throng to celebration. An impromptu feast was held in

Tjaden's honor. The residents of Shey's Orchard converged on the wabe, bringing food, music, and a euphoria that Tjaden had never experienced.

Despite his exhilaration, part of him questioned whether he had truly earned the invitation. Tjaden would never pass up the chance to become an Elite, but this was not how he had wanted it to happen. At least no one in town brought it up.

Elora arrived with her family, her wide smile even more full of life than usual. They hadn't seen each other since the Swap and Spar, and Tjaden still had no idea how to give her the ring—or if she even wanted it. Her parents congratulated Tjaden, and then Mirrorer Aker nudged Elora. "Lora, why don't you go tell our town hero the good news?"

Elora took Tjaden by the hand and led him away from the party. Unfortunately, she let his hand fall when they had some space. Like the scars on his right arm, the two seams across her face had lost the red swelling, but the sight of them made him want to apologize.

Curiosity won out over guilt. "What is it?" he asked.

"You're not going to believe it. Captain Darieus wants Father and me to go with you to Palassiren for the induction ceremony!" There was no sign of the self-consciousness she'd shown since the bandersnatch.

Tjaden, already slightly immobile in Elora's presence, was paralyzed.

She continued in an accurate imitation of Captain Darieus's voice. "I am to 'recount the heroic acts and selfless display of courage,' and 'relate the ferocious and brutal nature of the frumious bandersnatch'."

"No!" Tjaden exclaimed. The thought of being made an example to the other recruits mortified him.

"No?" Elora responded. She turned her head ever so slightly, making her scars less visible.

"No. Yes!" He was torn by conflicting emotions.

"Yes?"

"No . . . yes, you should come. It will be nice to have a friend there, but no, I don't want a big deal made. I know how competitive those men will be, and it'll just make my life harder."

"A friend." Her excitement escaped along with the word, but she straightened her shoulders and said, "Well, I'm proud of what you did. And I'll tell the whole world."

"Elora," Tjaden said awkwardly, "I didn't do it for the whole world. I did it because you . . ." he put his good hand on her shoulder and almost forgot what he intended to say when he stared into her brilliantly dark eyes. "You—not someone else, you—were going to die if I didn't do something."

"So the smart thing was to die along with me?" Elora's eyes somehow grew even wider, and he couldn't tell if she was angry or appreciative.

"What do you call clubbing a bandersnatch on the side of the head? If that thing had an ear it would be deaf now."

Elora grinned.

"You should have tried to run," he said.

"Even if I'd had a fast horse and some way to get to it, I wouldn't have left you to die alone."

"Well, I'm still alive, but I would have died for you." High on his recent success, he continued with uncharacteristic boldness. "For you I'd catch a Jubjub bird, tame it, and teach it to say 'Elora.' For you I'd fight a dozen bandersnatches using a fork for a sword and a corncake for a shield. For you I'd visit every town in the kingdom to prove there is no one to match your beauty."

Tears appeared out of nowhere. Elora wrapped her arms around him and disappeared in his embrace. In his experience, tears were a bad thing. He shouldn't talk about her beauty any more.

"For you," he said, thinking of anything to change the subject, "I'd hunt the mighty Jabberwock."

The hug got tighter and she rested her head on his chest. For the first time in his life, he wished he would never have to leave Shey's Orchard.

Knowing he might never feel as bold, Tjaden reached into his pocket for the pouched ring.

"There you are," said Tjaden's father, approaching them in the mid shadows. "Your admirers are waiting."

His mother was right behind him. "Mikel, don't you dare interrupt them right now. I'm sorry, you two. Go back to what you were doing."

But Elora had already slipped out of his arms. Tjaden let go of the ring and followed Elora back to the celebration. There were still six weeks before they had to leave. He'd have plenty of time for the ring.

For the rest of the night, his exultant mood had little to do with the festivities.

The next day, Tjaden asked Ollie to be his Fellow.

"Of course. The real reason they invited you was because they knew I'd be your Fellow."

Tjaden grinned. "Then why didn't they just invite you to be an Elite?"

"I'd make all the other recruits look bad. As a Fellow I'll be able to blend in. It's for the best." He nodded confidently.

Each day passed so slowly Tjaden felt like he was physically dragging time like a mule drags a plow. His wounds healed and the bone mended. The scars remained, like red tunnels made by something living under his skin. He continued to practice sparring and improve his physical condition. By the end of the six weeks, Tjaden felt stronger than ever.

Despite every attempt, Tjaden was never able to talk to Elora alone. He only saw her three times, and there was always a parent present, as if they'd conspired against privacy for their children. Ollie tried to get him to sneak out at night and throw pebbles at her window, but Tjaden didn't feel like it was the right way to do it. The right time never came.

The sun set on their final day in the orchards and he and Ollie returned home. His father gathered them. "After I escort you to Palassiren, it will be over a year until we see each other again." He paused. "I want to make sure you know I'm proud of you. Both of you."

His father's praise made Tjaden uneasy. There was something comforting in his father's usually stoic nature.

"Ollie," his father continued, "I have something for you." He went into his bedroom and came out holding the yew longbow from the auction.

Speechless, Ollie accepted the bow and examined the weapon. Tjaden noticed his glance out the window to see if any daylight remained. Surprisingly, there was moisture in his eyes.

Tjaden couldn't resist. "I don't know which surprises me more, you being speechless or you crying. I haven't seen you cry since you fell out of that grapefruit tree—how long ago was it? A couple of months?"

Ollie kept his eyes on the bow. "Shut yourself! This is the best bow I've ever seen, and easily the best in Shey's Orchard. Oh, and it's been six years since that tree."

Tjaden's father didn't intervene. Ollie could take a little of what he had dished out for so many years.

"Thank you," Ollie said as he embraced the closest person he had to a father. "I don't even know what to say."

"Wow, at a loss for words for the second time tonight," Tjaden said. "That bow has changed you already."

His father said, "We'll see how detached you act after you see this." He walked across the small dining area, reached behind the hutch, and withdrew a four foot long object draped in burlap. He held it out but Tjaden could only stare.

"Well?" said his father.

Tjaden walked forward and reached for it.

Please be a sword! Please be a sword!

He slowly pulled the burlap off and was not happy; he was thrilled.

Wrapping his fingers around the hilt, Tjaden slowly withdrew the blade from the hard leather scabbard.

The blade was not straight; it had wavy edges, giving it the appearance of a dangerous, meandering river. The steel itself was folded, a time-intensive method of crafting in which layer upon layer of thin steel was pounded flat, giving it an elegant, mottled look.

It was a masterpiece. Tjaden could only stare, mouth open.

"Who's speechless now?" said Ollie wryly.

Tjaden barely heard him. "Where did you get this? I've never seen a finer sword in my life!"

"I ordered it from Palassiren. It's a sword worthy of an Elite. What do you think of the hilt?"

Tjaden wrapped both hands around the hilt and extended the sword in front of him. Unlike other swords, this one was an exact fit in his large hand. "It fits perfectly! I've never held anything like it."

"I had them forge the hilt from a mold of my hand. The blade's lighter than a straight sword of the same width, but its reach is half a hand longer."

Tjaden continued to marvel at the excellent craftsmanship. Like a newborn foal testing its legs, he cautiously swung the sword. It scraped the ceiling. The close quarters forced him to be content examining it. He felt the edge with his thumb.

His father said, "Sharp, but not too sharp. Perfect for penetrating armor or bone, but the edge won't fold the first time you hit armor."

He longed to spend hours trying the blade, getting accustomed to the length and forging the metal into an extension

DANIEL COLEMAN

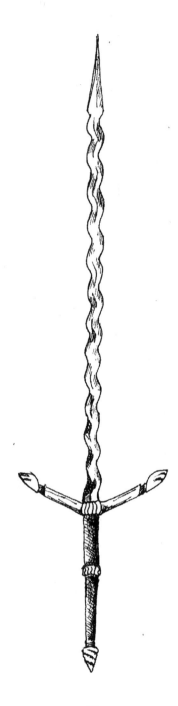

of his right arm. But night had fallen, and the Elites would be waiting for them at sunrise.

After another lingering look at the sword, Tjaden replaced it in the sheath. He leaned it carefully by the front door next to his father's bow and quiver then thanked his father as profusely as he knew how.

Ollie carried his bow into the small bedroom they shared. Tjaden's bed covered nearly half the room, and when they slid Ollie's trundle bed out, it only left two small walkways along the walls.

"You know that would fit better in the front room," Tjaden said when he entered.

Holding the bow protectively, Ollie replied, "Hey, your dad's habit of carrying his bow saved your life. Besides, I've never had anything nice *or* new. I plan on keeping this close."

Bracing one end of the bow with his foot, Ollie removed the string. Tjaden wondered if would be another fleeting interest, but just said, "Tough to argue with that."

The front door opened then closed. He'd been waiting for his father to go outside.

"Be right back," he told Ollie, and walked into the front room. "Mom?"

"What is it?"

Tjaden held out the ring and his mother came forward and picked it up.

"For Elora?" The look she gave him made it clear he'd have to answer to her if he had other plans for it.

Tjaden nodded.

"It's perfect. Where did you get it?"

"The Swap and Spar."

"That was six weeks ago."

Tjaden let out an exasperated sigh. "I know."

"Changed your mind?"

"No," said Tjaden immediately. "No way. I just haven't been able to talk to her alone."

His mother handed him the ring. "You should have told me. We wouldn't have worked with Aker and Adella to keep you two from being alone."

"You did that on purpose?"

"You'll understand why when you have teenagers of your own. You want to go over there right now?"

"Really?" Tjaden looked out the window into the darkness. "I do, but I don't think it's a good idea."

"Need me to go down there and see you off in the morning? Just to make sure you have a chance?"

"No," said Tjaden. "I have a week on the road to give it to her."

"If there's nothing I can do to help, why did you show it to me?"

"I thought you'd want to see it." He shrugged. "And know what I had planned."

"Look at you," she said and stepped forward to take his hands. "My boy has grown into a man, all considerate and tender."

Tjaden felt his cheeks redden. "I want to ask her to put my sword on me tomorrow morning. You're a girl. Is that a good idea?"

"Having a special young woman gird your first sword is a beautiful tradition. It's a brilliant idea."

If he could just find a way to ask her without sounding stupid.

"She's a good choice, Jay," said his mother.

"I know. I just hope she thinks the same of me."

They woke before sunrise. Tjaden's mother packed a breakfast of boiled eggs and salted pork. The food for the rest of the week-long trip to Palassiren would be provided by the soldiers' cook. Tjaden and Ollie each carried a small pack that contained the few items they were taking to the Academy.

Tjaden placed the strap attached to his scabbard over one shoulder as they prepared to leave.

"That goes around your waist," said Ollie.

"I'm going to ask Elora to do it," said Tjaden. He was prepared for a look from his father or a comment from Ollie, but neither said anything.

His mother held him back after the other two walked outside. She kissed him on the cheek and said, "Good luck with the ring. Of course, in matters of love it's best to not need luck. If Elora's anything like girls were when I was her age, you won't need it."

He hugged her again and wiped a tear from her cheek.

Then Tjaden the boy walked out of his house for the last time. The next time he entered, he would be wearing the Circle and the Sword.

"I wish I was going with you," said Lily.

"Me too," said Elora. Her grin widened and she felt the pull of the scar. "I'm sure your exceedingly rich and powerful husband will take you to see the capital someday."

"If he ever finds me! You have to tell me *everything* about it. Especially if you see any of the Ladies."

"Too bad we won't be there for Capital Day," said Elora, "or I could tell you about all of them."

She put her hand on Lily's arm and they slowed, allowing their father to walk a few paces ahead of them. He didn't seem to notice. Probably doing another checklist in his head to make sure everything they needed was in the packs he carried.

"It'll be good to be away from here for a while," said Elora. "Away from certain people especially." After her injury,

more than a few of her friends suddenly forgot she existed. Some awkwardly walked the opposite direction whenever they saw her coming. Others had started referring to her as 'Scratch' behind her back. How did she not realize her friends were so petty?

Lily squeezed Elora's hand. "There are lots more people who love you and still think you're beautiful. Including a certain soon-to-be Elite." Her voice rose in pitch and moonlight twinkled in her eyes.

"In fourteen months, he might not want anything to do with a girl from Shey's Orchard. Anything to do . . ." she thought for a second and decided to say it. "Anything to do with a girl who looks like me."

"I told you to stop saying things like that," said Lily, swatting Elora's arm. "Anyone who cares about stupid scars doesn't deserve you."

"What if the only ones who don't care are the dregs of Shey's Orchard?"

"Then who needs them? You and me can be old biddies together."

Lily was the last one in the kingdom who'd end up a spinster, but the thought made Elora smile. "What will our trade be?"

"Teach me what you know about herbals and medicines and we'll give the good stuff to people we like. We'll give the others bogus medicine that turns their skin blue. And laxatives!"

Elora laughed, and even the pull of the scar on one side of her smile didn't bring her down. She could never mistreat a patient, but she didn't put it past her sister to pull any manner of prank. Especially if it involved vengeance for Elora.

"There's something I didn't tell you," said Elora. "For that exact reason."

Lily rose up on her toes and turned toward Elora as they walked. "Well?" She squeezed Elora's arm with both hands.

"Right after it happened, when I still had the stitches in, I was on my way to Baker Hettie's. Even though I didn't like being alone, it was so close that I thought it would be fine. Brune was hanging around—doing nothing."

"As usual," interjected Lily.

"I won't burn your ears with what he said, but he told me exactly how he thought a girl with face scars would end up." Elora's own ears grew hot, and she shook her head to keep the vulgar words he'd said out.

"He didn't!"

Elora nodded. "He tried to grab at me so I hit him in the eye as hard as I could. Told him I'd scream if he didn't walk away." If she would have had the club Tjaden used on the bandersnatch, Brune wouldn't have survived.

"*You* gave him that black eye?"

"Yes," said Elora. "He deserved a lot more."

"Tell me what he said." There was none of the usual sweetness in Lily's voice.

"No."

"Tell me, Lora."

They had never kept secrets, but if Elora told her, Lily would do something regrettable.

"I wish I could forget it." She looked down at her hand, pale in the moonlight. "I don't know how men can hit each other like that. My hand hurt for days."

Lily breathed out slowly through her teeth and her eyes narrowed. "You know I'm going to make Brune pay."

"Tjaden already did. I asked him to at the sparring competition."

"That? That was *nothing* compared to what I have in mind."

"That's why I didn't say anything sooner," said Elora. "Promise me you'll wait until I get home." Maybe some time to think it over would temper Lily's mood.

"Don't try to talk me out of it."

"I won't," said Elora, "but I'll make sure you don't do anything too stupid."

"Fine. I'll wait. It'll give me time to think up something really good."

JABBERWOCKY

The wabe came into view as they rounded a corner. Tjaden, Ollie, and Grower Mikel were the only ones there. Enough light came from the moon that torches weren't necessary. The amount of darkness fit her perfectly. Tjaden acted as if he didn't care about her scars, but she'd take as much dark as she could find.

Elora pulled Lily to a stop and let her father go on ahead. "I don't know what I'd do without you, Lily. Having one person I can talk to makes it so much easier to deal with those other people."

"Always, Sissy." Lily hugged her and grinned a mischievous smile. "Now let's go find a good place for me to watch the Elites."

As she followed Lily toward Tjaden and Ollie, chills ran up Elora's arms, whether from the cool morning air or for other reasons she wasn't sure. Either way, it was a good excuse to raise the hood of her cloak.

Tjaden smiled and gave her a small wave. That was a face she wouldn't mind seeing every day for the rest of her life. He was holding a sheathed sword in his hand, the belt of the scabbard hung down to the ground. Elora smiled back and was glad the hood of the cloak hid her face.

Her father and Grower Mikel were already talking about work and days away from work. Elora and Lily walked around them and joined the boys.

Ollie pulled a bow off one shoulder and hung it on his other shoulder. Yawning, he said, "I don't think I slept at all last night."

Elora and Tjaden murmured agreement. Twinkling with excitement, Lily said, "You're so lucky! I want to see the palaces, the Ladies, all the shops with the pretty gowns, and—"

Ollie interrupted. "And the drill grounds and the insides of the barracks and probably enough classrooms to make us wish we'd never heard of Elites."

In the short silence that followed, Tjaden stared at his feet and kicked a clump of grass. He was obviously nervous about something, probably training. The conversation from the day Captain Darieus visited came to mind, and she wondered if he really was happy to have her along.

He looked up suddenly as if he just came up with something to say. "So, seven days on the road. Have you ever travelled that far?"

"Lily and I have never been past Stevva," said Elora. "Father had to borrow a pack to fit all of our things."

"You got me beat," said Ollie. "I've barely seen the Telavir Spoke."

Another short silence followed, but it was the time of morning that did not need to be filled with words. Tjaden stuck his free hand in a pocket and looked at the stars. Elora found herself wishing that his hand was still out, holding hers maybe. She considered saying something to fill the space, but sharing the unease offered her a comfort of its own.

Horses moved into the silence before voices did.

"Can I ask you a favor, Elora?" said Tjaden quickly. He looked in the direction of the approaching horses.

"Of course," said Elora. She looked over her shoulder, but the horses weren't in view yet.

"I got a new sword." He held it up. "There's that tradition of asking a girl to . . . gird it. I thought, maybe . . ."

"I'd be honored," she said. That must be why he'd been nervous. She had no idea how to gird the sword, but loved the idea of figuring it out.

The horses and riders came around a corner. Elora turned and stood next to Tjaden to watch them pass. A full squadron of Elites entered the wabe, eight Elites with eight Fellows, all wearing a patch on their shoulder of a large snarling cat with scales like a snake. Her father had mentioned that Scaled Tiger Squadron would be the one escorting them. Their leader peeled off and dismounted near the fathers as the others rode past and stopped a short distance beyond.

Lily's act was perfect. If Elora didn't know better, she'd think Lily had never seen the soldiers. The night before, however, Lily had told her she was sneaking out to see them arrive. Elora's choices were to either tell her parents or go with her. So of course she had gone with Lily to watch them ride into town and stable their horses at the Dusty Tunic.

Two other men had arrived with the Elites. They rode at the rear of the procession on horses that stuck out like swans among ducks. They were taller and sleeker and carried their heads higher than the others. The men on their backs matched them for poise and pomp. The moonlight shimmered on silky fabric, and one of them wore a cloak with a fine white fur lining. Elora was surprised to see men wearing such elegant clothing. Judging by Lily's smile, she approved.

The taller of the two young men was handsome in an opulent way, with curly blond hair to his shoulders. He led his horse, a beautiful bay, to Elora's group and said a word she didn't understand. The horse knelt on its front legs and put its head down in a bow. The young man dismounted as gracefully as if it were a dance step. With a flourish of a cloak that looked as though it had never seen a road, he performed a bow of his own. When he stood and clicked his tongue, his horse stood up again.

"Pardon my surprise, m'ladies, but I did not expect to find a pair of lovely blossoms so early in the morning and in such a remote location."

Lily curtsied as if she'd been raised at court. Despite her cotton dress, the nicest she owned, it was believable. The tug of her scar told Elora she was smiling inside the hood of her cloak. She simply nodded.

"I am Rodín, son of Paradin, Viscount of the South Region of Verinalia Province."

"I'm Ollie, son of the wind and chum of this guy." He stuck a thumb over his shoulder. "Tjaden."

"Hello," said Tjaden, and offered his hand.

Rodín looked down his nose at Tjaden's hand before accepting it. The smirk said he was amused in the same way he would be at a court jester who had slipped in manure.

He might be nice to look at, but his disdain for Tjaden was as ugly as the treatment she'd received from some of her friends lately.

Two months ago, when I was still beautiful, would I have been so put off?

She hoped so.

When Rodín noticed the bow on Ollie's back, his expression changed. He scanned it from tip to tip and gave the slightest nod.

"This is Elora," said Tjaden. "And that's Lily."

"Fitting names for such beautiful creatures," said Rodín. He took a moment to inspect each of them as he had Ollie's bow. Elora resisted the urge to shy away, but Lily smiled and stood a little taller.

Tjaden cleared his throat. "Elora's going with us to Palassiren." He seemed as uncomfortable as Elora felt.

"A pair of blossoms would make the journey more scenic, but one is better than none." He bowed shortly, then turned his back to the girls. To Tjaden, he said, "I have not lost at fencing or jousting in over sixteen months, inter-Provincial contests included. Lieutenant Markin himself offered my invitation to the Academy. Tell them, Valdrin."

"It's true," said Rodín's companion. They resembled each other, Valdrin being older and shorter and not as handsome. Brothers, probably. "And that's to say nothing of the dressage competitions he's won."

"You wear dresses in competition?" asked Ollie. The sun wasn't even up and he'd already started taunting.

"I wouldn't expect a clodpile like you to be familiar with highborn diversions," said Valdrin.

"Now, now," said Rodín. "Manners."

"Yes, Sir," muttered Valdrin. He stepped sharply back a step.

"And you?" Rodín asked Tjaden.

"I used to grow oranges. Now I'm going to be an Elite. I think that's about it."

Elora opened her mouth to tell Rodín about the bandersnatch, but Tjaden said, "Excuse us for a minute. We were in the middle of something when you arrived." He didn't seem comfortable, but at least he was standing up to the haughty recruit.

With pride, Elora accepted the sword Tjaden held out.

"I'm not really sure how to do this," said Elora.

Tjaden shrugged. "First time for both of us." He raised his arms to allow her access to his waist.

"What are they doing?" asked Valdrin.

"Quiet," ordered Rodín. "It's fascinating how they attempt to mimic courtly traditions."

Elora ignored the arrogant peacocks. Looping the belt around Tjaden brought her up next to him. Even under the scrutiny of the nobles it was enjoyable. Comfortable. As she buckled the strap, she said, "May your sword be true and your arm be strong."

Before she had a chance to plant a kiss on Tjaden's cheek, the lieutenant called, "Mount up!" Everyone hurried to obey. Within minutes they were riding. Tjaden rode on her right and Rodín on her left. Lily sat side-saddle on the back of the horse Elora was riding until they reached their home. She dismounted and blew a kiss to the group—to Rodín—and waved until she was out of sight.

With the Elite recruits riding on either side of her, Elora felt like a proper Lady. As long as she had the hood up, anyway.

Ever since the night at the celebration she had waited for Tjaden to show more interest in her. But the days leading up to the trip were busy for all of them, and they'd barely been closer than casual friends. The gesture with the girding of the sword was a wonderful way to start the journey. She hoped she'd be able to find out more of his feelings for her on the seven days to Palassiren.

The streaming light from the morning sun switched from their backs to their sides as the group turned their horses onto the Telavir Spoke, one of eight main highways that ran from the capital to the edges of the kingdom like spokes on a wheel.

"What a relief to sleep in an—" Rodín paused midthought. He strained to see into Elora's hood. "Ahem, an inn, as I was saying. Notwithstanding the, er, the quaintness of it." He blinked and stared at Elora's left cheek. At her scar. "Valdrin," he said and fell back to ride with his brother. They chatted in tones too quiet for Elora to hear, then he called to Tjaden.

Tjaden smiled at her as he stole a glance before slowing his horse. He and Rodín spoke some quiet words, not many, then Rodín maneuvered to her right side. Tjaden, looking slightly confused, took the spot on her left that Rodín had vacated.

Rodín leaned forward far enough to see all the way into her cowl. With a nod, he muttered, "Yes. That's better."

Perfect, thought Elora. *Just when I thought I was free of small-minded people.* She wanted to give him a black eye, but couldn't live the rest of her life punching everyone who was revolted by her face.

So the morning went. The boy she wanted on her right side always riding on her left. The one she didn't care for, insisting on the right. Her pretty side.

As the sun set, the lieutenant called for a stop and the Elites began laying out tents. The tent she would share with her father was located dead center of a ring formed by the others—a gesture intended to protect the only girl in camp.

Tjaden as an Elite became more and more attractive to her as she witnessed the chivalrous attitude of the soldiers.

As Elora bent to help her father unroll the thin fabric of their tent, Tjaden snuck in and grabbed the roll. "We can do this," she said. "Go help with your own tent." She hoped he wouldn't listen.

"I know you can," said Tjaden. "That doesn't mean you should. Not when there are twenty strong men around to do it for you."

"I'll settle for one strong man," she said. With Tjaden's back to her she couldn't see his blush, but she knew it was there. Three times she picked up a stake, and three times Tjaden gently removed it from her hand. Her father wore a smile as he watched their interaction.

She didn't force the issue. If Tjaden was gentleman enough to treat her like a lady, she would be lady enough to let him.

In no time the small tent was pitched and the stakes pounded. Six weeks of doubting her value were being erased in a day by Tjaden's simple acts.

"Be right back," said Tjaden. "I'll see if they have some extra blankets."

"You don't have to," said Elora. "The grass is soft enough for me."

"Not for me," he said. "I mean, it's not soft enough for you for me. I mean—" His face reddened. "You ought to have a softer bed."

"I know what you mean," she said, and he walked off.

Elora was carrying her pack to the tent when Rodín fell in on her right side.

"It's pure barbarism to force a lady to sleep on the ground without cot or pallet."

"I'll be fine."

"You'll be bruised, most likely. Lieutenant Serrill should be embarrassed."

Not far away, Valdrin was working alone to set up a tent. Elora pulled back the flap of her tent and grunted as she set the heavy pack down.

"As a future Elite, I offer my most sincere apologies." The anger on Rodín's pretty face made him look pouty. "I'll have Valdrin bring his cot."

"You don't have to . . ." but Rodín was already walking away.

Elora set her pack inside the tent and opened it. As she was laying out her nightshirt she heard someone approach. It was Tjaden, carrying two thin blankets.

"This is the best I could do." He handed them to her.

"Blankets," said Valdrin as he approached carrying a folded cot. "A poor substitute for proper etiquette." He ducked into the tent and set up the cot. "Compliments of the Honorable Rodín."

Tjaden was scowling into the tent.

"It's a noble gesture," said Elora, "but I will be fine with blankets."

"The Honorable Rodín anticipated your refusal," said Valdrin. "If you will not sleep on it, I am to break the cot and use it as kindling."

It was absurd, but Elora didn't put it past the pompous brothers.

As gracefully as she could manage, she said, "Thank you. And please thank Rodín for me."

Valdrin walked off. Tjaden scowled at his back.

"I didn't ask them for that," said Elora.

"No, I'm glad you don't have to sleep on the ground." Tjaden looked at the blankets as if he was embarrassed. "Is there anything else you need, Elora?"

"You've already done plenty," she said.

He looked into her face and smiled. Elora gave him a moment to start a conversation or invite her to take a walk, but the dinner bell rang and they went that direction together in silence.

The next day of travel passed similar to the first. Apparently the recruits were not welcome to fraternize with the Elites. Mikel and Elora's father kept close company, leaving the five teenagers to ride as a group.

Elora tried to avoid Rodín but no matter where she rode, he maneuvered to her right side again. He could probably tip toe a horse through a field of dandelions without sending a single seed into the air.

Unlike the horse, who did things she wouldn't have thought possible, the rider was ill-mannered. But she couldn't bring herself to return rudeness. So she was stuck listening to his stories of hunting prowess, contest victories, and future achievements. Tjaden usually rode at her left side, sometimes Ollie. With Rodín there, Tjaden was close-mouthed and timid. Ollie had a knack at saying just the right thing to quiet Rodín and give her a little peace.

They arrived at Stevva, a town she had visited once before, and slept in an inn. Just after sunrise they were back in their saddles and Rodín was nattering in her ear again. Her right ear, of course. The weather turned gusty, then cold. She raised her hood, but it didn't slow Rodín down. He was already beginning to repeat things he'd already told her.

If only Lily had come along. Not only could she advise Elora on how to deal with the unwanted attention, she would have happily distracted Rodín, and Rodín wouldn't have to worry about which side of her he was riding on. The trip was supposed to be a time for Elora to get to know Tjaden better. Find out how deep his feelings for her went. But Tjaden was as closed up as a flytrap with Rodín around.

Girding the sword was a great start, and gave her a lot of hope. Tjaden was obviously nervous about asking her and even though it was rushed, the experience had been pleasant. It made her wish she had thought ahead and brought some token to give him that he could keep with him. Perhaps in Palassiren or a town along the way she could find something suitable.

They made camp early the third day near a clear, blue lake. Mountains on the far side of the lake rose even higher than the clouds, and the trees in this area were three times as tall as any she'd ever seen. Elora couldn't wait to look around for new and interesting herbs and plants.

Ollie and Mikel finished setting up their tent at the same time Tjaden and Elora's father finished. A couple hours of sunlight remained and Tjaden and Ollie stole off with their sword and bow. Elora followed them, hoping for a few minutes alone.

Tjaden was still warming up when she found him, swinging his sword in long, slow circles. She stayed back and watched as he transitioned into patterns with exact footwork. Tjaden made the sword look like it didn't weigh anything, but Elora had held it. It would take serious arm strength to keep up so long. From the times they had embraced, she knew he was strong. After the bandersnatch, and at his celebration. The memories made her smile. Hopefully before they said farewell they would have more chances to be so close.

If I wasn't so ugly, Tjaden would probably—

Suddenly Tjaden was standing still, staring at her, catching his breath. He smiled, that shy smile that always seemed to appear when he saw her. Without looking down at his waist, he slid the sword into its sheath and walked toward her.

"Don't let me stop you," she said,

"I've got fourteen months to work on this," Tjaden said, still breathing heavy.

Elora sat down on a dirt embankment and patted the ground to her right. Tjaden acted like he didn't care about her scars, but she'd rather have him look at her pretty side. He sat, and they watched Ollie take aim with an arrow at circles of bark he'd hung from a tree with twine. The arrow flew from his hand and sunk into one of the chunks of bark.

"He loves that bow," said Tjaden.

"Looks like he's pretty good," Elora said.

"Not bad. The question is, will he stick with it long enough to become great?"

Now that they finally had a minute alone, Elora did not want to talk about Ollie.

Ollie hit another target and Tjaden said, "The real reason he's not missing is because he's too lazy to chase the arrows if they go past his targets."

Elbowing him in the side, she said, "Why are boys always so mean to each other?"

Tjaden smiled an easy smile, more relaxed than the one she was used to. He shrugged. "Makes us tough, I guess. I hope he does become great. Might save my life one day."

"Let's hope it never comes to that," Elora said. Mikel's bow was handy against the bandersnatch, but Tjaden would have saved her even if Mikel hadn't shown up.

"I'm glad we finally got a minute alone," Tjaden said. He stuck a hand into his pocket and fumbled around.

"Me too."

Tjaden pulled his hand out of his pocket in a fist and held it like that, not looking at her. After a minute he finally turned and looked her square in the face. Elora was tempted to turn her scars away from him, but he held her gaze.

"Elora," he said, and his eyes flicked past her. With a heavy sigh he dropped his eyes.

She glanced back to see what had deterred him.

Rodín.

Without horses to maneuver he couldn't squeeze between them. Rather than sit at her left, Rodín sat on the far side of Tjaden. It was all she could do to stay there and listen.

"Before I decided to be an Elite," said Rodín, "I was quite the archer. I have been using a man's bow since I was only eleven."

"Ollie's just starting," said Tjaden, "but he's got some natural talent."

"Such things need to be taught from boyhood. He'll never be better than middling."

Tjaden didn't reply.

Elora rolled her eyes. She couldn't sit any longer with Rodín showing by his position what he thought of her. She couldn't listen to Tjaden stay silent while the pompous donkey made sure everyone around him knew they were inferior. Even if Tjaden preferred to show instead of talk, she couldn't take it anymore. And it might be asking too much, but she wanted him to teach Rodín a lesson about manners and how girls should be treated. A lesson taught with words or fists, not by example.

There was no point in staying and growing more frustrated with both of them. If Tjaden had something important to say to her—or give her—he better get to it in the next four days.

She cleared her throat, stood up, and straightened her herbal belt. "If you'll excuse me."

Tjaden and Rodín stood when she did, but they didn't follow. As she paralleled the tree line toward camp, she spotted a patch of itch oak. Lifting her divided skirts to keep them clear, she ducked under some branches for a closer look. Whitehock, the best pain reliever she knew of, often grew close to itch oak. She never passed up an opportunity to harvest it.

With a stick, she pushed the itch oak leaves back, but didn't see any whitehock. The frustration she felt went beyond the lack of whitehock. At least she had something to take her mind off of everything else. She tried the next clump. Nothing. Deeper into the trees she went, checking patch after patch after patch. By the time she spotted the first bunch of whitehock, it was too dark too see whether it was ripe. Keeping the itch oak at bay with her stick, she reached for the whitehock.

A rumble, like a huge rock rolling down hill, shook the ground. Elora looked around. She was alone with that huge

noise and whatever had caused it. If it was an animal, it was bigger than any she'd ever seen.

She ran. With no concern for her skirts or herbs or how bad she would suffer later that night, she ran. No glances behind, no care for the path she had taken. The nearest light was seconds away. It felt like days.

As soon as she burst out of the trees she looked behind her. The only movement came from branches settling back into place. The rumble had moved farther away.

She got her bearings and didn't wait to catch her breath before starting along the steep embankment to where she had started.

The boys would be on the other side of the long mound of dirt. She considered calling to them, but remembered her frustration. Soon enough she would be safe at camp. The twang and thump of Ollie's bow told her that her bearings were correct. Voices followed.

The first words she understood were, "A bandersnatch? In truth?" It was Rodín.

"Yes," said Tjaden. "Meaner and faster than you can imagine."

Elora leaned closer, anxious to hear him brag about himself and maybe even her. Hopefully, her name would come up and she could find out what he really thought about her. If she was going to wait fourteen months for him, she deserved his candid opinion.

"A pity she was left with such terrible scars," said Rodín.

No surprise there. At least Tjaden had to defend her now.

"I know," said Tjaden, "Sometime I feel sick when I think about them. Like I've been gut hit with a staff."

When she heard that, Elora felt like she'd been hit in the gut herself. That explained all his attention to her—pity. Making himself feel better was what he cared about, not her. How could he? The pain moved from her gut to her chest. Tjaden was just like everyone else. He saw her scars and pitied her for being ugly. Lily would tell her to get away, to not let words like those into her ears. She took her absent sister's advice and hurried away.

"A terrible shame," said Rodín as she tried to outrun their words. "She might be attractive without . . ."

She left the biting words on the path behind her. And the tears that stung like the bandersnatch's claws. But there were always more to take their place. Tears in her eyes, words in her ears, lies and betrayal in her mind. Even after plunging into her dark tent she still felt ugly.

Her scars made Tjaden sick? Why would he squander their time and her hope with so much attention?

Rodín and his condescension weren't hard to put up with, but she cared about Tjaden, thought they had a long, happy future together. But she could never spend her life with someone who pitied her and got sick just looking at her.

Was there anyone in the world besides Lily that could see her without seeing the scars? The tears grew more powerful, racking her chest and stealing her breath. Elora didn't want to go on, not without Lily. But she did the only thing she could. She sobbed alone, not wishing this time that her sister had come along, but that she herself had stayed behind.

When someone tapped a knuckle on the post of the tent, she forced herself to quiet and take a breath.

"It's me." Her father. "Are you all right?"

She couldn't answer, and when he cracked open one of the tent flaps, she started sobbing again. "What happened?" His fists were clenched, and so was his face.

Shouting came from another part of the camp. Aker looked back over his shoulder.

"Daddy?" She hadn't called him that in years. When he looked in she said, "Are we safe?"

"Yes. It looks like the boys might be in some trouble, though."

Even if she cared about them at the moment, it wouldn't outweigh the crushing fear and sadness.

"Now, what is it?" he asked.

"I know I shouldn't care what people say about me." She held her breath to block the tears, but eventually lost the fight.

"Who was it?" It wasn't like him to be so quick to anger.

"There is no justice in revenge," she managed to say, repeating the words he had said to Lily so many times.

"I don't know how much I believe that right now," he said. After a few moments, he added in a softer voice, "What can I do?"

"Sit here?"

"Sure."

"Careful." She sniffed and wiped her nose on her sleeve. "I ran through itch oak. It's already starting to sting."

He stepped back and let the flaps close. "I'm right outside, Lora. Change into your nightclothes and I'll have someone take care of your skirts."

"Thanks," she said. "Ollie. If you can find him." Tjaden would volunteer, even act happy to do it, but whatever reasons he had for tagging after her, it wasn't because he cared for her. Other than her father, and probably Mikel, she only had one true friend in the camp.

She changed clothes and waited until she heard Ollie's voice outside. "Hello? Elora? It's Ollie."

"Sorry to take you away from your bow practice."

"I wasn't practicing. We were with the lieutenant."

She resisted the urge to ask if everyone was safe. "Can you soak these in the lake?" She pushed her skirts through the flaps. "They've got itch oak on them. Be careful. Only touch the waist."

"Is that all? Do you need me to find any of that jewel stuff?"

"No, I've got some here." Jewel weed was the best antidote for just about any rash. "I'll get my skirts when we leave in the morning. Thanks, Ollie."

Her father came back into the tent and sat on his bedroll while Elora applied jewel weed oil to her ankles. If only there was a salve that could soothe the hives on her heart.

"Do you want to . . . talk or something?" asked her father.

"I don't think so." After a pause she added, "I'm glad you're here, but I wish Lily was too." *I wish I was back there.*

He rubbed his chin. He'd never been one for talking. "I'll just stay here, then. I was thinking of turning in early anyway. If you need anything, I'm right here."

With him there, everything—life, the world, the lies—was bearable. Tears still threatened when her mind started down dangerous paths. Before settling in to try to sleep she repeated the application of jewel weed oil.

The night was restless. Rumblings like the one she'd heard in the forest came again and again, whether real or imagined. Huge and heavy, like a mountain had sprouted legs and started walking. In one nightmare, kids from Shey's Orchard turned into bandersnatches and chased her. Tjaden ran with her, but every time he looked at her face he clutched his stomach and turned green.

Half a dozen times she pulled back the flap to let in moonlight so she could make sure her father was still there.

"I'm right here," he said every time.

She lay back down and tried to sleep. Even the bad dreams were better than being awake, until one dream late in the dawn. She was trying to hide her scars from Tjaden but he insisted on looking at them. When she refused, he grabbed her shoulders and shook her.

"Lora," she heard. Her eyes flew open and she realized it was her father gently shaking her awake. "Grab your cloak and come with me."

The sky was light in the east only. They stopped at the cook's post, and Aker picked up a couple of oranges and some hard biscuits. He said a few words to one of the soldiers that Elora couldn't hear. They walked to the Telavir Spoke, and she slipped her arm into his. After walking a short distance, they stopped alongside the road at a spot where no trees blocked the view on the side opposite their camp. He sat and she sat next to him.

Her father offered her an orange, but the thought of eating it made her feel too much like she had the evening before. She nibbled on a biscuit and waited for her father to explain.

The pre-sunrise revealed land that stretched farther than

her eyesight did. Trees and tall dark mountains with wispy clouds. The only blemish in the landscape was a pool of green water half a mile away. It was the same color as Tjaden's sick face from one of her nightmares.

"I was up most of the night," said her father. "Wishing there was something I could do or something I could say. The sublieutenant showed this to me and Mikel yesterday. I hope it speaks for itself. It's all I have. I'm sure your mother or Lily could help you, but . . . anyway." He turned to his orange.

The view was majestic. Light dispelled the morning mists and brought out the blues and purples of the mountains. Birds took to the skies, some appearing to be soaring simply because they could. Elora almost felt as though everything would be fine eventually.

"Look," said her father, pointing. "A saccharox."

At the edge of a small meadow a large shaggy animal with a white head was grazing. It left a trail of fine white mist in the grass wherever it bent its head. Four more sacchraroxen grazed into the clearing. Supposedly their breath was sweet enough to stun predators. She'd heard it could knock a man unconscious.

That couldn't be what her father wanted her to see. The green pool maybe? It looked rotten, and even the soil around it was blanched and barren. It must have been poisoned.

After a while, sounds of camp being broken mingled with early morning birdcalls.

"Shouldn't we help at camp?" she asked.

"No, I've taken care of it. I don't know how long this will take, but we need to stay here."

For longer than a while, Elora studied the scenery. The pool and the barren ground around it began to stand out so prominently that she could barely see the beauty of everything else. The rest of the panorama was perfect, but she couldn't see past the one blemish on the landscape.

The wagons started down the road, followed not much later by the men and horses. Elora didn't turn to look, afraid of what might show on her face if she saw the wrong person. Twice her father motioned someone to keep going. When it sounded like they'd all gone, Elora peeked over her shoulder. One Elite and one Fellow waited up the road with two extra horses.

The rumble started, far off. Elora seized her father's arm and looked around. The noise and tremble were growing closer, but he was calm. The soldiers didn't react. Birds continued to fly and the saccharoxen munched.

As if thunder passed under them, the earth-shudder came and went, traveling toward the putrid pond. An explosion of water into the air forced a shriek from her mouth. A pillar of water rose a hundred feet into the air. Maybe two hundred. Feathers of mist fanned out. The first sunbeams of the day collided with the mists, creating rainbows that darted like hummingbirds. It was all the beauty of a flower's life, compressed into one minute.

Elora realized she'd been holding a hand over her open mouth. As tears ran down her face, the water misted to the ground. The water in the pool appeared as clean and blue as any she'd ever seen. Then the blue waters ran from the pool, leaving it as it had been. The water wasn't stagnant after all. It just appeared so because of the discolored earth.

Rays from the sun breached the mountain and spilled into the pool, illuminating it like a living emerald.

All that beauty from what looked like nothing more than an ugly scar on the earth.

A different kind of tears filled her eyes as she stood. Her father stood as well and looked down to see if she'd understood.

Elora could only nod. The sound of birdsong rang in the air. If her throat hadn't been full of emotion, she would have sung along. The beautiful view, the beautiful memories, the beautiful scar.

The girl, the beautiful girl, finally understood.

Tjaden rode with his father and Ollie behind four Elites that separated them from Rodín and Valdrin. In addition to sentry duty every night and bread and water rations, they'd been ordered to stay away from each other.

Something had made Elora mad, and Tjaden had a strong feeling that he was the cause of it.

"You didn't say anything to her?" Ollie asked.

"No," said Tjaden. "Rodín sat down and started talking about what a great archer he used to be, and I told him you were new to the bow."

"Not that new," said Ollie.

"You never took it seriously until you got that one."

"Yeah, but Mikel gave me some lessons."

"How long ago?" asked Tjaden.

"A few years."

"Exactly. Anyway, she walked off, and I think she was angry, but I don't know why."

"Is that why the fight started?"

"No." Thinking about it made Tjaden want to hit Rodín again. "He started bragging about hunting bears. He asked if I'd ever seen one and I said no, but me and Elora were attacked by a bandersnatch and we had to fight it off."

"Glad you finally said something," said Ollie.

"I don't know if he believed me, but he started talking about Elora's scars and I told him that I feel sick about what happened to her." It took effort to force out the next words. "Because it's my fault she has them."

"Could have been a lot worse, son." Tjaden's father said.

"Yeah, if you hadn't showed up," said Tjaden. "Anyway, he said the scars made her look ugly and it was too bad. I said, 'That's not what I meant. It's my fault it got to her.' And then he said, 'That doesn't mean you're stuck with her.'"

"Doesn't sound like something you'd start a fight over," said Tjaden's father.

"That wasn't when I hit him. I wanted to, but it got worse. I told him to stop talking about her, and I told him I meant it."

"But he didn't," said Ollie.

"He started to leave, but then he turned around and said, 'Play now if you like, but soon you'll be an Elite. I'd hate to see a brother of mine settle for damaged merchandise.' So I hit him."

"He deserved worse than a broken nose," said Tjaden's father.

"I was tempted to draw my sword," said Tjaden. He rubbed his jaw and stretched it. "If he's half the swordsman he says he is, that could have ended very badly for me."

In addition to the sore jaw, Tjaden had a black eye and some bruised knuckles from a few good shots he'd gotten in.

"Did Elora say anything to you, Ollie?"

"Not really."

"Well, son, I wouldn't worry too much. Women always react unpredictably when it comes to fighting. Give her a little while."

Tjaden hoped it didn't take too long. It had taken three days to get five minutes alone with her. In another four days they'd be at Palassiren.

Ollie tapped Tjaden's arm. "What's Lieutenant Serrill doing up there?"

The lieutenant was talking to Rodín and Valdrin, who were glancing over their shoulders in Tjaden's direction. The conversation didn't last long before the lieutenant left them and rode up to Tjaden.

"I've had a stroke of genius. The punishments I gave last night were drivel. Poorly thought out, with no correlation to your offense. How much more fitting would it be for you and Recruit Rodín to spend some time getting to know one other?"

Tjaden suppressed a groan. Out of the corner of his eye, Tjaden saw Ollie raise a hand to hide a smirk.

Lieutenant Serrill leveled his grey eyes on Tjaden. "Your new punishment is to stay close to him."

"Yes, Sir," said Tjaden. "How close? And for how many days?"

"Until neither of you has a bruise to show for your stupidity." Lieutenant Serrill snapped. "And close enough that when one of you farts, the other better be the first to smell it."

The lieutenant turned his horse to go back to the head of the formation and the three from Shey's Orchard followed him. Tjaden was tempted to ask Lieutenant Serrill if anything had happened to Elora, but the timing was wrong. Elora's father had waved him on when he tried to stop and talk to them. Tjaden may have imagined it, but the mirror maker's gaze had felt unfriendly.

Tjaden fell in next to Rodín, but neither one looked at the other. Tjaden thought about apologizing, but he couldn't bring himself to do it after what Rodín had said. By the midday stop, they still hadn't spoken to each other. The only glimpses he'd seen of Elora were over his shoulder to where she rode at the rear of the formation with Aker. She appeared healthy enough, but she wouldn't make eye contact with him.

The company stayed at an inn that night. After getting their things settled in their room, Tjaden spoke to Rodín.

"I need to talk to Elora." He wouldn't subject her to Rodín for long, but he had to know how she was.

Because of the swollen nose and bruises under his eyes, Rodín's smile showed none of the usual handsomeness. His stuffed-up voice didn't affect his arrogant bearing, however.

"Your needs are not my concern," He sneered. "Neither is your unsightly woman."

Tjaden clenched his fists and his jaw and stepped chest to chest with the dandy. Ollie was there immediately, pulling Tjaden away.

With an ugly laugh Rodín said, "Do you think I need this? I am the son of a Viscount. I could go home today and live a hundred times happier than you."

How could anyone give up after the work it took to be accepted to the Academy?

"You're the second son. You won't be able to command your older brother anymore."

Valdrin's eyebrows went up, but Rodín just shrugged. "No, but I'll have 10,000 yokels like you to command. So go find your horrid girl. I doubt I'll get dismissed along with you, but if I do, it's no skin off my back."

Tjaden shrugged off Ollie's grip and turned away from Rodín. It wasn't worth risking his Academy invitation. He still had three days until Palassiren. He'd just have to find a way to talk to her in that time.

Drizzly rain was falling when they started traveling the next morning. It was still falling when they stopped at midday and while they set up camp at sunset.

As Tjaden helped Ollie and Valdrin unroll their tent, he noticed Elora and Mirrorer Aker slowly getting their tent laid out while trying to stay covered from the rain. The entire camp was in for a miserable night, and if Elora and her father could ever use a hand, it was setting up a wet tent in the middle of a wet field.

"I'm going to help Elora and Aker with their tent," Tjaden said.

"Be my guest," said Rodín. "I'm staying right here." He was bundled in a thick cloak, watching the others work. Their punishment had included sleeping arrangements as well.

It was too far to go without Rodín and every Elite in camp would see them separated from each other.

"Ollie," said Tjaden, "Would you mind helping them? Tell her I'm stuck here."

"Sure thing," said Ollie. "You two behave while I'm gone."

Elora smiled when Ollie walked up. After a few words, Elora waved at Tjaden. The hood of her cloak obscured the expression on her face. He kept an eye on them as he helped Valdrin. Ollie was chatting like usual, and Elora laughed a few times. When the mirrorer's tent was up, Aker ducked inside with their packs. Elora stayed outside and talked to Ollie.

Standing in the rain and watching them felt awkward, so Tjaden climbed into his tent and lay down on his bedroll against one wall. It already smelled like wet, stinky men.

Rodín was dressing on the other side of the small tent. He said to Valdrin, "Give me some cotton for my ears so I don't have to listen to the farm boy cry himself to sleep."

Tjaden ignored him. He had more important things to worry about. Time was running out. If he only knew what he'd done wrong he could try to fix it. Could Elora really be so mad at him because of the fight? He thought about the conversation before she had stormed off, but couldn't think of anything that might have offended her.

Ollie's voice brought Tjaden out of a shallow daydream. "You want some food, Jay?" he said through the tent flap.

"No." What he wanted was to hear what Elora had said.

"Be back in a bit."

It seemed much longer than a bit.

When Ollie returned, he took his time outside the tent shaking off as much rain as he could. Droplets still splashed everyone in the tent when Ollie ducked in.

"My dog shakes better than you," said Rodín, patting the water off his face.

"I wish he was here," replied Ollie. "He probably *smells* better than you."

Tjaden asked, "What did Elora say?"

"You are pitiful," said Rodín to Tjaden.

"Biddiful?" asked Ollie in a nasal voice as he sat down and handed Tjaden an apple.

Tjaden ignored the banter "Well?"

"Nothing," said Ollie.

"She said *something*."

"Ok," said Ollie. "She said she's fine, and I believe her because she seems like it."

"One only has to look at her to see she's not fine," said Rodín.

Tjaden took a slow breath. Things would only get worse if he broke Rodín's nose again. He asked Ollie, "What do you mean?"

"She seems happier than any of us," said Ollie, "but that makes sense, considering the company she has the luxury of avoiding."

"Hick," said Rodín.

"At least I don't dress like a woman."

"What do you mean, 'she seems happy'?"

Ollie looked at Tjaden. "I wouldn't have gone if I'd known there was going to be a test. I don't know, she was humming when I walked up—"

"What song?"

Rodín put his hands in the air and said, "Oh, Lieutenant Serrill, how could you know the torture to which you were subjecting me?"

"Seriously," said Ollie. "I'm starting to agree with Lord Fancy Pants. Look, she said her and Aker are planning to ride with us again tomorrow."

That was the best news in days. Tjaden was ready to let the subject drop.

Rodín had other plans. He sat up on his cot and said, "I'll explain this once more for the benefit of dim, rural minds: An Elite uniform turns a man of average handsomeness—" he paused and looked pointedly down his nose at Tjaden, "—or below average, into a creature of immense allure to any person of the female variety. If you do succeed at the Academy (which I doubt, but for the sake of argument I will concede), you will have your choice of a thousand women who are not damaged."

Tjaden rose to his knees and stared at Rodín. He could feel his face burning and his hands automatically clenched into fists.

"He's taunting you," said Ollie. He knelt in front of Tjaden even though they both knew he couldn't stop Tjaden. "Keep biting and he'll keep baiting."

Tjaden wanted to knock the teeth out of Rodín's smug smirk. But Ollie was right. It would only make Rodín's taunting worse. Tjaden thought about what he wanted more than anything: to make things right with Elora and become an Elite. Starting another fight would take him further from his goals.

Ollie pulled a strip of dried meat from under his cloak and pressed it into Tjaden's chest.

"Thanks," muttered Tjaden, taking it and laying back on his bedroll. He closed his eyes and let his jaws take his frustration out on the tough meat.

The next morning, shortly after they started on the road, Elora and Aker led their horses to where Tjaden rode next to Rodín. A morning ray of sunlight broke through the clouds and her cowl. The small smile and bright brown eyes made Tjaden forget about the pain of the previous two days. Ollie was right. She held her head higher than she had in weeks, and her smile was full of confidence.

With Aker riding on Elora's right side, the only place near her was on her left. Tjaden worked his reins to make the horse take the spot, but Rodín was infinitely more skilled on horseback. His tall bay pranced in a backward diagonal directly to Elora's side. It seemed to take about as much effort as a yawn.

After an embarrassing display with his horse, Tjaden ended up on Rodín's left, forced to lean past him if he wanted to talk to Elora.

Tjaden wanted to say something thoughtful and intelligent, but he had to hurry before Rodín started talking. "Morning. Glad you're back."

Rodín gave Tjaden a quick smirk that made him feel like he'd said something stupid, then turned to Elora and said, "M'lady." He gave a small bow with his head. "The past days have been dark without you to brighten it for us."

That's what Tjaden wanted to say, exactly how he felt, but he'd never be able to think of anything that good. It was going to be impossible to really talk to her with Rodín around.

Elora greeted them both with a polite smile. She seemed to sit as tall as any of them. It reminded Tjaden of how she was before the bandersnatch. He was glad to see it, but didn't know how to tell her without offending her.

"How has the traveling been?" Tjaden asked.

"Quite enlightening, actually," she said.

"Don't be absurd," said Rodín. "The lady has borne up exceedingly well, but the treatment she has received is appalling."

"I am neither brittle nor soft," she said. "My strength and worth lie as deep as any man's."

A week before Tjaden would have expected her to glance away or absently touch her scars, but her hands remained in her lap, holding the reins loosely. Tjaden agreed entirely and tried to think of a way to say so without sounding insincere.

Rodín spoke first. "Is it difficult being in the open air?"

"No, I've enjoyed it," said Elora. "I wish I knew more about the herbs of this region, though"

Sounding puzzled, Rodín asked, "So the light, the people, being out of doors does not terrify you?"

"No. Why would it?" Elora mirrored Rodín's confusion.

"I feel I owe you an apology, m'lady." Rodín cleared his throat and made as formal a bow as the saddle allowed. "I have relied on what my fellow recruit told me about you."

"What!" demanded Tjaden. He felt his legs tense, ready to spring off his horse and tackle Rodín from his saddle. But another fight would just upset Elora all over again, so Tjaden forced himself to relax.

Rodín turned his confused face and his outstretched palms to Tjaden. "The hood. The scars. The attacks of panic."

"That's not what I—" He felt like he'd been hit in the face with a hornet's nest. "I didn't say anything like that!"

"It sounds like you two have plenty to discuss," said Elora. "If you will excuse me." She calmly pulled her horse to a stop. Aker angled his to block Tjaden's view of her. He glared at Tjaden, fiercely and full of disappointment.

"Elora, it's not true!"

Rodín kept moving, and conjoined as they were by the lieutenant's orders, Tjaden allowed his horse to keep pace. If he disobeyed, he could be dismissed from the Academy before even arriving. He'd have to sort everything out with Elora later, when Rodín wasn't there.

But the things she might believe about him. The poisonous seeds Rodín had planted. The daggers Aker stared at him. Her voice when she said, "If you will excuse me."

That's what she said last time.

Tjaden felt wounded on the inside as badly as the bandersnatch had done to his arms. The injury wasn't physical, but the pain might as well have been. He couldn't put up with it another minute.

Tjaden spurred his horse with both heels, almost falling out of the saddle when the horse shot forward like an arrow.

JABBERWOCKY

He reigned hard to the right and came around sharply. Away from the Academy was the wrong direction, but finally he felt like he was going the right way.

The words Rodín said as Tjaden passed him couldn't penetrate the shell of resolve. Even Aker's frown didn't slow him down.

"Elora," he said. "I have to tell you the truth."

Aker's jaw moved, but his lips were clenched tight.

"It's okay, Daddy. I can do this."

After another warning look, Aker rode on. Tjaden pulled the pouch from his pocket and gripped it in his closed fist. Whether he was able to give it to her or not, it might help him explain how he felt.

"I have to tell you how I feel. The truth." He led his horse so he was close enough to see into the shadows of her cloak.

Elora reached up with both hands and lowered her hood. Five days on the road hadn't diminished her beauty. He was about to tell her that, but she spoke instead. "Let me talk first, Tjaden. I heard what you told Rodín before your little fight. You made it very clear how you feel about me. We should stop pretending that you feel the same about me as I do about you. I've given up on things I thought were as sure as the sunrise. I think you should do the same. Anything else you say will just make it more difficult." And then, with the poise of a queen and a smile full of pity, she rode past him.

Words failed him. Tjaden could do nothing but stare after her.

"Hey, boy," said an approaching Elite. "Where's your twin?"

Tjaden didn't even look at the soldier.

Elora knew? Of course she knew. She had to know. But after all the hope she had given him, why was she rejecting him now? Something had changed. Somehow, he was not the man she wanted.

"Back to your post, recruit," the soldier barked.

She knew how he felt. And she did not feel the same. He never claimed to know anything about how girls thought, but how had he misinterpreted her so completely? Maybe it had something to do with Rodín. She had seen that there was more out there than simple town boys.

He would not embarrass himself or Elora by saying anything else. She had made her decision.

Two Elites rode toward him out of nowhere. One passed on each side, and they slid their arms under his, dragging him out of his saddle. They carried him like a child between them. Right past Elora.

He looked away from her. Even though Elora didn't feel the same, she was the girl he loved and he hated being humiliated in front of her.

The Elites did not stop until they caught up with Rodín, who had continued as if nothing had happened. They dropped Tjaden next to Rodín's horse, and he fell onto his backside in the muddy road. Rodín sneered at him. Tjaden looked away and noticed his father and Ollie had stopped to see what was happening. The shame was ten times worse than losing at the Swap and Spar. He forced himself to stand even though he wanted to wallow in his misery.

The Fellow continued on while the Elite pulled his horse up to face Rodín. "Is something funny?" he demanded.

"No," said Rodín.

"Where are you going?" asked the Elite.

"With the camp."

"Do you think it's wise to leave your favorite soldier behind?"

"No, I was just—"

"I didn't ask for excuses, recruit! You'll explain it to the lieutenant."

Seeing Rodín humiliated was a small victory, but any pleasure Tjaden felt disappeared when Elora and Aker rode past. Tjaden kept his eyes off of them. From the corner of his vision, it appeared they were keeping their gazes on the road ahead of them.

The storm of the previous day was nothing compared to the storm in Lieutenant Serrill's grey eyes when he rode up. He looked at Ollie and Valdrin. "You two are dismissed. Continue marching."

They didn't wait to be to be told again.

"Grower Mikel," said the lieutenant. "If I may speak with these boys in private."

"Of course." Looking at Tjaden, he slowly shook his head and turned his horse.

Lieutenant Serrill didn't wait for any of them to be out of earshot. "You must have a remarkable nose, Rodín."

"I'm afraid I don't understand."

"Don't understand or don't know how to follow orders?"

"Sir?"

"How are you going to smell this recruit's farts from up there on your high horse?"

Rodín grimaced. "He rode off without warning."

"Why didn't you follow?"

"He seemed intent on being a nuisance to the young lady. I did not wish to impose on her."

"Is that an excuse or a lie?"

Rodín wasn't stupid enough to respond, but his eyes narrowed as he stared back. In nineteen years of life, he'd probably never been spoken to like that.

Lieutenant Serrill must have noticed the arrogance because he kept pushing. "Are you waiting for Tjaden to join you in the saddle?"

A frumious bandersnatch was less red than Rodín's face as he dismounted and stood at Tjaden's side.

"Obviously," said Lieutenant Serrill, "this is regarding the young lady."

"No," said Tjaden. The word came out before he could bite it off.

"Hm. You two are more alike than I realized. Not only do you lack the ability to follow orders, you both have the same lying tongue."

Rodín didn't pass up the opportunity to slander Tjaden. "It was regarding the girl, Sir. He did not want me to talk to her. He said, 'What's the point of being an Elite if you can't impress girls?'"

"That's a lie!" said Tjaden. "Recruit Rodín—"

"Enough bickering," snapped Lieutenant Serrill. "I was unaware that they now accepted girls into the ranks of the Elites. And he is Rodín, not Recruit Rodín. You have both lost the right to that title unless Captain Darieus or Lieutenant Markin decides to reinstate it after I've delivered you. The Circle and the Sword does not give you license to swagger and try to impress women. Captain Darieus is going to regret inviting her to the induction ceremony."

As much as he wanted to, Tjaden couldn't regret having her along. The chance to be so close to her for seven days was worth almost anything, even with the unhappy results.

The Fellow who had ridden off in search of Lieutenant Serrill returned, holding two pairs of shackles.

"Put them on," said Lieutenant Serrill.

Tjaden reached for a pair, but Rodín objected. "I assure you that is not necess—"

"For once in your life, follow an order, you over-prissed peacock!"

It took a few breath's time for Rodín to decide to obey, but he eventually accepted the metal chain from the Fellow.

One of Tjaden's shackles was in place and he held his arm up for the Fellow to lock it. He began to put the other in place, but Lieutenant Serrill said, "Just one."

On the spectrum of unusual punishments, dragging an empty shackle around ranked only medium. When Rodín had one shackle around a wrist, Lieutenant Serrill told the Fellow, "Link the other shackles together. If the boys can't follow orders, we will force them to stay near each other."

The Fellow wore an amused smirk as he locked the empty shackles around each other, giving Tjaden and Rodín about five feet of chain between them. "They will stay in place until we reach the training grounds."

"That's not—" said Rodín, but thought better of whatever he was about to say and shut his mouth.

"Sir," said Tjaden. It was worth taking the risk. "May I have permission to remove it to practice the sword in camp?"

"Are you going to practice on Rodín?"

"No, Sir."

"Very well, then. It may help you focus and release some tension in a healthy way for a change." The Fellow handed Lieutenant Serrill the key. "March."

Rodín looked around. "Where's his horse? Sir." The tone of voice was the same one he'd use on a servant.

"You'll find it at the Hopps Inn tonight if you can find a way to get to Borca. And no more problems. I've been more lenient than I've had to." He rode toward the front of the column.

"We can either walk or we can ride double on your stallion," said Tjaden. He had no more fight in him.

Rodín made a choking noise. "I'll carry him on my back before I allow him to carry you."

Tjaden started walking, followed by Rodín who was followed by the horse.

The stallion seemed to be the only one content with how the morning had turned out.

Tjaden and Rodín walked into the Hopps Inn well after dark. Borca was a city twenty times the size of Shey's Orchard,

but it was too late to see anything more than its lights. They spread out for miles, blending in with the stars on the horizon. They had walked through the midday break just to catch up to the others. Rodín remained stubborn regarding his horse, even when the weight of the shackle made Tjaden's arm feel twice as long as the other. After lunch they quickly fell behind the rest of the group, except for one Elite and one Fellow who stayed behind, probably to make sure Tjaden didn't strangle Rodín.

The Fellow unlocked the shackle in the dayroom of the Hopps Inn. Rodín went off toward the room while Tjaden went outside. The inn was located next to the wabe, which offered plenty of room to safely swing a sword. After doing some slow warm-ups, Tjaden let loose, vigorously performing the few forms he knew. After the weight of the shackle, his right arm didn't last long so he switched to the left. When his left was exhausted, he used both arms. It didn't take long for both to grow too heavy to lift the sword.

Behind him, someone said, "Hark how heavy his hatchet hangs." Ollie stood there next to Tjaden's father.

"This is called a *sword*, Ollie. A Fellow should probably know that."

"Aren't you tired from walking?" asked his father.

"No. More frustrated than anything. Did you see the city?"

"No," said Ollie. "We arrived with an extra hour, so he was teaching me everything he knows about archery."

"I did that in the first five minutes," said Tjaden's father.

A silence settled, but Ollie dispelled it. "Unless either of you need something, my belly needs seeing to."

"Grab some chow for me," said Tjaden. "I'll be in soon."

When Ollie walked away, Tjaden's father said, "Are you . . . is everything all right?"

It was, but it wasn't. "I don't know. I thought me and Elora might, you know? It just seemed so, well so much like . . ." He stopped, defeated. Was there even a way to say what he wanted to? Would his father even understand? He'd never given advice about girls and he probably wouldn't start now. "Training. That's all I have to worry about now."

His father nodded. After some time he said, "I suppose that's a good way to look at it."

Tjaden sheathed his sword.

"What about Rodín?"

Tjaden groaned and slumped onto the grass. "Smother him in his sleep, maybe?"

A small smile played momentarily on his father's lips. "Did you ever hear Jolan talk about enemies? Something like, 'When you start digging your enemy's grave, he's not using his own shovel to plant flowers.'"

"Yeah," said Tjaden. "I always thought it was a strange thing for a soldier to say."

His father shrugged. "I guess there's more than one way to beat your enemy."

"We shouldn't even be enemies," said Tjaden. "We both want to be Elites."

Some crickets chirped and a toad croaked. Sitting in the grass and the quiet with his father, worn out after a long day, life almost felt normal.

"Thanks," said Tjaden.

"You done out here?"

"Not yet."

He nodded and gave Tjaden's shoulder a small squeeze before walking back to the inn. Tjaden stood and tried the weight of the sword. It had lightened to a heftable level again. He held the wavy blade up in front of him to admire it in the moonlight. In the distance beyond the sword, in a window of the inn, he saw the outline of a girl or woman. Or young woman. Short. No, petite. Watching him?

You're imagining things. Gonna make yourself go mad over things that are in your head but not hers.

He forced his eyes away from the window as he exhausted each arm again.

The following day, Tjaden was allowed to ride. Both he and Rodín still wore bruises from their fight and still wore shackles. The only glimpses Tjaden got of Elora were faraway ones. The shackles between him and Rodin might as well have been a brick wall for the attention they paid each other. Tjaden was allowed sword practice again that night, but he didn't last as long as the night before.

His exhaustion was a sign that his body was obeying and learning. If only he could get his mind and heart to do the same.

The sun hung high the following day as Palassiren came into view. Neither the capital nor the mountain behind it appeared as big as he'd expected. Over the course of half a day and a dozen miles of farmland, he realized how grossly he'd misjudged the distance. The immensity of the city sank in as they neared the gates at sunset.

Tjaden had imagined cities, had heard descriptions and stories, but Palassiren was an entire world crammed into four giant walls and stacked high. The whole town of Shey's Orchard would fit in the open space between the inner gates and the palaces. Many of the buildings were three or four stories high, twice as high as the Dusty Tunic. It was like he'd never seen an animal larger than a mouse and was suddenly face to face with an elephant. Even with a proper description, it had been impossible to imagine. There was no space between the buildings, no fields, no orchards. It seethed like an anthill laid out in perpendicular lanes of travel.

Tjaden felt small and out of place. How could he ever hope to defend an entire kingdom when a single city could be so large? The clinking chains between him and Rodín made him look over. It had been almost two days since they had spoken to each other. Eventually he'd have to rely on other Elites and they on him. He should make some sort of peace before the city gates swallowed them.

"Rodín? What do you say we put everything behind us?"

"Did you hear a noise, Valdrin?" asked Rodín. He was still looking forward at the city. "It had the sonance of a cow belch."

Why couldn't he have started ignoring me before *we alienated Elora?*

"As far as I'm concerned," said Tjaden, "it's all forgotten." It was a total lie.

Rodín made a sour face and covered his nose with a handkerchief. "No, Valdrin. I was mistaken. That was a horse breaking wind. It's horrendous."

Fine with me, thought Tjaden. He turned his attention back to the grey walls.

At the city gates, sentries called, "Elites!" and banged staffs and swords against shields or wall or each other. Shackled and bruised was not the way Tjaden ever dreamed of arriving at the Academy, but between his coat and Rodín's cloak, hopefully it wasn't noticeable.

Citizens rushed along without stopping to chat or even greeting each other, though they parted as the soldiers and their companions passed. Some called, "Elites!" and clapped as they continued on their way. Others saluted the Elites by tapping walking sticks on the ground or whatever else they had at hand—a knuckle on a pot, horseshoes against each other, hammer against the frame of a roof under repair—all as they went about their business.

The sights that made Tjaden's jaw drop seemed as unremarkable to them as the cobbled streets or stars in the sky. Even with nightfall approaching most shops remained open and many vendors still lined the streets. The sheer diversity of

shops astounded Tjaden. They passed cheese shops, butchers, candle makers, and leatherworkers who sold only saddles. Tjaden noticed his father's gaze linger on a fruitstand with dozens of varieties of produce.

One shop sold an assortment of live animals. Displayed in front were two Jubjub birds in adjacent cages. Tjaden had never seen one alive, but it was impossible to mistake the red color, substantial size, and the intensity with which they attempted to break through their respective cages to be together.

Elora would have more stories to take back to Lily than she'd be able to remember. Tjaden stole a glance at her, wondering what she'd make of the city, but she didn't return his glance. Even though the evening was cool enough to ride with her hood up, it hung limply behind her head. Elora wore a smile as she examined every shop and sight they passed.

It was a straight course from the city gate to the inner gates, but it took nearly an hour for the horses to carry them there.

Tjaden asked a nearby Fellow, "Are these walls here in case the outer walls fall?"

He shook his head. "That'll never happen. The inner gates keep the populace out of the palaces and away from the military grounds."

Just inside the inner gates lay a huge courtyard. Seven palaces were lined up on the far side.

"Why are there so many palaces?" asked Tjaden.

The Fellow rolled his eyes and muttered, "Why are there so many nobles?" He pointed at the one in the center. "King Barash and Lady Palida live in the largest one. The one with all the red stone is Lady Cuora's. That one on the end is Captain Darieus's."

None of the soldiers had demeaned himself enough to talk casually to a recruit the whole trip. They had barely noticed Tjaden. He kept pushing while the Fellow was being civil. "Why is she Lady Palida and not Queen Palida?"

"She's from the Provinces. Don't ask me why that matters. Their son, Antion, is a prince, so he'll be king someday."

Next to the last palace was a collection of large gray buildings. "Is that the Military District?"

"Yep. It can easily house and train a thousand soldiers."

The Military District occupied as much space as Tjaden

had imagined the entire capital covering. He marveled at the huge barracks, stables, drilling grounds, warehouses, and other buildings whose purposes he couldn't even guess. In a courtyard in front of the buildings stood a huge Circle and Sword monument, taller than Tjaden. He didn't know how he missed seeing it earlier.

The largest building was their destination—a giant grey cube near the center of the District. Groomers took the horses as Lieutenant Serrill led the new arrivals into the building. In the huge entrance hall, Elora and Tjaden's father gave Tjaden and Ollie small waves as more servants led them to their quarters. Aker didn't wave, and his nod seemed to be directed only at Ollie.

Lieutenant Serrill pointed to two spots on the floor in front of him. Without speaking, Tjaden and Rodín stood where he indicated. Rodín held out his shackled wrist, but the lieutenant ignored it.

A door opened and the First Knight, Captain Darieus, walked quickly in, flanked by a pair of Elites. Tjaden and Rodín both saluted, bringing both fists to the center of the chests. The chain rattled and went taut and rattled more when they relaxed the salute.

Captain Darieus stood directly in front of them and gave them each a stern look before speaking.

"I am not in the habit of offering leniency to recruits. Fighting is one thing, but disobeying orders is another matter altogether. It is commonly said that recruits are one hiccup away from being kicked out of training. Consider this your final warning." He held out a hand and Lieutenant Serrill placed a key in his open palm.

Tjaden already felt like he was on shaky ground since he hadn't won the competition in Shey's Orchard. Captain Darieus was probably regretting the invitation already.

As he unlocked Rodín's shackle, the captain went on. "You

do not have to be friends, you do not have to like each other. My advice is to ignore one another as much as possible."

"Gladly," said Rodín. His shackle fell loudly to the ground.

Captain Darieus glowered at him. "You are dismissed, Recruit Rodín."

Rodín saluted then followed a servant down a hallway opposite the one leading to the guest quarters. Valdrin scooped up their belongings and hurried to keep up.

Captain Darieus reached for Tjaden's wrist, but Tjaden hesitated. He didn't want the First Knight acting like a lowly guard on his account. Captain Darieus cleared his throat and Tjaden lifted his arm.

"Some say women are only good at causing dissension in the ranks." The captain looked into Tjaden's eyes, but Tjaden couldn't tell if a reply was expected. "I say a soldier needs a reason—something for which he would give his life and the lives of his brothers."

So Captain Darieus knew about the fight and arguments, but didn't know about Elora's decision regarding her future with Tjaden. Still, the words were meant to be encouraging, and Tjaden took what hope he could from them. Even after everything that had happened between him and Elora, Tjaden would still give his life and the life of every Elite to protect her, even if his feelings were never reciprocated.

The shackle fell to the ground with a bang. "Dismissed."

"Thank you, Sir," said Tjaden. "Thank you." He and Ollie saluted then followed yet another servant through stone halls. They were shown the hallway that led to the dining area then taken to a stark room with two narrow cots, two small closets, and two wooden chairs. Even after adding two recruits and two travel sacks, there was still space to walk through the center of the room from one stone wall to the other.

"It's like a cave in here," said Ollie.

"Guess they never have to worry about fires," said Tjaden.

"What now?" asked Ollie. "Find out where Rodín's quarters are so we can shave his eyebrows off while he's sleeping?"

Tjaden laughed. It felt good. "How about we start with dinner?"

Tjaden and Ollie retraced the path to the dining hall. Despite the late hour, dozens of soldiers were spread throughout the large room, seated on benches alongside tables of sanded pine. Ten round tables near the front of the chamber stood out from the rest. Surrounded by chairs instead of benches, these tables were made of an ornate polished wood with natural streaks of blue. Sitting in pairs around two of them were about fifteen un-uniformed men and boys, talking in the animated manner of children before a Swap and Spar. Their fellow recruits.

A heated debate was underway as Tjaden and Ollie sat with their food at one of the Elite tables. Tjaden kept his arms in his lap when he wasn't taking a bite. The scars and story would come out soon enough. He didn't want any more attention.

One boy, a year or two younger than Tjaden, interrupted the debate to make introductions. He started by telling them his name was Brin-Dar. They went around the table saying their name and where they were from. A few recruits were younger than Tjaden, but most were a few years older. Two were in their mid-twenties, and one man with long, unkempt white hair looked old enough to be Tjaden's father.

The dispute began again quickly. A few of the recruits tried to convince the others that the best soldiers came from large cities. Others made the point that small towns produced better soldiers. The younger boys only listened for the most part.

"We have access to the best teachers, private lessons, and battalions of soldiers to observe," said a pale, young man with blond hair.

A well-tanned, wiry man spoke up. "Boys in cities grow up soft, selling trinkets in Daddy's shop or living in mansions with servants to do the real work. Try turning a copse of trees into a home for eight people. Takes three months but makes you into a man overnight."

A few in the group chuckled. Ollie jumped in. "Let me ask a question—Where did Captain Darieus come from?"

Half of the group answered, "Oblahar."

"Right," continued Ollie. "It's a small town in the western mountains. Most of the residents either raise cattle and horses or grow wheat. No nobles or easy living there. And what about King Barash?"

This time all of the recruits spoke at once. "Palassiren."

The pale kid asked, "What's your point?"

Tjaden wondered the same thing, but knowing Ollie, he had something in mind.

"Well," said Ollie. "One is perfectly suited for military life and has protected the kingdom for two decades. The other is better suited to sitting on a throne and ordering servants. I think the answer's obvious."

The dispute erupted into a free-for-all, each recruit trying to be heard above the others. Tjaden listened to the conversation with one ear, but his real interest was in his fellow recruits. They ranged from confident and friendly Brin-Dar to the pale, haughty, young man to a rigid, subdued eleven-year-old named Chism.

The old man, who was probably in his late thirties, sat next to Chism. Tjaden couldn't figure out why anyone, even a wild man, would pick such a small boy as a Fellow. Until the boy grew half a foot, he wouldn't match up with the next smallest recruit in the group. As he tried to figure out the kid, Tjaden noticed that he ate meticulously. Pick up fork, then knife, cut meat, stab, lift to mouth, lay down fork, lay down knife, wipe mouth twice. He repeated the pattern with every bite. Each time he laid down the knife and fork, they were perfectly straight.

If the boy had learned any swordplay forms yet, they were probably as sharp as a razor. There were things he could learn from each one of the recruits, whether Elite or Fellow.

Rodín and Valdrin joined the group, sitting as far as possible from Tjaden. Again Brin-Dar made introductions. As soon as the last recruit was finished, Rodín went to work like a bear with a barrel of salmon. Rodín and Zarin—Tjaden caught the pale young man's name the second time around—became instant friends and rivals. For some time, the only interruptions in Rodín's recountings of valor were Zarin's tales of incomparable skill.

They droned on and on.

"That's almost as good as the time I rescued a baby black bear from a cougar. Its mother came along thinking *I* was the threat! I fought her off without injuring her too badly."

"That's nothing. When I was hunting a pair of Jubjub birds I stumbled into a grizzly den—"

"And I once slew eight giants with a single arrow!" Ollie interjected loudly, referring to the legend of Bindle Surebeam. Everyone laughed and finally used their mouths for eating instead of talking.

Tjaden didn't speak much throughout the remainder of the meal. It was enough to finally be at the Academy among boys and men who, for the most part, weren't much different than the people he'd grown up with. With his recent luck it wouldn't have surprised him to be required to go through training with twenty people like Rodín.

The next morning, Tjaden and Ollie donned their new, pale blue uniforms. They weren't the hallowed colors of Elite or Fellow, but a peacock with a thousand tail feathers couldn't have been prouder than Tjaden was to be outfitted in soldier's garb. After inspecting every inch of each other's rough-fitting uniforms for dirt, scuffs, and stray threads, they made their way to the auditorium of the Assembly Hall.

Massive columns lined the front of the building. Tjaden's jaw dropped when he entered the hall and gazed at the huge vault of the auditorium. He'd never seen a room so large. How did the ceiling stay up, even with the columns spaced throughout? The walls and columns were adorned with pale blue matching the recruit uniforms and the midnight blue of the Elites.

A half-dozen Elites stood at attention along each wall. Their patches identified them as Wasp Squadron. Tjaden had heard of Wasp, but knew nothing about them. On the stage of the Assembly Hall were two rows of twenty-one chairs in front of a large Circle and Sword tapestry. Some of the recruits were already seated in front of their Fellows. Tjaden was shocked to see the young boy, Chism, in the front row and his gray-haired companion in the rear with the Fellows. Ollie gave Tjaden a little shove from behind, and Tjaden walked to the stage and took a seat alongside Chism.

Tjaden was still studying the soldiers from Wasp Squadron when Elora walked in. He couldn't take his eyes off of her. The dress she wore was deep green and fancier than anything he'd ever seen in Shey's Orchard. The long sleeves were wrapped with flowery white and yellow embroidery. Flowers had been braided into her hair, which was wrapped and stacked on her head. Not stacked, placed. Arranged. She wasn't even wearing her herb sash. Ollie pulled Tjaden back down to his seat, and he realized he'd stood up to see her better.

Under different circumstances, the ring in Tjaden's pocket would be a perfect complement to her gown. She smiled at him, and whatever small progress he'd made in forgetting about her was completely undone. Even the way the scars tugged at her confident smile made him wish he could stare at her all day. He forced himself to look at the other people who filed into the hall, but whenever his concentration lapsed, his eyes jumped in Elora's direction like iron filings to a magnet.

Around two hundred people, mostly citizens, came to see the ceremony. The hall could have held ten times that number.

Lieutenant Markin, second in command of the Elites, opened the ceremony by reading the names of the twenty-one recruits. Citizens clapped and snapped while soldiers tapped hard sheaths against the floor or the benches. Lieutenant Markin introduced Captain Darieus, and as he stepped to the podium, the applause grew thunderous.

"Ladies and gentlemen, family and friends, the young men seated behind me have been chosen from thousands of candidates across the kingdom. Each one has already proven himself to be a superb fighter. They will soon join the preeminent fighting force not only in the kingdom of Maravilla, but in the world."

More applause.

"Even at their young age, these recruits have accomplished many admirable tasks. Collu endured twelve rounds in Palassiren's tournament this year, winning every match. Polane single-handedly killed a voracious wolf while defending his family's flocks. In T'lai, our youngest recruit, Chism, won championships in javelin, archery, staves, and daggers."

Chism scowled and looked down at the wooden stage.

At least I'm not the only one being singled out, Tjaden thought. *If I'm lucky, some of them brought people to tell about it.*

Captain Darieus continued. "Countless witnesses could stand and relate examples of the bravery and skill of these recruits. I have brought one in particular. This young lady from the town of Shey's Orchard was attacked by a bandersnatch, and the actions of one of our recruits saved her life. I give you Miss Elora."

A few whispers passed through the audience as Elora glided to the stage. *Most likely commenting on her beauty,* Tjaden thought. As she climbed the few stairs to the stage, she gave Tjaden a friendly wink. The only good thing that might come from her change of feelings for him was that she might underplay the event. He didn't deserve gushing praise. He hadn't saved her and hadn't even won the sparring competition in his tiny town.

"Tjaden would never brag," she began, "but he has always been the type of person to help and protect others."

So much for toned-down. Tjaden's face began to burn.

After reaching the point in the story when the bandersnatch became frumious, she said, "I wanted to run. For a moment I considered jumping off the cliff into the river. But when Tjaden gripped his club and charged, the bandersnatch looked like it was thinking the same thing. Tjaden gave me the courage to fight."

Tjaden expected his face to burst into flames. On the stage, in front of hundreds of people, there was nowhere to hide.

From behind him, Ollie whispered, "Sit still. You're wriggling like a worm."

After another minute or two of bragging, she closed by saying, "If these other young men are anything like Tjaden, the kingdom is in very good hands."

More applause.

Elora turned from the podium. She paused and smiled at him. Smiled as if it was the only thing that needed to happen in the world at that moment. And he smiled back, because nothing else mattered.

Too soon, she broke the smile, started walking back to her seat. Tjaden remembered the crowd and his fellow recruits looking at him. He remembered that even if the smile implied otherwise, Elora didn't feel *that* way about him. And he realized that he always would feel *that* way about her.

At least the worst of the embarrassment was over. He'd rather face another bandersnatch than be singled out again.

As Captain Darieus returned to the podium, Tjaden wiped away the sweat trickling down his temples.

"Thank you, Miss Elora," said Captain Darieus. Something

in his tone and his bearing made every other man in the hall seem inadequate. "Assembled in front of you today is the greatest young fighting talent anywhere in the world. Every one of them has shown skill, valor, and dedication. I present to you the future protectors of Maravilla!"

When the applause died, Captain Darieus indicated the banner that hung behind the recruits—a white circle bisected vertically by a sword against a dark blue background. "The Circle and the Sword. The Circle represents the continuous connection between every individual in the kingdom—from a wheat farmer to a trader to a royal procurer to the king himself. The Circle returns to that farmer complete by virtue of the Sword. The Sword connects the king to the citizenry by offering protection against disorder, savage beasts, and would be invaders such as the Western Domain."

Leaving the podium, he slowly paced the stage. "This holds true not only for farmers, but for craftsmen, hunters, nobles. For the newest baby and the oldest woman in the kingdom. Everyone is connected in an unending circle to each other and to the king, and only through the strength of the Sword can the Circle exist. Remove the Sword, and the Circle collapses. Likewise, if the Sword is wielded outside of the confines of the Circle, it becomes a destructive rather than a sustaining force.

"Each of these young men will brandish the Sword because they understand that their mothers and fathers, their brothers and sons, and everyone they care for is part of the Circle."

Tjaden caught himself staring at Elora and quickly ducked his head. When he looked back, she seemed to be studying him, as if he was a riddle she couldn't solve.

Captain Darieus concluded, "If your young men can complete the rigorous training, they will pledge their lives to the support of the Circle and the Sword. I commend them for the dedication necessary to reach this point and encourage them to persevere in the months to come. Thank you."

The audience rose and cheered as Captain Darieus returned to his seat.

Lieutenant Markin spoke next. In contrast to Captain Darieus's uplifting comments, he was practical. He told them that up to half of the recruits would not finish training. The next fourteen months would be the most grueling of their lives and would include demanding daily schedules, tests of knowledge, and physical evaluations.

Those who completed training would be involved in daring rescue missions, drawn-out battles, injuries, and hardship. The Elites often completed specialized missions that swayed the course of battles.

Lieutenant Markin spoke of protecting citizens from barbantulas[1], bandersnatches, and targus. By the time he talked about hunting the Jabberwock, the only noises heard were nervous breathing and worried fidgeting.

He finished by saying, "Those that are strong and determined enough to endure the next fourteen months will swear loyalty to the Elites and Captain Darieus in defense of the king and the kingdom."

Undaunted by Lieutenant Markin's remarks, Tjaden thought to himself, *I will pass the training. I will be an Elite.*

As soon as the ceremony ended, Lieutenant Markin told the recruits, "Take three minutes for farewells if you have people here, then dress in practice uniforms and meet behind this building. Dismissed."

Tjaden didn't wait for Ollie, but his Fellow was right behind him as he walked up to the Shey's Orchard group.

There wasn't much time. He told Elora, "You were every bit as brave as I was when we fought the bandersnatch."

---

[1] **barbantula**: A giant spider that hunts with barbs instead of webs.

"When I become an Elite, you can tell everyone about it," she said with a smile.

Tjaden's father put a hand on Tjaden's shoulder. They faced each other, eye to eye. Man to man.

"No more trouble, son. Stay away from Rodín. Work hard." He clasped Tjaden's hand and shook it firmly. They'd never shaken hands before; Tjaden realized at some point he'd become a man in his father's eyes.

Aker also extended his hand. "Good luck. The whole town is proud of you." He looked at Ollie and Elora and added, "All three of you."

It was Elora's turn. She stepped forward and gave Tjaden a light, friendly hug. It felt stunted. Nothing like the hug after the bandersnatch fight or the night Captain Darieus had given him the invitation. She pecked his cheek and said, "I'm proud of you."

Tjaden angled his head toward the kiss and held the embrace a moment longer than Elora did. Without her, the approbation he'd received meant much less.

"You, too," said Tjaden. "I mean—" It hadn't been what he'd meant to say, but he couldn't take it back. Even though he was an idiot, he still felt ten feet tall in her presence.

He wanted to hug her again, but forced himself to step back.

When she hugged Ollie it looked different. More friendly, less fondly, but only very slightly. Or maybe it was the same. What did it matter? The difference wasn't enough to justify giving her the ring.

"Well then," said Tjaden's father.

"See you in fourteen months," said Tjaden. He turned to leave. After a few steps, he felt someone tap his shoulder.

It was Elora. She handed him a folded piece of paper and said, "There were a few things I had to say." On tiptoes, she kissed his cheek again. It was a lingering kiss, as warm as the coals of a bonfire. She turned away and walked back to her father.

As desperately as Tjaden wanted another glimpse of her face, Elora kept it turned away.

Tjaden followed Ollie toward their quarters, but a wrong turn took them to the wrong wing of the building. Minutes they didn't have to spare slipped away. When they finally reached their quarters, they hurried out of the dress uniforms, but they still weren't dressed when a man in the hallway shouted, "If you're still in your rooms in one minute you owe me an hour of chores tonight!"

By the time Tjaden got into pants, tunic, and boots, Ollie was just starting on boots.

Read the letter or help Ollie? If he hadn't already been in so much trouble, the choice would have been easy.

He knelt and laced one boot while Ollie did the other. Then they raced for the door.

A young Elite, twenty maybe, stood in the hallway. "There's two hours right there. Thank you, hiccouts."

Tjaden groaned as he ran. If he was going to be late, he might as well have read the letter.

When they were out of hearing range, he asked Ollie, "Hiccout?"

"Remember what Captain Darieus said? One hiccup away from being out of here."

The Elite from the hallway, who introduced himself as Elite Loil, lined up the recruits. An hour spent learning to stand at attention. Two hours standing at attention during the instruction on expectations. Then they finally got to fight. Elite Loil called Chism, the smallest recruit, to the center of the ring and tossed him a padded staff.

"Can any of you hiccouts beat Recruit Chism?" asked Elite Loil.

A few recruits raised their hands, but Rodín stepped forward and said, "Bah. How old are you, boy? Ten? Eleven?"

Chism stared evenly at Rodín without answering. The small Elite's mood was as dark as his eyes.

The old man, Chism's Fellow, smiled and asked, "Care to put some money on it?"

Elite Loil ignored him and said, "Standard staff fighting rules. First one to five." He backed out of the ring and said, "Don't hurt him too bad."

"I can manage that," said Rodín.

"I wasn't talking to you," said Elite Loil. "Fight!"

I wish I was in the ring with Rodín. Tjaden wanted to make him pay for all the problems he'd caused with Elora.

Chism took a defensive stance and waited. Wearing a cocky smirk, Rodín slowly approached and swung his staff to test the smaller boy. Chism blocked, side-stepped, swung, spun, jabbed, spun back, hit Rodín twice more then swept his legs out. One, two, three, four, five points. If Tjaden didn't know about Rodín's pride he would have sworn it was a staged demonstration.

Every recruit had wide eyes and an open mouth, including Rodín, who lay on the ground looking up at the sky.

Nope, thought Tjaden. *I'm glad it was Chism.*

"I'm fourteen, boy," Chism quietly told Rodín. He handed the staff to Elite Loil and took the empty spot in the circle next to Ollie.

"Skill simply surpasses size," said Ollie. "Way to make us little guys look good." He reached to pat Chism on the back, but Chism turned and slapped Ollie's wrist sharply.

"Please don't touch me," he said. Staring forward, into the ring, he added, "And thanks."

Elite Loil set up a rotating arrangement of rapid-fire sparring. Two hours of that felt like two days worth of fighting.

An hour of balance and strength training. Dinner. An hour with shovels in the stable for their extra chore.

An eternity. But it could not last forever.

When they returned to their quarters, Ollie dove onto his cot. Tjaden dove into the letter.

Dear Tjaden,

I should start by saying something I somehow haven't told you. Thank you. I know you think nothing of risking your life, but you've given me every experience for the rest of my life. Do not mourn over my scars. Be happy for the life I've been granted. That is what I will do.

I hope you don't mind me being open and honest.

Despite what Brune or Rodín or you see when you look at my face, I know I am beautiful.

Tjaden reread to make sure he'd understood. *Brune or Rodín or you? How could she lump me with* those *two?* He clutched his gut and looked around for somewhere to throw up. The sick gut stayed, but the light-headedness went away when he sat on his cot.

He kept reading.

My scars tell the world that something that thought it could beat me was wrong. Because I didn't let it.

I misunderstood your feelings for me, and I'm sorry it led to unspoken promises and shattered expectations. You are not stuck with me. How could you owe me anything after you've already given me so much?

You deserve someone you can love without regret or disgust. And I deserve someone who can not only see past my scars but can see the beauty in them.

Wishing you the best today and tomorrow and always,
Elora

Tjaden stared at the words. What they seemed to say was impossible.

"That bad?" asked Ollie.

"What?" He'd forgotten Ollie was there. Tjaden could hardly speak. "Worse. The worst possible." He didn't know how to explain it, so he held out the letter.

Ollie groaned in pain as he reached to take it.

Tjaden was stunned. He didn't know if he wanted to hit something or just lay back and die. The most beautiful girl he knew, the most beautiful he'd ever seen, somehow believed that he thought her scars were ugly and disgusting? A pain was growing in his chest that was worse than the bruises he'd collected during sparring.

Ollie whistled in surprise. Tjaden saw his eyes pass over a few more lines, then he whistled even louder and looked up, eyes wide. "This is bad."

"I'm going for her," said Tjaden. "I can't let her think that's how I feel for even one more night."

"Bad idea," said Ollie. "Even by my standards."

"How could this happen?"

"I don't know. Things seemed fine when we left Shey's Orchard."

The memories of hope Tjaden had felt just made her words burn more. "It changed the night I fought Rodín."

"When you two talked—before you tried to kill him. Was she listening?"

"She wasn't even there. She said, 'If you'll excuse me,' and walked off."

"Where'd she go?" asked Ollie.

"How should I know? I was busy trying to kill Rodín."

With effort, Ollie sat up. He drummed fingers on his jaw. "While you were trying to be the first one to get kicked out of the Elites before even starting, she was running through itch oak. Remember, she had me soak her clothes in the stream?

She could have eavesdropped. Something upset her enough that she ran without caring about itch oak. This is the queen of all things green we're talking about."

"She wouldn't eavesdrop," said Tjaden. "And if she did, she heard me defend her. Fight over her."

"Even if you said what you think you said, that's no guarantee she heard the same words."

"Words are words, Ollie."

"Are you kidding? Do you remember when I told Kaila she had pretty eyes, cute ears, and a beautiful smile?"

"I wasn't there." It sounded vaguely familiar, but Tjaden didn't have a lot of patience for Ollie's stories. He just wanted to figure out why Elora thought what she did.

"She said, 'What's wrong with my nose? You think it's ugly?'" Ollie threw his hands into the air, then grimaced. "Trust me. Words spoken by a boy and words heard by a girl are two different languages."

"Elora can't really believe that looking at her makes me sick. That's the opposite of what I think!"

"Jay." Ollie waited until Tjaden looked into his face. "Listen to me. She's a *girl*. Misinterpreting and overreacting come as naturally as breathing." Tjaden read the letter again.

"I have to go right now."

"Where?"

"To tell her the truth and give her the ring I should have given her weeks ago."

"Like I said, where?"

"She's somewhere in this city."

"So are a hundred thousand other people. You don't know if she's down the hall or downtown. If we walk out now, we'll never be invited back in. A hiccup, remember?"

Tjaden knew that was true. He'd more than used up any leniency Captain Darieus might give him.

"So what do I do? Let her think I think she's repulsive for the next fourteen months?"

"Do what she did," said Ollie. "Write a letter. You know where she's going. Her Sixteenery isn't for months. So you write a letter, then write another one the week after that. And another and another. If I survive another day like today, I'll make sure you say what you mean and don't say anything she'll take wrong. With me coaching and editing, it'll be way better than anything you might think to say in person."

Tjaden blew his cheeks out and rubbed his forehead. His thoughts refused to fall into order. Precisely why it was better to act instead of sit around thinking.

"Take advantage of the free couriers," said Ollie.

When Tjaden didn't argue, Ollie said, "Stay here. Think about what you want to say while I go find some paper." He looked at Tjaden for agreement. "The letter will be waiting for her when she gets back to Shey's Orchard."

Maybe Ollie was right. If Tjaden tried talking to her, he'd just make it worse somehow. He nodded and Ollie limped out of the room. By the time he came back with paper, ink, and quill, Tjaden only had one line written in his head. He picked up the quill but hesitated before dipping it.

"My letters look like they're written by a chicken with a tic," said Tjaden. "If I tell you what to write will you do it?"

"You're hopeless," said Ollie. "What would she think if you sent a letter in my handwriting?"

"Ugh." Tjaden inked the quill and slowly wrote:

RODÍN IS A LIAR.

Ollie peeked over his shoulder and laughed. "Nope. Don't start off your first letter talking about that cretin."

"What do I say, then?"

"There are two things you can talk about—her or your feelings for her. Don't talk about other people, and don't be a Rodín and tell her everything you've ever done."

"I know that much, at least." He leaned over a new sheet of paper with his pen poised. There were no words in his heart, only feelings. Feelings so vast they'd never fit on a sheet of paper. The uneven sliding of Ollie's feet on the stone made it hard to concentrate.

"Listening to you pace back there isn't helping," said Tjaden. "Go to sleep. Maybe I'll let you look it over in the morning."

Ollie had his boots off and was stretched out on the bed before Tjaden finished talking.

"Tjaden."

"Yeah?"

"Keep it simple. And short."

Simple and short.

Tjaden dipped the pen, but changed his mind and let the ink drip back into the well. Ollie began snoring quietly. Tjaden wrote Elora's name at the top of the paper, then poised the pen under it but still didn't have the right words. His body and mind were completely exhausted. Even though he needed sleep, there was no way he could rest until he got the letter done.

The candle on the desk next to him shrunk to a nub as Tjaden spent hours in which he should have been sleeping. One thought at a time he came up with a few lines:

Elora,

I don't know what I said or did. But I'm sorry.

All I feel for you is love. I would do anything to prove that. Anything. Even give up Elite training if that's what it takes.

I want to marry you, if you'll let me.

I want to see your smile every day of my life.

Tjaden

As he lay down to sleep, an image of Elora danced inside his eyelids. Hair flying, brown eyes afire. Unafraid. Club raised above her head. She wasn't running. She was fighting, and she was staying with him.

Half a day wasn't long enough to see a tenth of Palassiren. The palaces, street performers, new foods, unending marketplaces. Elora tried to memorize everything so she could tell Lily. Colorful fruits and vegetables; intricate jewelry and wood carvings; shoes, hats, and clothes of various fabrics; and countless other goods. When merchants and traders visited Shey's Orchard, they always brought a variety of items for trade, but their wagons couldn't hold a fraction of what Elora saw as she wandered the streets of Palassiren with her father and Grower Mikel.

A scabbard shop made her think back to how proud she was to gird Tjaden's sword and she wished he was with her. The intense feelings of betrayal after she'd overheard his conversation with Rodín had faded. He didn't have to be in love with her for them to be friends. She wondered if she'd ever stop loving him deep down.

It didn't matter. Apparently fate had plans for her that did not include Tjaden.

Lieutenant Serrill had given them each ten pennies "for incidentals."

The men bought a few small tools and gifts for their wives. The first thing Elora bought was a book entitled *Healing and Helpful Flowers and Plants of Maravilla*. For Lily she found a floral perfume that the perfumer said would drive the boys mad. When one vendor demonstrated a matchstick that ignited simply by dragging it against rough stone, Elora knew her mother would love them. She spent her last two pennies on two dozen matchsticks and tucked them into an empty pouch on her herbal sash.

Her father browsed every mirror shop they passed. Before leaving Shey's Orchard, Elora didn't like to spend time in the shop, but her image no longer bothered her.

A handheld mirror in one shop near the end of the day caught her eye. Fine leaves were carved into the pale wood of the frame. If she had any money left she would have splurged and bought it for herself. Her father must have seen her admiring it because as they walked back to the inner city he pulled it from his sack and gave it to her.

"Thank you," she said, hugging him. She looked at the gift and realized the mirror had been removed.

"I can't make frames like that one, but the first glass I'll pour back in Shey's Orchard will be to fit your frame."

They hadn't talked about what she'd learned on the trip, and even though he probably couldn't explain it, he knew.

It was hours after dark when they returned to the guest quarters of the military building. She wanted to find Tjaden and hear about the first day of training, but no one offered or invited. He would seek her out if he was allowed to, right? And if he wanted to. They were probably sleeping in the same building, after all.

But he did not come.

The next morning she was packed and ready for the trip home at sunrise. Horizontal sunbeams fell on the huge Circle and Sword statue in front of the military headquarters. It consisted of a perfect circle carved from dark blue granite with an oversized white granite sword inside that supported the upper arch of the circle. Sadness at not being able to share Tjaden's life was tempered by the fact that they were still linked by the Circle. She could still feel pride for Tjaden even if it wasn't the kind of pride she had imagined.

When she pulled her hand away from the cool granite to follow her father and Grower Mikel, she whispered, "Goodbye, Tjaden."

Even with a busy training day, Tjaden had surely had time to read her letter. The way he had looked at her at the ceremony the day before made her wonder if she was wrong. She'd told herself she had given up on him, while really she was still holding on. Waiting for him to give her any sign.

But he hadn't come for her. He hadn't sent for her. Hadn't even replied with a letter of his own.

So she left him behind. As he had done to her because of the scars.

They met up with a sublieutenant named Aislin, who waited with three other Elites and their Fellows. Each of them wore a patch with the number 1 on his shoulder. Captain Darieus's personal squadron. The same men who had visited Shey's Orchard to deliver Tjaden's invitation.

The horses and supplies were already outfitted, and the party wasted no time in leaving the city. The half squadron of Elites was on their way to an assignment and would be passing near Shey's Orchard. They didn't bring cooks or grooms like Scaled Tiger Squadron did on the way to Palassiren.

Elora read her new book as she rode. The feeling that she was wrong to just leave Tjaden behind kept nagging her, distracting her. But what could she do? Tell the soldiers and her father they had to go back and make Tjaden tell her to her face that he didn't love her?

All that time on the road to Palassiren she could have confronted Tjaden, but she was too busy being offended.

Just read, she told herself.

By the time they stopped for camp she'd skimmed every page and was starting over at the beginning. In the sunlight that remained, she was determined to harvest something new for her herbal sash. She'd probably never be in this part of the kingdom again. As if that wasn't enough reason, keeping busy was better than sitting around feeling bad about Tjaden.

The soldiers set up camp near a grove of trees that her book identified as black walnuts. The leaves contained an oil that could inhibit other plants from growing—which appealed little to her—and treat infections caused by fungus or mildew. Ringworm, yeast rot, and the like.

The Fellow who was cooking let her borrow a mortar and pestle. Until the light became too scarce, Elora crushed enough liquid out of the leaves to fill a medium sized vial. If she harvested something every day she'd fill nearly every vial in her sash by the time she got home.

The smell of beef, potatoes, and turnips filled the air. Elora returned the mortar and pestle then walked up to the fire. A young Elite with dark hair and dark eyes was stoking it. Elora warmed her hands.

"Where is your assignment taking you?" she asked the soldier.

"Southwest," said the soldier, poking at the fire.

"What about after Shey's Orchard?"

"I couldn't say, miss."

Her father joined them. "Is it normal to be in the dark regarding your destination?"

"No, Sir. This assignment is, eh, different than most." The Elite spoke slowly and his words blended together, marking him from far in the East. He didn't maintain eye contact with either Elora or her father.

Something had him very nervous. Probably his thick accent.

"How long will you be away?" she asked.

He shrugged and raked his fingers through his hair.

"Been a soldier long?" asked her father.

"Almost ten years," answered the young man. He couldn't be more than twenty-five years old.

"So you've almost earned your ten-year commission?" asked Elora.

The Elite nodded and said, "This will be my last mission with the Elites."

"Where will you be assigned after that?"

"I'll be Sergeant at a post in Yaltua, where I'm from." He kicked at a log in the fire.

"Are the other Elites close to ten years also?" asked Aker.

The soldier nodded. "The eight of us here, yes. Excuse me," he said and went off toward the horses.

Not long later, a Fellow brought bowls of stew. He returned shortly with a small bowl of fresh berries with sweet cream.

"Compliments of Sublieutenant Aislin, and fit for a lady," the Fellow remarked with a small bow.

The food was gone before she realized it. After dinner, she sat listening to her father and Mikel, but her eyelids grew heavy and she couldn't stay upright on the log she used as a stool. Excusing herself, she stumbled the short distance to her tent. More than mere exhaustion, a heavy sleepiness had settled over her. Without changing her clothes or removing her bandolier, she sprawled onto her blankets.

Aker and Mikel were left alone with the coals of the fire.

"How would it be spending your life crafting trinkets and knick-knacks?" Aker asked.

Mikel shook his head. "I don't understand those snobbish folk. Some of them must spend what I earn in a month on one set of clothes."

"Two months," said Aker. "Shey's Orchard suits me just

fine. No one lines up to buy baubles, but we've always been well fed, shod, and sheltered."

Grunting in agreement, Mikel said, "It'll be nice to get back to work. It's barely been a week and I already feel soft."

"I hear you," said Aker. "Riding horseback beats up your body, but it sure does it at a lazy pace."

They talked about weather until the coals stopped giving off heat. Aker hadn't said anything to Mikel about the hard night Elora had gone through. It had probably been some thoughtless comment by a teenage boy. Time and distance had softened Aker's protective instincts, but if Elora hadn't asked him to stay close that night, he might have gone and started a fight. A fight he would have lost, but a fight that might have meant something to Elora.

Whatever it was, she'd come away from it more confident and happy than he'd seen her in months. He ducked into the tent and saw Elora sprawled onto the top of her bedroll. Careful not to wake her, he covered her as well as he could, then climbed under his own blankets.

Just when he was halfway into a dream, a commotion outside the tent brought him up with a start. The sound of tent poles cracking was the first noise he could put a name to. It was soon followed by men shouting and arming themselves. Having barely slept, he was disoriented and couldn't make out the words through the clamor.

Extricating himself from his blankets, he tried to shake sleep from his brain. The first words he understood were the last words he wanted to hear.

"Jabberwock! To arms!"

Despite the commotion, Elora still slept. He had no weapon, but if there was anything to be done to protect Elora, he'd do it.

Aker crawled to the tent's entrance. As he opened the tent

flap, a blow to his head sent the world spinning. He just had time to worry for Elora before darkness closed in.

Tjaden's body screamed at him as he pushed himself out of bed. His body longed for sleep, but every inward part of him needed to get his letter to a courier immediately. If the first day of training had been a full day instead of a half day, he might not have survived.

"Wake up, Ollie." Tjaden lit a candle.

"I can't move," said Ollie. "You're going to have to leave me behind."

Tjaden didn't plan on being the first to discover what the punishment was for arriving late or showing up without his Fellow.

"Get up," he urged. "We need to stop at the courier before breakfast. Unless you don't want to eat before training."

With more grunts and whimpers, Ollie swung his legs over the side of his bed. "I swear someone came into our room and beat me up while I was sleeping. Even my eyelids hurt." He blinked slowly and winced.

"You and me both. You hit like a girl compared to a group of first day recruits trying to impress the lieutenant. I feel like a bandersnatch kicked me in the chest. And the legs. And the arms."

Ollie stretched, winced, and said, "From what I saw when I wasn't being thumped, you gave your share of bruises."

Tjaden wasn't the worst, but he was far from the best.

They dressed, moaning as new sore muscles were discovered. As they jogged to the courier, since recruits were required to run everywhere, Ollie asked to read the letter.

"No point now," said Tjaden. "Too late to change anything."

Handing it to the courier felt like turning a corner. Hope that he'd given up, was back. There was nothing more he could do for a few weeks. Elite training would be a perfect distraction in the meantime.

In the mess hall, all of the recruits seemed to move as gingerly as Tjaden and Ollie. None of them spoke much, and Rodín didn't say a single word. He still hadn't climbed back on his high horse after being knocked off it by Chism.

After eating quickly, the recruits split up for an hour of chores. Tjaden and Ollie did laundry detail then jogged to their classroom. Each day would start with instruction on history, tactics, geography, or leadership. Growing up so far from the capital, Tjaden felt like he knew nothing about any of those topics. He couldn't wait to learn about the Knights and other heroes of the Elites.

When Lieutenant Markin and Elite Loil entered the classroom, the recruits all stood rigidly behind their chairs. Noticing Captain Darieus trailing them, Tjaden attempted to straighten even further. He hadn't expected instruction from the First Knight himself.

"Sit," said Lieutenant Markin.

They rushed into their seats, and Captain Darieus approached the podium. His stare made Tjaden's exhale sound like a whirlwind in his ears. He held his breath and the silence returned.

Captain Darieus spoke in an even, restrained voice:
"A soldier's life is fraught with peril;
Viscera, scalp, tendon, and bone.
Targus[1] wizened, lions feral;
Gryphon in packs or alone.
Yea, heed my words, for 'pon the land

---

[1] **targus**: A short creature that looks like a cross between a monkey and a crow. They are reported to eat dreams.

DANIEL COLEMAN

Roam beast and bird, you yet shall find,
More dang'rous fiends than fellowman
That feed on humankind."

Captain Darieus's focused eyes scanned the room. His voice gained intensity:

"Beware the Jabberwock, my son!
The jaws that bite, the claws that catch;
Beware the Jubjub bird and shun
The frumious bandersnatch."

The bandersnatch. Elora.

No. Focus.

The man in front of him had not only seen but fought beasts that Tjaden had only dreamed about.

Captain Darieus went on to instruct the recruits on the last fifty years of Maravilla's history, placing special emphasis on the twenty years since he had organized the Elites. The recruits sat enraptured, not moving, barely breathing.

Darieus told of Anselm the Intrepid, who stole into an enemy's fort, lowered the drawbridge, and disabled the mechanism so it couldn't be raised. His fellow fighters entered and took the fort, but Anselm died in the raid.

Then there was the account of Captain Hunbold, captured by the Western Domain and held hostage under deplorable conditions for seven months. He overcame his guards and instead of fleeing, he found the warehouse of war supplies and torched it. The Domain invasion ended that night. A single soldier stopped the advance of the barbarians and defined the borders of a kingdom. Thousands of lives were saved.

Ulibear the Unflinching, Gralfax the Iron Knight, Poatric the Vigorous. Each account surpassed the prior.

'Captain Darieus, the First Knight' could be uttered in the same breath as any of those, thought Tjaden.

His thoughts were interrupted by Captain Darieus's voice. "Upon completing your training, your true test will begin. Will you rise to the level of the task that faces you? Will future recruits hear your name and keep it in awe after being told of your deeds? It's possible to live forever through the memories of your accomplishments.

"But one tale remains to be told. In a week's time I will return to detail my encounter with, and slaughter of, a Jabberwock."

A few low murmurs came from the back of the room. Shock and confusion showed on most faces. Tjaden had always assumed there was only one Jabberwock.

"Yes," said Captain Darieus. "The Jabberwock can be killed, and it was not always alone. I personally led the assault that claimed the life of this vile creature's mate."

The recruits' eyes grew even wider.

"Such is the legacy that you have inherited. Now, I ask, are you worthy to embrace such a heritage?"

Half of the recruits, including Tjaden, shouted, "Yes, Sir!"

"Will your courage match that of Anselm, Hunbold, Ulibear, and Poatric?"

All of the recruits answered in unison. "Yes, Sir!"

Captain Darieus nodded. "Such deeds are required of those who wear the Circle and the Sword. Each of you at some point in your training will question your dedication. You will doubt yourself and wonder if the life of an Elite is right for you. But I want you to remember how you feel at this moment. I promise you the sacrifice will be worth it in the end."

Captain Darieus walked out, and the room breathed again. They had one more class before rapid-fire sparring. Collu and his Fellow were missing at lunch.

"Quit," was the only explanation when they asked about them.

The next morning at breakfast, Goelvy and his Fellow were absent. Tjaden ran to make sure they hadn't slept past the bell and found their room empty. Elite Loil came into the mess hall and informed the rest of the recruits that Goelvy and his Fellow had been caught in an undignified location in the city after curfew. Before walking away he added, "They hiccoutted."

Ollie didn't say anything with his mouth, but his eyes reminded Tjaden of how close they'd come to the same fate. Tjaden wiped sweat from his brow. It would have been worth it for Elora, but he was relieved it hadn't quite come to that.

Somehow even more sore than the day before, Tjaden sat in Lieutenant Markin's discourse on the history of weaponry. Captain Darieus again surprised him by attending the class as an observer. The lieutenant had just started speaking when an Elite from First Squadron rushed into the room in full riding gear. He was dusty and out of breath, but he scanned the room intently. Markin paused.

After saluting to Captain Darieus, the Elite spoke. "Captain Darieus, Sir. An urgent message." He had a slurry accent that ran the words together. Captain Darieus followed him out of the room.

Tjaden wondered what matter would arrive with such immediacy. War? Some other mission that required Elites?

Fourteen months. Fourteen months he had to spend in training instead of completing missions and soldiering. Though Lieutenant Markin continued his lecture, the recruits shifted in their seats and glanced frequently at the door. When Captain Darieus came back in, the angle of his eyebrows made it clear he was concerned about something. It was a small change that made a large impression.

"Recruit Tjaden. A word with you and your Fellow, please."

Elora.

It had been less than forty-eight hours since they'd said goodbye. What could have happened so close to the capital? Tjaden understood she was to have an Elite escort. Maybe it was his father, but that didn't feel right.

If Elora needed him, Tjaden would leave the Academy immediately. He'd promised in his letter after all.

Captain Darieus did not keep them in suspense. "I have unfortunate news. The company of Elites escorting Elora and your father to Shey's Orchard was attacked last night. Just after nightfall they were beset by the Jabberwock."

Tjaden's knees went weak.

Captain Darieus continued. "Your father and Mirrorer Aker were both knocked unconscious, but they will be fine."

"And Elora?" Tjaden blurted in the brief pause.

"Unfortunately, the soldiers were unable to withstand the beast. The camp was ravaged, and soldiers were killed." He paused and his face became more grave. "Elora was abducted."

The physical pain from two days of training disappeared, replaced by an agony far, far worse. He saw Ollie's hand on his shoulder, supporting him against the wall. His gut turned sour, and his vision wavered.

Jumbled words clustered in Tjaden's mouth as he struggled to come up with a question that made sense. "How did that happen?" He had to do something.

"The Jabberwock targets maidens. With nearly every attack, it carries off one or two unfortunate lasses. She was the only female in the party." When Tjaden failed to respond, Captain Darieus continued. "It is a tragic loss, Tjaden. Elora was as fine a young lady as I have ever met. The kingdom mourns with you."

Tjaden didn't bother with tears. Decision. Action. Find the Jabberwock. Fight it. Kill it.

"I'm not mourning," Tjaden stated. "I'm going. I've got to save her. I . . ." He still had trouble forming words.

"I'm going with you," Ollie said.

Tjaden barely noticed.

"I don't doubt your courage, and I know you're willing to singlehandedly confront the Jabberwock. However, you would be dead before you had a chance to unsheathe your sword. There are alternatives that afford you at least a small chance of survival."

Tjaden shook his head at Captain Darieus's words. "You said you killed one. How'd you do it? Where is it? You have to tell me."

"Do not forget your place, Tjaden," Captain Darieus cautioned. "I'm offering to help you, but remember that you are a recruit with less than two days of training. Listen to me."

"Yes, Sir," Tjaden replied, partially returning to the moment. "How can the Jabberwock be killed? Sir."

"I can teach you. I've spent two decades puzzling it out, and I have the means. But it will require trust on your part."

"Anything, Captain. I'll do anything."

"First, you need to commit to two weeks of specialized training before you rush off—"

"Two weeks! I can't wait two weeks, I need to—"

"Recruit!" Captain Darieus spoke firmly, and Tjaden immediately stopped protesting. "Elora may already be dead. However, if she survived the first day, she will most likely survive a month. We don't know the Jabberwock's motives, but we do know that the unlucky maidens sometimes survive for months in captivity."

Tjaden felt even sicker at the thought of already being too late. *That's not even a possibility,* he told himself. *Elora's alive.* The words did little to soothe him, and he had to restrain himself from running to find her.

Captain Darieus's gaze took in both Tjaden and Ollie. "Continue to attend your morning classes and exercises. In the afternoons, I will personally train you. I will teach you the secret of the vorpal blade and the other keys to defeating the Jabberwock. There is no foe more manxome[1] anywhere in the

---

[1] **manxome**: More than fearsome.

world." He placed a strong hand on Tjaden's shoulder. "Lucky for us, there is no man as determined as you."

Tjaden hesitated. Studying out problems and using unconventional means to overcome them was not his way. Sword-swinging, straightforward action had always worked better. He hated to leave Elora with the creature for even one more breath, but his failures against the bandersnatch and in the tournament made him wonder if there was a better approach. Even attacking Rodín had turned out nothing like he'd expected.

This new battle was one he could not lose. There would be no second chances. Walking straight into the Jabberwock's gaping jaws would not accomplish anything.

"You know where it is?" asked Tjaden.

Captain Darieus nodded. "It lives in a forest a few days north of here."

Ollie spoke up. "It's suicide to go without training, Jay."

But what about Elora? How could he just leave her there to suffer? If he would have been with her, he could have protected her.

Tjaden looked back and forth between Captain Darieus and Ollie. He hated to depend on someone else and hated endangering his best friend even more. But simply wanting to kill the Jabberwock wouldn't guarantee success.

Ollie nodded encouragingly, and Tjaden knew what he had to do.

For the first time he could remember, he was unable to control his emotions. Anger, fear, and anticipation welled in him, filling his eyes with tears. The tears flowed over, but he didn't care. Only one thing mattered—he had to find Elora.

She had to know the truth.

In a broken voice he said, "Two weeks."

PART III

> He took his vorpal sword in hand:
> Long time the manxome foe he sought—
> So rested he by the Tumtum tree,
> And stood a while in thought.

Elora's eyes were open. Slowly she realized she was awake. How long had she been staring at that tree? How long had she been awake?

Small bits of earth stung the side of her face where they dug into her cheek and temple.

Why am I laying on the ground?

She still didn't feel like getting up.

There was something about that tree. It looked like a tree, but it was so big. As big as the whole world.

Maybe not quite that big. Haze in Elora's head made it hard to make sense of anything around her.

"Sit up," she said, and lifted her head, then her torso. She had to close her eyes and let her head adjust. When she opened them, the surroundings were still unfamiliar and she had no idea how she had arrived. She blinked more, shook her head, but still felt befuddled.

She was sitting in a clearing. The woods surrounding it were as thick as a wall, and in the center of the clearing was the

largest tree she'd ever seen. It was as big around as a house and three times taller than any other tree in the forest.

Where am I? How did I get here?

Elora remembered traveling with an Elite escort toward Shey's Orchard. They made camp, ate dinner. And then . . . she couldn't remember. *Did I feel sleepy after dinner?* The image of a tent came to mind, but it might be from the trip *to* Palassiren. Her father and Mikel were in the camp with her. She ate dinner and . . . *now I'm here.*

"So where is here?"

She didn't feel as if she'd slept. For one thing there were no dreams, only blackness. Struggling to puzzle through the situation made her head throb. It was useless.

Hunger gnawed at her belly. It could have been days since she'd eaten. Weeks. Examining her sore body, she found broad, but minor, bruises. Her muscles felt as if she'd been working them. The clothes were her riding dress with divided skirts. The herbal sash was in place across her chest.

It can't be the same day. It was night when I was in camp. But how many days have passed? Her confusion and the unfamiliar surroundings were beginning to scare her. Trying not to think about being alone only reminded her that she was alone.

She had to do something.

The enormous tree stood twenty paces from the crowded woods which formed a circle around it. The only sign of human life was some kind of diagram on the ground near where she was sitting. She shook her head but it didn't help make sense out of the scrapings in the dirt. It reminded her of a wagon wheel. Protruding from the center was a tall wooden stake with a dark blue bandana attached to it. A small branch stuck out of the ground not far from the center, close to one of the spokes of the wheel. The diagram was large—if she stretched she could barely reach from one side to the other—and had been etched deep into the dirt.

Elora stood for a better angle and the world nearly went black again. When her vision cleared, the figure still didn't make any sense to her.

The clearing was entirely free of any other form of life as well, plant or animal. At first she saw no roads leading out of the clearing, but after walking around the massive tree she found a small path, just big enough for a horse and rider, leading into the woods. Judging by the sun's position, the path either led east or west. It would take some time to figure out if the sun was rising or setting.

Apart from its size, the tree itself was nothing special. It could have been elm or oak or ash or something else altogether. Hardwood trees didn't grow around Shey's Orchard so she'd never learned to distinguish them. This one just looked like a tree. A lone leviathan of a tree. The bark was so rough and exaggerated she could climb it if she had to, but the path looked like a better option.

Taking one more glance around, she called out. "Father! Mikel!" There was no response. Trying once more at the top of her lungs she called, "Father!" Indistinct forest sounds were the only answer.

"The path it is." She started into the cave-like trail. The plants lining the path were as tightly woven as a wall. Entwined. Impenetrable. Tulgey[1].

As she waited in the darkness for her eyes to adjust, faint noises came from the clearing. Being alone in the light was better than being alone in the dark, so she decided to go back and investigate the noise before plunging into the tunnel through the trees. Trying to stay hidden on the path, she peered carefully out but saw nothing. Sure she had heard movement, like an overloaded wagon crossing an old bridge, she warily entered the sunny clearing. Staying close to the outer perimeter, she circled the forest cavity.

The clearing was still empty. Just as she passed the odd diagram in the earth, a rushing wind washed over her. It smelled like the downwind side of a rotting animal. As she glanced into the sky, she realized how she had arrived at such a remote location. The Jabberwock. It was worse than she could have imagined.

She sprinted for the tunnel in the trees. The ground shook

---

[1] **tulgey**: Thick, dark, and entwined.

as the Jabberwock landed clumsily in the clearing and slammed its tail to the earth, blocking her exit like an enormous writhing snake.

Escape through the thick forest wall was impossible; she couldn't even fit an arm between the crowded trees. She turned to face the beast. Its head bobbed like a bird discovering a worm in its nest.

Is it really so stupid it doesn't remember bringing me here?

The Jabberwock moved its head toward her. Its forceful, rancid breaths made her sway both from their force and their stench. The beast was every bit as manxome as the stories described. Nothing seemed to make sense with it. Most of its appendages were scaly and twisty, but its trunk was solid and covered with leather-like skin. It looked like rotten spinach and smelled even worse. Its head was large and roundish like a squat egg. The heavy-lidded eyes glowed with a dull fire as it examined her from different angles. Sweat from its face mixed with saliva on its teeth and dripped to the earth.

Her bowels threatened to empty, and she was sure her stomach would have lost whatever it held if she had eaten anything. Staring at the sweaty-toothed monster, she told herself, *I've survived before. I'll live to tell this story as well.*

Elora looked around for a weapon or other means of escape. She was too far from the tree to climb, but the stake in the center of the diagram was within arm's reach. It took effort, but she wrenched it from the ground. Holding it like a staff in front of her, she tried to look menacing. The dark blue bandana hung limply from the end of it.

The bandersnatch bled when I hit it, but I don't know if this thing will even notice.

She still wasn't ready to give up.

Quick as a viper, the Jabberwock latched onto her weapon with its mouth and ripped it from her hands, filling her palms with splinters. Before she could move, it shot a reptilian arm forward and trapped her in its claws. Its speed was impossible. Scaly fingers ended in claws almost as long as her arm. At first she struggled to free herself, but her movement caused the rigid claws to dig into her. If she pushed too hard, the claws would slice her open.

Tossing the stake to the side, the Jabberwock lowered its head to her level. Stringy, reptilian protrusions from its fleshy cheeks dragged on the ground like tentacles, leaving a juicy trail.

The Jabberwock froze. Its eyes lost focus. An agonizing length of time passed. The Jabberwock breathed raggedly, like an old man snoring and its scent kept her stomach sour. Though it still held her fast, the Jabberwock turned its attention to the discarded stake and bandana.

It sniffed the dark blue material, eyes opening wider and red irises burning brighter. A strange sound started low in its throat, and when it reached its mouth it was an unpleasant gurgling sound. Not earthy like the rumbling that caused the water fountain, but sickly and wet.

The beast tensed, then swung its head to the other side of Elora. It focused on the diagram of the wheel on the ground. With effort, Elora calmed her breathing and continued to stand as still as possible, hoping to be forgotten.

The Jabberwock studied the tracings, looking at the image from every viewpoint. Still making the awful gurgling noise, it lowered its oblong head to the ground, breathing in dirt along with every detail. The noise stopped, and the beast raised its head and howled. The howl turned to a roar, and the Jabberwock cast Elora aside, then tore at the ground in front of the diagram. Its claws churned the hard earth like plows, showering the clearing with dirt.

Stomping powerful, awkward legs, it bellowed and burbled[1]. Elora shrank against the trees in fear. The Jabberwock

---

[1] **burble**: A mixture of a bleat, murmur, and warble.

inhaled an immense breath that came out as a thunderous roar. It bent trees and sent Elora crashing to the ground. With a clumsy lunge, the beast took flight.

Elora almost thought she heard a word in that groan as the creature flew away: "Revenge."

Elora raced toward the trail. No matter what might be waiting for her in the dark tunnel through the trees, it couldn't be as bad as the monster out here.

Tjaden's individual training sessions started with instruction about the Jabberwock. On the first day, Captain Darieus dispelled myths: the Jabberwock is not immortal, it does not breed unnaturally with the maidens it kidnaps, and it is not a creation of other kingdoms designed to wreak havoc on Maravilla.

Captain Darieus described the Jabberwock from the rounded tip of its tail to the gelatinous protuberances that hung from its cheeks. The creature's dull, oversized eyes came to life when enraged, glowing with hate-fueled intensity. Its quickness was unexplainable. Though the Jabberwock seemed awkward, it moved with viper speed.

In addition to classes, Tjaden went through specialized physical training while Ollie worked to improve his archery skills. Instead of sparring against men, Tjaden faced specialized training equipment designed to simulate a speedy, oversized opponent able to attack from any direction. At first he got knocked down or tripped up almost immediately. As he improved slowly, hour after hour, he began to build confidence. Or at least a glimmer of hope that he might actually succeed.

He collected bruises like Elora used to collect herbs. But for her he gritted his teeth and stood up to collect another one every time he fell.

On the third day of their private training, Captain Darieus led him to yet another contraption. "This will imitate the Jabberwock's many means of attack. Its tail is powerful, but more fearsome still are its jaws and claws. One bite will easily splinter a man's spine. Once grasped in its claws, you are helpless—wholly in its power. As I mentioned, the Jabberwock is as quick as a lightning strike. You must have reflexes to match."

Tjaden stood, sword drawn, on a narrow beam. He faced three padded, spring-loaded boards that would swing randomly. If the highest board activated, he ducked. He blocked the middle board with his sword and jumped over the lowest. Or at least he tried to. The first board swept his legs out and he landed hard on his back. Yet again, he didn't stay down.

After hours with the device, Captain Darieus said, "That's satisfactory improvement. You're ready to see more."

A soldier fetched Ollie from the archery grounds. He joined Tjaden and Captain Darieus as they exited the exercise quad. Captain Darieus explained, "I had not yet reached my thirtieth birthday when an expedition I commanded came across two Jabberwocks. With the safety of the citizens in mind, my brigade of two hundred attacked. We took them by surprise. We surrounded the first one and badly wounded it before they fought back. I lost half my men, but we succeeded in killing one of the beasts. The other was badly wounded and fled. It is that monster that plagues us to this day."

Tjaden didn't know what to ask first. "How'd you kill it? Why doesn't everyone know that? Why haven't you gone back to kill the other one?"

Captain Darieus waited until he finished. "All in good time. Since that time, the forest that surrounds the glade where he lives has changed. Only one or two men can approach at a time now, so ambush is no longer an option. The Jabberwock knows our intent, and its vengeance is fierce."

Ollie asked, "But why not tell the citizens about it? It would give them hope to know it *can* be killed."

"If the citizens of Maravilla knew that we were powerless to confront the beast . . . gone would be their hope. The crucial support we've always counted on would disappear. It's vital that they continue to have faith in us to protect them, to believe that once we confront the beast, we will come off conquerors."

It was difficult for Tjaden to follow the politics behind such maneuvering. If something threatened people he was supposed to protect, he took the necessary steps to protect them. That's why he was going after Elora. What was the point in deception and dragging it out? And why send a couple of new recruits?

"Sir, how can Ollie and me succeed where fully trained soldiers have failed?"

Captain Darieus stopped and turned to face them. "A prudent question. But it must wait."

They had arrived at the entry to Captain Darieus's residence. It was lodged in between the military quadrant and the palaces of the king and other nobles. A tiled fountain and sculpted hedges decorated the exterior.

The three walked through an enormous door and turned left, passing under a stone arch. Tjaden was stunned by an oversized hall lined with dozens—no, hundreds—of preserved animals. Near the entrance he saw smaller game like dormice, squirrels, crows, scalidinks, and borogoves. As they continued, the animals grew larger. A fawn, a small pack of coyotes, a pair of tusked peccaries, an elk, an olifant, and every animal in between—all frozen in lifelike stances. It was an impressive collection, and even though Tjaden knew the animals were dead, he felt more comfortable gripping his sword hilt.

The sheer waste which Captain Darieus displayed with obvious pride surprised Tjaden. The pelts of the animals in this room would keep an entire town warm through a bitter winter. Not to mention the uses for the horns, hooves, claws, and scales.

At the end of the hall was a large oak door. Captain Darieus opened it with a key. On the other side was a smaller hall than the previous one, though still impressive. Instead of being lined with common animals, Tjaden realized that it was filled with rare and implausible creatures.

He recognized almost all of them, some only by legend. Two bandersnatches stood menacingly near the door. The spines on their backs were raised, and their skin had a red tinge.

Quietly, he said to Ollie, "Not quite as frumious as ours, but close."

Next to the bandersnatches crouched a pair of barbantulas—great hairy spiders with legs as thick as Tjaden's and twice as long.

Tjaden smiled and looked at Ollie, who gawked at the barbantulas. "Still say they don't exist?"

Ollie muttered, "I respectfully rescind rashly recited rantings."

A small flock of Jubjub birds hung suspended from the ceiling, peering down with glassy eyes. Their red wings were angled backward in a lifelike dive. Tjaden's hand tightened on his sword, and he kept his eyes on them until he was clear.

They passed a short, shaggy animal with oversized paws that he assumed was a feriwumpus. The next animal was squat and wrinkled. It resembled a mix between a monkey and a crow. "Is that . . ."

"A targus," said Captain Darieus. "Yes, indeed it is. Notice the advanced age. The elder targus are much more deadly. I took this one with a single arrow.

"I have hunted extinct animals," he said, pointing to three dodos and a gryphon, "terrible creatures," now signaling the bandersnatches, "and even some that any reasonable person would swear do not exist." He indicated a brilliant white horse with a solitary pearly horn.

Tjaden had never even heard of such a collection. Hunting animals for food and clothing was a way of life everywhere, but it seemed like Captain Darieus killed for self-gratification and not on a small scale.

Everything Tjaden had seen in the inner city of Palassiren seemed to indicate that status was based on how much each noble could waste, or how opulently they could live. As if the more they spent on frivolity, the more important they were. For the cost of one palace, how many villages could be fed during drought years? How many additional soldiers could be retained to defend Maravilla?

Captain Darieus's display really wasn't different than the grand staircases, the elegant servants' garb, and the enormous palaces of the other nobles. At least Captain Darieus's collection demonstrated his own skill and determination over decades to accumulate.

"This is not why we are here," said Captain Darieus. He led them through another arch into a room with only one trophy—a full skeleton of a Jabberwock.

"Behold your enemy."

The bones looked like an oversized snake skeleton with arm, leg, and rib bones extending from it. Tjaden immediately noticed a problem.

"Where's the head, Sir?"

"Ah, the one flaw in my collection. We were able to disassemble the body and bring it back in pieces, but the skull was damaged so severely in the battle we couldn't salvage it. I've been waiting two decades to finish this skeleton. I'm counting on you to complete my collection."

Whatever reasons Captain Darieus had for sending him instead of other Elites, Tjaden was just glad for the opportunity to go after Elora himself. Nodding, he said, "I'll bring you the head."

As long as that doesn't interfere with rescuing Elora.

The following day, Ollie practiced at the archery range. Both he and Captain Darieus felt his time would be better spent practicing with his bow than doing physical training with Tjaden.

He took careful aim.

"Not going to get the bull's eye again," called Egden, a fellow Fellow recruit.

Thwang, thunk.

Ollie's arrow found the bull's eye, joining two of his other five arrows in the tight circle.

"I'll be hornswaggled. How do you do that?" asked Egden.

"It's all about breathing," answered Ollie. "That's the first thing I learned. Out. In. Release. I've known that longer than I've known that you should never run to the privy."

"Never run to the privy?" asked Shen, a Fellow recruit from Palassiren.

"That's right," Ollie said with a smile. "That's the last place you want to try to catch your breath."

When Ollie started training, he had good basic skills that he'd learned from Mikel. Since becoming a recruit, all of his precious free time was spent on the range, shooting and picking up tips from more experienced archers. He had distinguished himself as the best archer among the Fellow recruits.

A week into the specialized training, Ollie awoke excited at the prospect of a small break. It was Capital Day, a holiday commemorating the building of Palassiren. This being the fiftieth anniversary, the king and many nobles would spend

the day greeting subjects in the open square in front of the palaces. The fiftieth year being a Jubilation year, a feast was to be provided as well. The Elite recruits and their Fellows were to form part of the honor guard for the king.

Tjaden had been excused from the honor guard; neither he nor Captain Darieus was willing to lose even a few hours of training.

"Too bad you don't get a day off, Jay," Ollie said the morning of the Jubilation.

"In another week we'll both have a few days off to travel."

"I can't believe Captain Darieus is missing it."

"I was surprised too," said Tjaden. "I'm just glad he's taking my training so seriously."

"Did you hear about the cloak?"

"What cloak?" asked Tjaden.

"Some Elites were talking at the archery range. I guess King Barash is a huge military enthusiast. He gets so excited about all the pomp and ceremony that it's silly. Well, Captain Darieus offered a formal request to be excused from the festivities and of course King Barash approved it. By way of paying respects to the occasion, the First Knight offered the king his Elite cloak to wear as a symbol of Maravilla's military might."

"And he accepted?" asked Tjaden.

"With tears of joy or honor or something in his eyes. If we actually succeed in our mission he'll probably be the first one lined up to kiss our feet when we get back."

Tjaden chuckled.

"I wonder if I should go practice instead of going to the Jubilation," said Ollie. He wanted more time at the range, but the Jubilation was a once in a lifetime opportunity.

"From what Captain Darieus told me, you can afford to take a day off. He said there isn't much left for you to learn on the range."

Ollie was shocked. "He told you that?"

Tjaden nodded. "He knows you still have room to improve, but he hasn't seen many recruits that can shoot like you."

With a smile, Ollie said, "Yeah, me neither."

Tjaden didn't let him off that easily. "I'm glad you're my Fellow, Ollie."

"Enough, I get it. You're proud of me. You're not going to kiss me now or anything, are you?"

"No, I'll save that for Elora."

"One week, Jay," said Ollie. "We'll go get her in one week."

Ollie wore his pale blue recruit uniform, but Darieus insisted Tjaden wear a dark blue Elite's uniform for the Jubilation day. Neither he nor Ollie understood the reason, since Tjaden wouldn't be involved in the festivities, but he didn't object. They bid farewell. Tjaden went off with Captain Darieus, and Ollie left to join the honor guard.

Ollie had never seen anything like the crowds that assembled before the gates had even opened. Carrying his bow over his shoulder, Ollie walked past the Circle and Sword sculpture and into the plaza, which was filling with citizens and soldiers. Some of the Elite recruits wore swords or axes, but most of the Fellow recruits hadn't bothered to bring their bows, crossbows, or javelins. The regular soldiers would provide crowd control, so the honor guard duty didn't necessitate being armed.

Some of the other recruits teased Ollie as he walked out to the courtyard. "It's an *honor* guard," said Zarin.

"You're not going to war," added Wenn.

Ollie shook his arm, but the bow stayed in place. He made a mock attempt at pulling it off, grunting. "Hmm. Guess it wants to stay with me."

The others chuckled and dropped the subject.

The day started to drag after standing for an hour. The citizens that filed past the king became a steady stream of repetitive faces. Ollie's mind drifted to the range. If he couldn't practice with his bow he would practice with his mind.

Breathe. Raise bow. Draw. Aim. Out. In. Release. Bull's eye. He went over and over it in his mind.

As he was about to mentally release another arrow, a shrill scream startled him. Lifting his eyes and his bow, he saw a huge, dark shape descending on the courtyard. In the commotion of the celebration, everyone had failed to notice the Jabberwock until it was in their midst.

The earth shuddered as the Jabberwock crashed to the ground, landing on some Elites a mere twenty paces from King Barash. Ollie was at least that far away from the king in the other direction, but he still caught the Jabberwock's stench, like rancid tallow. Citizens fled in every direction and nobles ran with their escorts toward the palaces. Soldiers drew weapons and surrounded the king.

The Jabberwock scanned the crowd as if looking for someone in particular. It seemed to be inspecting the assembly with both its fiery eyes and flat nostrils. It locked onto the king and bounded toward him. Soldiers attacked, but were only able to land superficial blows.

How does it move so fast? Ollie wondered as he nocked an arrow. Soldiers were thrown aside or crushed by the creature's approach.

Ollie took aim and let fly. His arrow glanced off the Jabberwock's chest as it loomed over the petrified king. While Ollie readied another arrow, this one aimed at the curvy neck, the Jabberwock paused to inhale King Barash's scent. Ollie drew back again and his arrow flew true, lodging in the outstretched neck just under the head. The monster's threatening growl turned sharp in pain for a moment, but it was not long distracted by the arrow or the infrequent soldiers who got past the thrashing tail. It didn't seem to mind the minor wounds inflicted by the soldiers' weapons, and no one could get close enough to strike deeply.

The Jabberwock opened its mouth, bit down on the blue-clad king, and lifted him as effortlessly as a girl picks up a baby doll. It slammed the king to the stone courtyard, and his body bounced, lifeless. Lowering its head, it inspected the corpse.

While its tail kept the soldiers at bay, the Jabberwock's attention stayed on the king, barely flinching when Ollie sunk another arrow into its neck. After a short time inspecting the king's body, the Jabberwock's eyes opened in an expression of shock. With a powerful bellow, it turned on the attacking soldiers. Tail whipping, claws gouging, and jaws biting—any soldier within reach was thrown violently to the side or left lifeless on the ground.

Ollie changed tactics and aimed for one of the creature's too-small wings. They were stretched wide for balance. Aiming for the intersection of supporting bands of cartilage, Ollie focused on remaining calm. His arrow passed through the glutinous wing and tore a chunk of waxy flesh as it exited. That got its attention. It grasped a fully armored corpse in its claws and hurled it in Ollie's direction.

The throw was on target. Ollie was knocked down and pinned to the ground by the dead soldier. Severe pain shot through his left leg. From his pinned position, Ollie lifted his head and saw a light blue uniformed leg emerging at an angle from under the heavy soldier.

I wonder whose leg that is.

Movement had died down around the Jabberwock, but it continued to scan the crowd. When there were no more soldiers within striking distance, it took flight, barely wounded.

Pain dragged Ollie into unconsciousness, but not before he witnessed the Jabberwock's unsteady flight.

I got him . . .

Tjaden expected commotion on the day of Jubilation, but the sight as he entered the plaza with Captain Darieus was pandemonium. Enough so that he heard it from deep inside the training grounds. Thousands of citizens swarmed out of the inner city, through the gates into the city proper. Fellows and physicians attempted to aid fallen soldiers and a large, unorganized group surrounded King Barash's throne. Tjaden's hand went to the hilt of his sword, but Captain Darieus was calm, even unconcerned about the devastation.

Tjaden followed Captain Darieus to the edge of the king's dais. Bluish and still, the king lay on top of Captain Darieus's Elite cloak, his physicians helpless to do anything. They directed a blanket be placed over the body.

King Barash was dead.

Even though he hadn't been assigned to the guard and was only a recruit, Tjaden felt a pang of guilt. In his heart he'd already taken the oath to defend the man that lay dead in front of him.

Captain Darieus addressed a nearby Elite, "Soldier?"

With a salute he answered, "Sir, the Jabberwock. It came out of nowhere. Went straight for His Majesty. It didn't care about anyone else until after it killed him. Left with some minor wounds, a few arrows stuck in. We have dozens dead and at least as many injured."

"Prince Antion and Lady Palida?"

"They are safe, Sir." The soldier pointed at the palaces to the north. The upper patios were full of people watching the scene from a distance.

"The beast grows bolder," Captain Darieus said loudly. In a rising voice he continued. "He must be destroyed. We *must* have order!"

He stepped onto the platform and shouted, "People of Palassiren and citizens of Maravilla!" The push of the crowd diminished and many turned to listen. "The Jabberwock has struck at our very heart. It has discovered our capital and taken the life of our beloved sovereign. This deed will be avenged, and the people will be safeguarded."

Shouts arose from the crowds. Angry, demanding, supportive, and scared.

"I have groomed a hero to hunt the Jabberwock!" The crowd quieted and began moving inward again. "To discover its lair. And to slay it!" He pulled Tjaden up to the platform beside him.

Tjaden's mind felt like it was spinning in a whirlpool. If the Jabberwock could do all this, what chance did Elora have? What chance did he stand of killing it? In the plaza there were more people than he'd ever seen. Many of them were staring at him, waiting for something.

Captain Darieus shouted, "I present—Sir Tjaden, the Vorpal Knight!"

Everyone in the crowd, many with tears still staining their faces, craned their heads for a look at him. Some applauded and called for the Jabberwock's head.

A Knight? He wasn't even an Elite yet. Never in his life did he think he'd earn that title, and the fact that it had been granted before he had a chance to actually do anything struck him as wrong. Irritation joined his shock. The mission was supposed to be quiet, no fanfare.

"Draw your sword," Captain Darieus whispered.

"What?" answered Tjaden. He glanced up to see if the Jabberwock had returned.

"Draw your sword and raise it over your head," said Captain Darieus slowly. "These people need to believe."

Tjaden slowly obeyed, ready for boos and cries of "Imposter!" He hadn't beaten the bandersnatch. Hadn't even won the Swap and Spar. Wasn't even an Elite.

The crowd didn't care. The moment his sword was in the air, they exploded in cheering. The sound of clapping and tapping was deafening. Tjaden was thankful to be wearing dark blue instead of his pale blue recruit uniform. Captain Darieus was right. The people needed to hope.

"I swear," shouted Tjaden, taking a breath so he could come up with more words. "I swear that the Jabberwock will find its demise at the hands of my vorpal sword!"

His statement was met with more enthusiastic cheering.

"Good enough," Captain Darieus commented quietly.

"Thank you, Sir. I just wish I knew what vorpal meant."

"In good time, Tjaden." Captain Darieus stepped forward to the front of the platform and raised his voice. "In two days time we will send off our hero! He will carry our vengeance to the Jabberwock!"

Two days? I'm not ready. Thoughts of Elora came to mind and he wished they could leave immediately. Ollie was as ready as—

Ollie!

Tjaden looked around, embarrassed he hadn't thought of his friend sooner. Recruits were easy to spot in their pale blue but he didn't see Ollie anywhere. A few recruit uniforms stood out among the ranks of the dead and wounded.

"Excuse me, Sir, I need to find Ollie."

Captain Darieus didn't hear. He continued in his booming voice, "In this time of danger the kingdom needs strong leadership. Prince Antion is obviously too young to provide this. I will step into King Barash's place and serve as King Regent until Prince Antion has reached an age appropriate to serve as Ruler and Protector."

Lieutenant Markin stood near Captain Darieus, visibly shaken. He wiped tears from his face and shouted, "Citizens of Palassiren . . . your King Regent!" He went to one knee and a ripple spread outward through the crowd.

Tjaden, who had been moving through the crowd, knelt near a fallen soldier, twenty paces from the spot of the melee. The soldier had deep gashes from his waist to his shoulders, but Tjaden spotted swathes of blue-gray fabric underneath the body.

A familiar voice sounded from under the dead soldier. "Looks like you'll be embarking solo on this one, Sir Tjaden."

Tjaden had begun to think he'd imagined the part about being a Knight.

Ollie lay trapped by the bulk of the dead soldier and his armor. Sweat soaked his uniform and he spoke through clenched teeth.

"What do you mean solo? What happened to you?" He started to roll the limp body off his friend.

Grimacing in pain, Ollie pointed to his left leg. The leg was bent sharply above the knee, obviously broken. Ollie was breathing rapidly and gripping his upper thigh with white knuckles.

"Physician!" Tjaden yelled as he continued to pull the dead soldier's body free.

Just as Tjaden finished extricating Ollie, a physician arrived and cut the pants from the injured leg.

"Your femur's definitely broken. I'm going to straighten it to relieve the pain."

Ollie's eyes widened. "What? No!"

Tjaden held his friend by the shoulders as the doctor grasped Ollie's ankle and knee firmly. He slowly pulled the leg into alignment, leaning back to use his weight. Ollie screamed in pain. When the physician had pulled sufficient traction, the bones folded back in line.

Ollie took in a large gasp as if preparing to scream again, but released it slowly and said, "Well, hello. That does feel a lot better." Most of the strain disappeared from Ollie's face. He looked up at Tjaden and said, "I got it, Jay." He had never looked so proud in his life and Tjaden wondered if he was hallucinating.

"Huh?"

"The Jabberwock. Stuck some arrows in its neck and poked a hole in one wing. It was flying unsteady when it left." He cocked his head and said, "With wrecked wing the wretch withdrew."

"I wish I would have been here, Ollie. I could have helped. Maybe even prevented this."

"Or you could have gotten squished. Even with all the training in the world, I don't know how a man can expect to kill it."

"Thanks for the vote of confidence," said Tjaden.

"Except you," said Ollie. "It, uh . . . it doesn't stand a chance."

"You're lying, but I don't care. I'm still going after it."

"I heard. Five days sooner than planned."

Tjaden nodded. "That's right. I still don't know how, but I'm going to bring Elora back." It felt so good to say her name out loud. Looking over his shoulder to where Captain Darieus continued his speech, Tjaden added, "Who knows? I might even bring back the Jabberwock's head."

Later that day, Tjaden was summoned to Captain Darieus's audience room. He was shown into the chamber as the new king regent sat behind his desk listening to Lady Cuora, one of the most powerful nobles in the kingdom, who also had one of the shortest tempers.

"A Council should be assembled to advise the young king!" Lady Cuora's snaky black hair encircled her head and red-clad shoulders, bobbing in every direction. "The military will certainly play an important role but by no means should be the sole ruler."

"I assure you, Lady Cuora, my position as regent is temporary. When the current threat has been eradicated, we can discuss other possible arrangements. Now if you will excuse me, I need to see to that very issue."

Lady Cuora followed his gaze to where Tjaden stood. Under her gaze, he definitely didn't feel like a Knight.

"A boy. That's your grand plan? Bah! You make me wonder if you even want the *current threat* to be eliminated."

Before Captain Darieus could reply, she spun and stormed from the room. She didn't look at Tjaden again, but she did mutter, "Vorpal Knight. Nonsense."

Captain Darieus dismissed the Elite and Fellow that remained behind as his guard, and motioned Tjaden forward. "The burdens of leadership," he said with a sigh. "But we have more urgent matters, don't we?" He placed his hand on the hilt of Tjaden's sword and asked, "May I?"

Tjaden nodded and Captain Darieus pulled it from the scabbard.

"This style of sword is called a flamberge," said Captain Darieus, tracing the undulating edge with one finger. "It means flame sword. The wave-like blade inflicts as much damage as a wider sword, but allows a faster strike due to the reduced weight."

"But you said I needed a vorpal sword to kill the Jabberwock."

Nodding, Captain Darieus said, "Yes. Vorpal, meaning truth and flame. You have the fire. Now it's time for the truth."

"So I had the vorpal sword all along?" Tjaden asked. It was an impressive weapon, but he never imagined it holding any magic.

Captain Darieus shook his head. "The flame sword is appropriate for your mission, but the fire to which *vorpal* refers is in here." He tapped Tjaden's chest. He rapped a knuckle on the flat of the blade and said, "Not in here."

"But, Captain—"

"You are a Knight now, Sir Tjaden. It's best if you adhere to propriety. The proper title for a king regent is Lord Protector, or Highness. Lord Darieus is also appropriate. Now, no more questions until you hear the rest." He returned Tjaden's sword and walked to a cabinet at the side of the room, which he unlocked, removed a glass container from, then locked again. The glass, approximately the size of a grapefruit, was filled with a murky, brown substance. The stubby neck was sealed with thick wax.

"Sir Tjaden, the Jabberwock that plagues our land is male."

"Male?" People always called it an *it*.

"The creature I killed was female. This globe contains musk from that female. The Jabberwock has overly keen senses. This is the truth you need to defeat him."

"The truth is a putrid jar of . . . musk, Sir?"

"When did the Jabberwock start attacking our towns?"

"Generations ago." Everybody knew that.

"That is exactly what most people believe." Captain Darieus smiled down at Tjaden. "The truth is the first Jabberwock attack occurred twenty years ago. With soldiers stationed across Maravilla it was a simple task to spread the tale of our enemy and unite the populace against it. The accounts of the Jabberwock almost always came from a far away town, but over the years he has terrorized widely enough that people at least know the beast is real."

Tjaden nodded slowly as he worked to figure out the significance.

"If you ask any citizen how many people have been snatched by the Jabberwock over the years, they'll say hundreds. Thousands. The truth, as near as we can tell, is closer to three dozen."

"I still don't see what any of that has to do with me. I just want to get Elora back." As an afterthought he added, "And kill the Jabberwock."

"That is the thinking of a farmer. You can't kill a creature like the Jabberwock with wishes and dreams."

Lord Darieus carried the glass bulb to his desk and sat down.

"I have been entrusted with the daunting task of protecting an entire kingdom and making a million people feel secure. But it is a delicate balance. If we have no enemy, the king has trouble collecting taxes. People complain that the army is too powerful, and we end up with an insufficient number of soldiers, which places the kingdom in true danger. The easiest road to peace is through a common enemy. Now that I am king regent I need to consider these things more than ever. For the well-being of the kingdom."

That didn't seem right to Tjaden. It sounded like manipulation.

His face must have shown something because Captain Lord Darieus asked, "Have the sixteen years of your life been lived in relative peace, Sir Tjaden?"

"Yes, Sir."

"Taxes are reasonable, the army is strong without being oppressive, and the losses inflicted by our enemy are not more than we can absorb. No one could have established a more favorable balance than I have done."

That made sense. Without being a nuisance or an oppressor, Lord Darieus had protected the kingdom all of Tjaden's life. In a way, he had created the monster the Jabberwock had become, but not on purpose. And it wasn't like he wanted it to live. He and the other Elites just hadn't succeeded in killing it yet.

Tjaden could never come up with logic like Lord Darieus's, but he also couldn't argue the fact that life was very good for most people in Maravilla. Unfortunately, that didn't include the person he cared about more than anything.

"That makes a lot of sense," said Tjaden. "But how does it help me rescue Elora?"

"Good, back to the point. Based on what I've told you, do you have any idea why we have been under attack for the last twenty years?"

After a moment of thought, Tjaden said, "You killed his

mate. He wants revenge." It was a sentiment with which Tjaden could identify.

"Correct." Lord Darieus leaned forward on his desk and stared up into Tjaden's eyes. "If you knew how many times I have regretted killing its mate . . ." The regret was clear on his face. "But that does not excuse it for two decades of murder, kidnapping, and terror. Today alone the beast killed our king and close to fifty of our brothers-in-arms! How many more maidens will we allow him to carry off? How many of your brothers must die? How much longer must he be allowed to exact a vengeance long since earned?"

Lord Darieus stood and fixed Tjaden with his penetrating gaze. "You will face the Jabberwock with fire in your heart, bearing the truth. And the truth is this: the Jabberwock's true nature is a creature of peace. Losing its mate transformed it into what it is today."

Holding the sealed jar he continued. "This is the secret behind your vorpal blade. In the moment before you approach him, you will coat your sword with the pungent fragrance of the female. It will awaken the creature's true disposition. And you will slay him."

Boyhood images of killing the Jabberwock were turning to mist in his mind. It wouldn't be through swordplay and bravery, but through trickery. Like something Ollie would pull.

But it didn't matter. The path ahead was simple—rescue Elora.

Tjaden nodded.

"Very well," Lord Darieus said. "You will find him near the Tumtum tree. Travel the Harbinger Spoke for four days and you will find a pathway leading into a particularly tulgey wood. The path passes under a canopy so thick it will feel like night. Two days on that path will bring you to the Tumtum tree. It is a tree as big around as a wabe and ten times as tall as the city walls. Climb the bark and you will find an opening in the tree near the first branch, a chamber. If you happen to arrive at night, sleep inside the chamber, not in the clearing. There is a ladder in the corner of the chamber that will take you downward to another tunnel that leads to the glade where the Jabberwock lives. There you will find Lady Elora."

Tjaden broke concentration to smile at the title. Elora wasn't a Lady, but if she married a Knight, she would be.

Lord Darieus asked Tjaden to repeat everything he had said. As Tjaden repeated what he could remember, Lord Darieus corrected, filled in gaps, and gave much more detailed explanations of every step. When he was satisfied, he gave Tjaden the flask and dismissed him.

Later that night, Tjaden talked with Ollie in their quarters. Ollie had spent most of the day in the infirmary, but there were so many injured soldiers that stable patients had been moved to quarters. A large splint held his leg in place, and he was confined to his bed for at least two weeks.

Tjaden told Ollie what he'd learned. The truth about the Jabberwock's mate and his true nature, and how Tjaden would use the female's essence to slay the Jabberwock. With each tidbit, Ollie pushed himself to a more elevated sitting position, as much as the leg would allow.

"I knew it, Jay! I told you back at home there was something suspicious about how it always attacked far-off places. Soldiers have been exaggerating the attacks our whole life."

"Alright, genius, use that amazing brain of yours to tell me how that helps us now."

Ollie drummed his fingers and stared at nothing.

After a minute, Tjaden said, "What does it matter? At least with this plan I'm less likely to get squished."

"No one's happier about that than me," said Ollie, "present company excluded. But the rest of that sounds pretty suspicious."

"We're soldiers. Not nobles. Let them figure it out."

"Captain Darieus has sure benefitted from everything that has happened."

"That's crazy," said Tjaden. "You think the Jabberwock is his pet monster or something?"

Ollie shifted to a more comfortable position. "No, but you weren't there this morning. You should've seen the Jabberwock. It—he—was definitely looking for something specific. After he killed the king, he inspected the body. I don't know why, but after he sniffed it, he went berserk. He changed from satisfied to enraged faster than a frumious bandersnatch."

"I wish you would have been there tonight, Ollie. Captain, I mean, Lord Darieus explained it much better than I can."

From where he lay, Ollie made an exaggerated salute and said, "Lord Protector His Protectorship Captain Regent Darieus. His Eminency."

"Funny," said Tjaden.

"Fine, just tell me this. If all you need is this magic potion, why waste all the time training with machines?"

"Confidence?" said Tjaden. "Appearances? I don't know. The only reason I'm leaving so soon is because the Jabberwock happened to show up today. I appreciate the concern, but unless you've got something that will help on my mission, I should get some sleep."

Ollie lay back in bed. "Try to figure out a way to get at the Jabberwock's belly or neck. I don't know how you'll get close enough, but those were the only parts any of us could pierce."

"If I can find a way to get Elora out without fighting him, I will. She's all I care about."

"You might lose your title if you come back without the head."

"He can have it," said Tjaden. "By the way, I'm leaving first thing tomorrow. Not in two days like he said. I told Lord Darieus I don't want to bother with well-wishers crowding the streets. He agreed, and he said he was going to suggest it to prevent other would-be rescuers from following me."

Elbowing up in bed again, Ollie said, "I'd tell you to take any Elite who would go along if I thought it would do any good. But I don't think all the Elites in Maravilla could kill that thing."

"More encouraging words," Tjaden said with a smile. "Thanks."

"Like I could stop you from going if I tried. It'll work, Sir Jay. Captain Darieus wouldn't waste his time just to send you to your death."

"I hope you're right. Because I'm going either way."

Tjaden mounted before sunrise, ready for whatever lay ahead. He paused at the Circle and Sword sculpture. His entire life, it had been all he cared about, all he had ever struggled for. That desire was a pale shadow of how badly he wanted to find Elora and make sure she knew how he felt.

A dark-haired boy stepped out from the far side of the statue, holding a sword.

"You off?" he said quietly. It took Tjaden a moment to realize it was Chism. The words were more than the boy had ever said to him.

"Yeah. Don't tell anyone."

Chism asked, "What will I talk about all day then?"

Tjaden smiled. He wished Chism had opened up earlier. They probably would have gotten along pretty good. "Getting some early sword practice in?"

The boy nodded. That explained part of his skill with the sword. He was probably out here every morning, but with so many designated practice areas, the location was a strange choice.

"Want some help?" asked Chism. "I don't need a fancy title or anything, but you could use better odds."

Other than their small size and dark hair, Chism and Ollie had exactly nothing in common. Even so, with Ollie bedridden, Tjaden couldn't think of a better partner than Chism. Quiet, serious, and deadly with a blade. But if something was afoot, as Ollie suspected, he didn't want to put anyone else at risk. Especially Elora. If he changed the plan now, it might endanger her.

"If it was up to me," Tjaden said. "But this is Lord Darieus's mission."

Chism made a disappointed noise and glanced to the bluing eastern horizon. "Come down here. Hurry."

Not even on his way and already facing delays. For most people he would refuse, but the young recruit intrigued him. He dismounted and walked over to Chism.

"Climb up on top of the Circle."

"Why?" Maybe there was some rule against it and Chism was trying to steal his mission. Or maybe he wanted Tjaden to fall and break his arm. Or maybe—

"Climb up. Trust me."

Anything to get it over with so he could start the trip. It was not an easy ascent, but Tjaden managed by using the crossbars of the sword hilt as footholds. Asking Chism for a hand was out of the question; the boy had an irrational fear of touching people.

From the vantage point, the view was all-inclusive. He felt like he could see every building in Palassiren. That made sense. They probably chose a spot for the statue that could be seen from the most possible locations.

"Look," said Chism, pointing east.

Tjaden looked up just in time to see a tiny slice of sun rise between two peaks. One single ray streamed directly toward him, hitting him full in the head then chest. The entire sun seemed intended for him only. Out of everyone in the world, he alone felt its warmth.

Within the space of a few breaths the ray became a blanket, and began rolling down over the inner city. Tjaden didn't have to ask if that was what Chism had intended for him.

He climbed down and asked, "That's why you practice here, isn't it?"

Chism nodded.

"That sunbeam was supposed to be yours, wasn't it?"

"Some people say the first rays are lucky," said Chism, avoiding Tjaden's eye. "You need luck more than I do today."

Lucky sunbeams? Magic Jabberwock musk? A tree as big around as a wabe? Definitely not the type of mission he'd always envisioned.

"Thanks," said Tjaden. He settled into his saddle. "See you in a couple of weeks."

With his head still down, Chism waved. It was comforting to find out that even stoic Chism held boyish superstitions about lucky sunbeams.

But if it was so ridiculous, why did Tjaden feel like he could accomplish anything? The last time he'd felt so invincible was when Elora smiled at him on the stage at the induction ceremony. When he made it out of the city without being recognized, he wondered again if there was something to it.

With two horses and enough food for three weeks, Tjaden traveled in the brown workman's clothes he'd arrived in plus a plain cloak. The journey would only take one week in each direction, but he needed enough food for two people on the return trip. Though the path ahead would be thorny, it was better than waiting and planning.

Tjaden had asked Lord Darieus about the possibility of a contingent of soldiers as an escort, but Lord Darieus said he had ample faith in Tjaden's abilities. Any danger he faced along the way would be minor compared to his final goal.

The moon that rose at the end of the day shone brightly so he was able to ride into the night. Hours after sunset, he set up his bedroll under a large willow. As soon as the sun rose the next morning, he was on his way. When the Harbinger Spoke ran through towns, Tjaden found paths that skirted it so he could keep to himself.

After riding a couple of hours on the second day, the road entered a forest of tall trees that he couldn't name. Not more than a hundred yards into the woods, Tjaden came to a fork.

He paused in the center of the road to consider his options. Darieus hadn't mentioned any splits in the road. There were no signs, no tracks in the road, and no indication of which way was correct. He nearly fell off his horse when he heard what sounded like a boy clearing his throat. Ripping his sword from its scabbard, he demanded, "Who's there?"

He looked around and saw no one. He was alone on the road. The sound repeated itself, and he leaned forward to see past the foliage of a tree. Lounging in the branches was a large cat. It was grey with broad black stripes, plain except for a wide smile that extended past the borders of its face. The teeth were sharp like any other cat's teeth, but it had way too many of them.

"How do?" annunciated the cat.

Tjaden stared in surprise.

"I say, how . . . do . . . you . . . do?" it repeated.

"I, ahem. Did you say something?"

"No, I did not say 'something.' I merely inquired after your current state of well-being. Or poor-being, as the case may be."

The animal continued to smile a ridiculously wide grin.

Tjaden had no idea how to answer. "I'm, uh, a bit confused, I suppose."

"Oh, wonderful!" said the strange cat. "Imagine the two of us meeting in the exact same state of mind. Forgive me, I've forgotten your name already."

"I haven't given it," replied Tjaden.

"I don't want you to give me your name. I've a perfectly good one, after all. And besides, I have nothing to give you, and *Cheshire* simply would not work for you. You're much too serious."

Still trying to figure out the strange creature, Tjaden asked, "Are you a cat?"

"Heavens, no. I am a Cheshire Cat."

"A Cheshire Cat is still a cat."

"And a sea horse is a horse. A prairie dog is a dog. And a woman is a man."

After pausing to consider, Tjaden said, "I see your point. So you're not a cat."

"And you're not a cat either. That makes four things we have in common—confusion, the name Cheshire, not being a cat, and having four things in common with each other."

"I believe that's only three things," started Tjaden. "Wait, my name's not Cheshire. It's Tjaden."

"What's Tjaden?"

"I'm Tjaden."

"Oh dear. Well, do you like to scratch behind your left ear like so?" The curious animal reached its right front paw around its head and scratched vigorously.

"Not really."

"Aha! Me neither. That's three things again!"

Frustrated, Tjaden asked, "Can you just tell me which way to go?"

It chuckled and in its pleasant voice answered, "They always want me to tell them which way to go."

"Who do?"

"You do."

"Who's you?"

"You who ask me which way to go, of course! My dear boy, I would not say you are confused."

"I assure you, I am." Tjaden rubbed his temples.

With a thoughtful look on its smiling face, the cat-like creature replied, "Discombobulated, maybe. Flummoxed, perhaps."

Tjaden ignored that. "Can you at least tell me where I am?"

"Whatever for? After all, it matters much less where you are than which direction you are going." Its smile seemed to broaden even more.

Determined to get some guidance, Tjaden asked, "Which of these is the Harbinger Spoke?"

"Is that a riddle?" Its eyes brightened. "Let me see . . ."

Tjaden interrupted, "No, it's not a riddle. I just want to know which of these roads will take me northwest."

"This road," it answered, signaling to the right with one paw, "will take you west. And this one," pointing left, "will take you north. So, to go northwest you simply must take both of them. Now I'm catching onto your riddles, my boy."

"No, not really."

"I have an idea. A perfectly wonderful idea! If you wish to go northwest simply go back the way you came, turn around, and walk toward me."

Tjaden tried once more, "Which of these roads will lead me to the Tumtum tree?"

After clearing its throat, it answered:

The Tumtum tree, the Tumtum tree,
King of forests, quarry's bane.
Arrive in peace; there'll be a feast!
And there you shall remain.

Tjaden decided that the Cheshire Cat made less sense the longer the conversation continued. Very pleased with itself, it went on. "And you'd do well to remember that, lad."

"I give up, I'll just choose one."

"We all make choices," said the Cheshire Cat. "We just don't make consequences."

Shaking his head, Tjaden started on the northward fork.

"A fine choice, Sir Tjaden," the feline affirmed.

Sir Tjaden? Is there any way it knows about the whole Vorpal Knight thing? It wasn't a topic he was comfortable with so he asked, "What if I would've gone the other direction?"

"Do you like stories? A *whatif*, a *shooduv*, a *round tuit*, and a *diddit* all started down a path much like the ones you see before you. I'm not going to say how the story ends, but even a muddled youth such as yourself should know who reached their destination first."

Curiosity outweighing his frustration, Tjaden switched directions and started down the westward path.

Again the animal complimented him. "Might I once again commend you on a fine choice?"

More confused than ever, Tjaden continued. After traveling less than a mile, the road angled to the northwest and soon merged with an identical road he could only assume came from the fork where he'd seen the Cheshire Cat.

There was no time to go back and ask, but Tjaden said anyway, "Why didn't you just tell me they led to the same place?"

"Why didn't you ask?" One second there was only a voice next to the trunk of a tree, then Tjaden noticed the smile, and then it was sitting there. Smiling.

"What would have happened if I'd taken the other road?"

"I am not a dealer in would-haves. Sorry."

"How about possibilities? What possibilities did I avoid by taking that road?"

Somehow, the Cat's smile shrugged. "Perhaps there was a targus down that road. Perhaps your eyeballs were eaten. Or perhaps it was cruel and left your eyeballs but ate your dreams."

"You can't eat dreams," said Tjaden.

"I wasn't talking about myself." The Cheshire Cat stood and stretched. "Besides, you probably think it's impossible for the dead to sniff and the tamed to bite."

"The what?"

"Why haven't you ever been nipped by a dead snake?"

Tjaden considered for a moment. "Because I don't get close enough to the head for it to get me." He'd seen plenty of headless snakes strike out of reflex up to an hour after dying.

No one he knew was stupid enough to get bit. "What are we even talking about?"

"Nonsense," said the Cheshire Cat as it started to fade away. "Always remember that nonsense can be your deliverance. It's unfortunate that even if you happen to survive, you'll see before you understand."

Just as it had appeared, it disappeared. The last Tjaden saw of it was the silly grin.

Good riddance, thought Tjaden. It had wasted enough of his time and the words that sounded like some kind of warning were already a muddled heap in his head.

Two and a half days later, just past a small road leading to a town called Silhaven, Tjaden reached the path that led to the Tumtum tree. Lord Darieus had described it perfectly. The forest had been sparse yet evenly wooded until this point, when for no apparent reason the trees along one side of the Spoke clumped closer and closer together until there wasn't enough room for a man to walk through. The thick portion only stretched a hundred paces along the Harbinger Spoke, but there was a single path directly in the middle of it. Night was approaching, and Tjaden was reluctant to enter the dark path at dusk, so he made camp.

The exhaustion of four days hard travel helped him fall asleep, but the nerves from what lay ahead made his rest fitful. Part of his brain worried over what he'd find, like a dog worries a bone. Nothing could keep him from continuing, but with each passing day he wondered if there was any way Elora could still be alive. It would be his fault if she wasn't—she'd never have left Shey's Orchard if not for him.

Tjaden didn't know how he'd live with that. With the ring stuck in his pocket and the words stuck in his heart. Well, not words, not exactly. Hopefully those would come if he needed them.

Almost as soon as he was on the path the next morning it became as dark as a moonless night. The canopy was just barely tall enough for him to travel on his horse. Minute specks of light occasionally shone through like sporadic stars. The path seemed straight, but in the darkness he couldn't be sure. A slight bend would change his course considerably over the miles.

The absence of forest sounds was almost palpable. There was no room for birds or animals to move around in the woods, and the thick foliage kept any wind out. The sensation was so foreign that he almost felt like he was wandering through an underground cave.

Hours passed. Tjaden stopped occasionally where small streams crossed the path and let the horses drink. Sparse grass lined the edges of the trail and the horses devoured it every chance they got. Tjaden wondered how grass could grow with no sunlight. Hunger for the thin grass led the horses forward on the trail, but Tjaden couldn't take the sluggish pace for long. Only with a lot of coaxing was he able to draw the horses away from the grass.

Into the forest he traveled, deeper and deeper like a hare in a burrow. When the specks of light overhead disappeared, he assumed it was night, so he slept. At some point he woke up and saw pinpricks of light, so he resumed his journey. The passing of time was impossible to track, but eventually a hazy light appeared in the path ahead. The opening was not directly ahead of him, as he expected it would be; instead it shone from behind a bend in the path. When the full light came into view, he realized the path had a significant curve.

I've probably been walking in a tightening spiral this whole time.

His exhaustion faded as he pushed forward, yearning for light and freedom from the oppressive forest. Despite his desire for open sky, he entered the clearing carefully. It was mostly empty. There were no trees or other vegetation in the

twenty paces between him and a gigantic tree that reached higher than Tjaden could see.

The Tumtum tree. It had to be.

He drew his sword and examined the rest of the clearing. In one area the ground was disturbed, having recently been plowed but not by human hands or tools. The Jabberwock must have done it. Adjacent to the churned up dirt, Tjaden saw a faint imprint of a wagon wheel with one bent spoke. A wooden stake, a strip of dark blue cloth, and a small branch lay near the center.

How would anyone get a wagon in here?

After inspecting the clearing, he sheathed his sword, leaned against the tree, and pondered his options in the fading light. He could go immediately and look for Elora, possibly rescue her. At least find out if she was still alive. But he only had one chance, and he didn't want to waste it with the low light in the Jabberwock's own territory.

Within a day he would find Elora and lead her home. The anticipation he'd felt about making it to the Academy was nothing compared to this new feeling.

A faint sound, like breathing from a distance, brought him upright, listening. Slowly, he drew his sword and stood ready. Time passed, and the sound did not change. He circled the clearing as silently as possible, looking for the source of the uneven rush of air, but he was still alone. Twilight played games with his vision.

Looking up, he noticed the tree tops swaying in tune with the sound.

The wind, he thought with relief. The confinement of the dense forest had made him extra sensitive.

Tjaden led the horses back into the path where he could still see them, but where the Jabberwock couldn't reach them if it happened to come. He shouldered his pack and scaled the rough bark of the Tumtum tree to the first branch. Near the fork of the wide branch was an opening in the tree like a hole that a squirrel would live in—if that squirrel were the size of a man. Just as Lord Darieus had described. Tjaden squeezed through the opening and found a chamber inside the tree that was almost tall enough to stand in.

He dropped his traveling gear on the pulpy floor. In the far corner of the cavity was a hole with a ladder that led downward through the pith of the tree. Again he resisted the urge to rush to Elora. It would be better to rescue her in the morning than die with her tonight.

The chamber felt as oppressive as the forest had for the last two days. Even though Lord Darieus had recommended he sleep there, Tjaden wanted nothing to do with the cramped quarters.

This is my *mission now.*

Taking only his bedroll, dinner, and sword, he climbed down into the clearing. Night had fallen, but it wasn't nearly as dark as the tunnel had been. Leaning against the base of the huge tree, Tjaden ate a cold dinner. He visualized his sword piercing the Jabberwock's heart. Elora was watching, and he finally felt like a hero.

When his thoughts and dreams began to merge he pulled the bedroll up. Leaning against the massive tree, he slept.

PART IV

**And, as in uffish thought he stood,
The Jabberwock, with eyes of flame,
Came whiffling through the tulgey wood,
And burbled as it came!**

Tjaden walked through the dense tunnel of trees. Instead of stillness, malice surrounded him. The forest sent probing vines that snared him and tried to choke the life out of him. Terrified, he remained still, without resisting or drawing his sword as the forest claimed him. All the while, the Cheshire Cat trilled, "Arrive in peace; there'll be a feast!"

Tjaden's horses shrieked, yanking him from the dream. Shooting up to a seated position, he looked around. The horses sounded like terrified women. Tjaden grabbed his sword and tried to stand, but he was attached to the ground. There was enough moonlight in the clearing to make out what looked like roots that had grown over his legs while he slept.

From his awkward position he hacked at the plants, which began to constrict as soon as he fought against them. Unable to use the full range of his swing, it took ten or fifteen strikes to chop through a single root. More tendrils came out of the ground to replace the ones he hacked through. Tjaden intensified his slashing, all the while hearing the shrill cries of the horses. When all but one ankle was free, he stood, nearly exhausted, and three swipes later he was clear.

Tjaden rushed to the entrance to the path and saw that the animals were much more entwined than he had been. In addition to roots like that those that had bound him, the horses were being wrapped by vines extending from the trees. All of their legs were caught, and a few vines reached completely around their bodies and necks. The vines weren't as hardy as the roots, but they moved much faster, writhing and slithering in the air. In between screams, the animals bit at the vines, but they were quickly losing the battle.

As soon as Tjaden began hacking at the plants, two vines released one horse's leg and moved quickly along the ground, sniffing out Tjaden like blind snakes. He swung his sword and cut the tip off one, but the other wrapped around his wrist. It was as strong as a rope. With his free arm he swung and severed it, but more vines were coming after him. In the dimness he couldn't tell how many.

He backed up and fought them off, shocked at how fast they moved. Even with so many vines coming after him, the horses were more entangled than ever.

Tendrils and roots writhed at his feet. The area where he stood was filling with them. He tried to run to the tree, but two roots had already wrapped one ankle. He chopped through the roots and sprung in four long strides to the base of the tree. It pained him to abandon the horses, but there was nothing he could do for them. With sword in hand, he scaled the tree and sat defensively on the first branch. No roots, vines, or tendrils attacked him.

Why hadn't Lord Darieus warned him? Maybe there was something he could have done to save the horses. Tjaden was still out of breath when the horses went silent. Sounds of wringing and an occasional crack of the animals' bones filled the clearing, and he ducked into the cavity of the Tumtum tree to escape the grotesque noise.

It was free of roots and vines. As far away from the door as possible, he leaned against the wall of the tree with his sword still drawn and cursed himself for not being able to do more. Unable to think of anything that would have made a difference, he cursed Lord Darieus for not telling him how to avoid it.

The sickening noises continued. Tjaden did not sleep again that night.

When a good amount of sunlight reached into the Tumtum's interior, Tjaden crawled out onto the branch with his sword in hand. The clearing was vacant. No sign of his bed roll or the horses, and no sign of struggle. The ground appeared undisturbed. Tjaden's heart sank, but he forced himself to focus on the reason he was there.

Back into the Tumtum tree he went. Luckily, he had left his pack inside instead of taking it into the clearing. Kneeling next to it, he removed the glass container that held the female Jabberwock's scent. After unwrapping the padding, he tied it to his belt, then climbed down the manmade ladder. The climb was much longer than the climb up the bark to the branch. He had to be below ground.

The passage at the bottom of the ladder felt like it had been scraped with tools long ago. The walls were woody. Not hard like a branch, but soft like the inside of a root. He had to rely on his sense of touch, for the passageway was as black as the path through the tulgey woods.

He kept one hand on the stringy wall of the corridor and the other on the hilt of his sword. With each step he felt the weight of the sealed container that held the Jabberwock essence. Lord Darieus obviously believed in the musk, but it had never been tested. Tjaden couldn't help but wonder if the tincture in the flask would have any effect on the Jabberwock—or, worse, bring the Jabberwock right to Tjaden in a rage.

Hundreds of paces later, the passageway began to narrow and angle upward. An opening ahead admitted light. He slowed his pace, his heart racing and a sheen of sweat forming on his brow.

Creeping within an arm's reach of the narrow opening that led into daylight, Tjaden didn't dare peek out. He didn't need to. Standing near the mouth of the tunnel he felt a slight breeze start and stop in rhythm with the sound of resonant breathing. The rotten air current revolted him even as it cooled his sweaty brow.

With determination, Tjaden loosened the tie on the container at his hip. Sweaty hands made it difficult, but he peeled away the wax seal.

Clenching his teeth and taking a deep breath, he grasped the lid and heard a voice. A human voice. Someone was singing, and as he listened to the melancholy song, he realized it was Elora. Tears of relief sprang to his eyes. Everything in him wanted to burst out and rush to her, or at least peek around the corner and see her face. Her voice was pure and pleasing, and it made him long for her face that much more. With effort, he retreated and sank to his knees to consider his next move.

It surprised Elora how many of the songs she knew had sadness at the core. Love songs, nursery rhymes, even lullabies. Somehow the songs made her feel heavyhearted and hopeful at the same time. She wasn't one to give up, but after nearly two weeks in captivity, her options hadn't broadened.

She sang.

Again the dark night presses, presses on thy soul.
Pierces hope and dreaming, he's never coming home.
'tever path he's trodden, trodden free or bond
Onward he'll continue, the pathway still is long.

Ay dah la dee, ta loo ree
Ay dah la tee, lo ray
Ay dah la dee, ta loo ree
Ay dah ta ree ta lay.

Ere she 'proaches smiling, smiling pure as gold
Nights and years a' crying, countless ye shall know.
The vanished know no comfort, comfortless are ye
Yet continue waiting, tho' live or dead she be.

Ay dah la dee, ta loo ree
Ay dah la tee, lo ray
Ay dah la dee, ta loo ree
Ay dah ta ree ta lay.

The song was a common lullaby in Shey's Orchard, but Elora had never imagined being one of the vanished. Her imprisonment wasn't physically hard to bear once she learned she was safe, but she wouldn't last much longer.

The glade she shared with the Jabberwock was much larger than the one around the Tumtum tree. The trees that enclosed the clearing were a closely knit wall, the same as the rest of the tulgey wood. Besides a few large boulders, soft grass covered most of the open area.

The only water supply was a spring that formed a pool at the center of the glade. The water appeared crisp and clear, but it was laced with mercury. Every time she took a drink she could taste the quicksilver. It was similar to an iron taste, like a bloody nose, but she had enough experience with mercury from helping in her father's mirror shop to sense the difference. If it was strong enough to taste, every drink was poison, even if it took weeks or months to affect her. She drank only once a day to avoid the symptoms as long as possible.

Elora spun the gold-tipped red ribbon around her wrist. The ribbon was the only human item she'd found in the glade, most likely left behind by a former captive. Since Elora was months away from her Sixteenery, it wouldn't be proper to wear it in her hair. But somebody once had.

"Did anyone try to rescue you?" she asked the ribbon. "Did you even have anyone to dream about?" They were bleak questions. No one had ever survived being abducted.

"When I escape, I'm going to find out where you lived and take this to your family."

Each town's ribbons were slightly different. Finding out where this one came from would be a daunting task, but if tasks gave her a reason to survive, all the better. She could rule out the twelve Provinces on the outer border of Maravilla. Girls there wore white ribbons instead of red.

So, somewhere in the interior. Half of the kingdom eliminated was a good start for a morning's work.

The Jabberwock stood and lumbered toward her. She didn't flinch. She hadn't flinched for days. Satisfied that she was still there, the Jabberwock lunged into the air, leaving her alone for as long as it took to find a meal.

The hole in his wing made flying difficult. How he had received the wound was a mystery, but it happened after he left her in the clearing by the Tumtum tree on the first day. His flight was uneven, more like a bat than a bird. She wondered how much of that was due to the wound.

The matchsticks she'd planned on giving her mother had proven to be a boon the first time the Jabberwock dropped the hindquarters of a deer in front of her. She'd only used one so far, then made sure the fire never went out. Twenty-three matchsticks left for her mother.

"What are you going to bring me for breakfast today?" she said, though the Jabberwock was far out of hearing range.

"I have some dried meat and flat bread."

She jumped. By the time she realized the voice was familiar, she was halfway hidden behind a boulder. Looking for its source, she saw the most welcome sight of her life. Tjaden was walking out of the tunnel. Was he truly shining, or did her imagination just make it seem so?

Elora ran into his arms and felt as safe as their embrace after the bandersnatch.

"What are you doing here?" she asked in amazement, still clinging tightly.

"Um, rescuing you," he said. As smooth with words as always. "Did you get my letter?"

"What letter?" she asked.

"Elora, this might not be the right time, but if we only have a little bit of time together, there's something I *have* to tell you. Those things you thought that I thought about you—I, that wasn't what I thought at all."

The words were awkward, but the sentiment was clear. She had been wrong after all. More importantly, he was there, with her. No one else had come to rescue her. She didn't want anyone else.

"Tell me this." She leaned back so she could look up into his face. "What do you feel like when you look at me?"

"Ten feel tall," he said without delay. "Like I could pick you up and fly out of here. Like I can do anything in the world."

"No guilt?"

Tjaden shook his head.

She smiled as wide as she could, so the scars caught it and made it lopsided. "No disgust?"

Tjaden winced. "Never. The only thing prettier than you is you when you smile."

Her smile widened. How could it not?

One of his hands slid off of her back and into his pocket. He fumbled around and pulled the hand out in a fist. He opened his mouth, but closed it without saying anything. With his free hand he turned her palm up and dumped a ring out of a small black pouch.

A ring! It was formed by a circle of gold leaves and strong vines. Entwined among the leaves were flowers, also gold but with green and pink tints.

She couldn't have chosen a more perfect ring for herself. "I love it!"

"Does it fit?" asked Tjaden.

She slid it over the knuckle of her middle finger. It wasn't tight, but it wouldn't fall off unless she shook her hand hard. "Close enough." Even if it didn't fit, she would have found a way to wear it.

Tjaden's smile seemed uncertain.

"What is it?" she asked.

"Oh, nothing, it's just that now that I see it next to you, it doesn't look as pretty as I thought it was this whole time." He looked up to her face, saw the happy tears in her eyes and said, "I picked it because, you know, you like leaves and flowers and stuff."

How had she ever doubted him?

"Tjaden, it's perfect." She spun it on her finger, admiring the never-ending bouquet. "How long have you had it?"

"Since the Swap and Spar."

"How come you never gave it to me?"

"I never had a chance. Our parents never left us alone back at home, and I was about to give it to you that night I punched Rodín."

"*You* started that fight?"

Tjaden's ears turned red and he looked away. "I'll tell you about it later. We should go."

"One more thing," said Elora. "If we only have a little time together, there's something you need to know." She went up on tiptoes and kissed him. It lasted less time than a shooting star. He barely had time to kiss her back, but it was long enough for her to know everything would be all right. Not just that day, but for the rest of her life.

Tjaden stood there with a shocked smile on his face. Elora reached for his hand, and led him into the hollowed root.

"Why didn't you run away?" he asked. "And how are you possibly still alive?"

The dark air was humid and cool. "We can't get out this way. The Tumtum tree, it eats people and animals. Anything unlucky enough to wander near."

"I know. I barely escaped last night." He stopped and turned toward her. "It got the horses. I tried to fight them free."

The horses? How horrible. Saying anything about it would only make him feel worse, but she couldn't get the image out of her head.

Tjaden said, "It doesn't attack during the day, does it?"

She shook her head. "No, but it has vines that trap whatever wanders in. When prey approaches, the way is open, but when it tries to leave, the path out is blocked."

As if talking to himself, Tjaden recited, "Arrive in peace, there'll be a feast. And there you shall remain."

"What?"

"Something I heard," said Tjaden. "I'll explain when there's time."

"Anyway," said Elora, "the only way out of the clearing is through the Tumtum tree, which leads to that glade. And the only way out of the glade is through the Tumtum's root, which leads to the clearing."

In the darkness she looked up at him and felt his eyes looking down at her. Just the smell of him, sweat and travel dirt and all, meant everything would work out.

"At least you found the tunnel and avoided the Tumtum tree," said Tjaden. "I always knew you weren't the kind of girl to give up easily."

She grinned in the dark, laying her free hand on his arm. "No, I pretty much get what I'm after."

Predictably, Tjaden had no comeback. He cleared his throat. Signaling the direction of the glade, he asked, "No way out through the glade?"

"No. It's surrounded by trees just like the other clearing. I can barely fit my hand through most places."

"We'll have to try the path. With my sword maybe I can cut through."

"Give me your dagger. I can help or at least defend our ankles if the vines come out." She felt his spine straighten and knew he was as proud of her as she was of him.

They started down the corridor again, and Tjaden asked, "Why did the Jabberwock let you live?"

"The Jabberwock isn't like you think. He's not like anyone thinks. Where do I start? First of all, he can talk."

"You mean like a human?"

"Yeah. He struggles, but he can do it."

"What does he say?"

"He just can't stand to be alone. He used to have a mate. Before she was killed, the two of them lived here alone. They never left except to hunt. Animals, not people. When he lost her, his entire life changed. He changed. He became the monster everyone fears."

"Lord Darieus killed her," said Tjaden. "He gave me a flask of her musk. That was going to be the secret behind my vorpal blade, but it looks like I won't need it now."

Elora was shocked. "*Lord* Darieus?"

"That doesn't sound nearly as strange as *Sir* Tjaden."

It had a nice ring to it, but it had to be a joke. "One week in the Academy and they already made you a Knight, huh?" she teased him.

Tjaden stopped momentarily in the darkness and said, "Actually . . ."

"I thought you were joking! A Knight? Really?"

"Trust me. No one was more surprised than me. But back to Lord Darieus."

"Oh yeah, the Jabberwock told me about a man he hates, a man he will kill before he ever rests. It has to be Captain Darieus." The thought of the hatred that had emanated from the Jabberwock made her shiver. It was a thousand times stronger than anything she'd ever felt from Lily. Next to the Jabberwock's rage, Lily's was like a spark next to a bonfire.

"He's not Captain Darieus anymore," said Tjaden. "It's Lord Darieus. Or King Regent, anyway. The Jabberwock killed King Barash on Capital Day. Right in front of everyone."

"But he's never attacked the capital before. Why would he suddenly go there the one time the king was vulnerable all day?" she asked.

"I don't know, but Ollie claims it worked out perfectly for Lord Darieus. He swears he'll relinquish the throne once Prince Antion is old enough, but Lady Cuora doesn't seem to believe him."

Elora could tell he had more to say, but he was reluctant to continue. "What is it?" she asked.

"I don't know, maybe it's just this tight tunnel and all the stress, but I can't help wondering about Lord Darieus. He's not really the kind of man who gives up power." They reached the ladder. "It doesn't matter. We can worry about it after we get out of here."

They quickly climbed.

"Elora, this could be a hasty and dangerous escape. Are you healthy enough? He didn't hurt you, did he?

"Not at all. I had as much meat as I could eat every day. He isn't cruel by nature, but once he spends too much time alone, he goes mad. Having someone with him keeps him sane; he sees his mate in the young women he kidnaps. I don't think the mercury in the water helps his sanity either. That has to be why his captives never survive."

"One of them is going to survive." He pulled her toward him and she savored the feeling of safety. "I've had enough of planning and plotting," he said. "Action, finally." After kissing her again, he ducked out onto the branch.

Tjaden led Elora out of the tree's interior and onto the branch. Having her near him again renewed his determination. There was no way they could fail. With the Jabberwock off somewhere, it would be an easy escape. Just like he'd told Ollie, he wouldn't fight if he didn't have to.

They climbed down the rough bark of the Tumtum tree, Tjaden much more wary of the huge, carnivorous beast in disguise than the first time he'd descended. Safely on the ground, he untied the glass container and handed it to Elora so he could be unencumbered for whatever lay ahead. After a deep breath and a look into Elora's smiling eyes, he started toward the path.

Elora pulled him the other direction. "Wait. Did you see this? I couldn't figure it out when he first brought me here." She led him to the wagon wheel diagram. "It's faded. When I woke up it was more pronounced. The cloth was on the stake and it was in the ground right here," she pointed at the center of the wheel, "and the branch was over here."

With the markers in place Tjaden recognized it instantly. "It's a map. An exact copy of the one Darieus showed me, but instead of a stake and branch there were markers for Palassiren and the Tumtum tree. But why . . ."

The leaves on the branch matched the Tumtum tree, but what about the strip of cloth? It was the deep blue color of an Elite uniform, and it smelled strongly of sweat. The sight of dead soldiers in the plaza came to mind.

Exactly like the king's torn cloak, he thought. *No, exactly like Captain Darieus's cloak that he gave to the king.*

And Tjaden understood.

The Jabberwock hadn't brought Elora to the Tumtum tree. Darieus's soldiers had. They left her and a shred of Darieus's cloak with his scent to lure the Jabberwock to the capital, where the king would be conveniently waiting. The branch was placed where the Tumtum tree appeared on a map, and the cloth was staked in the center—Palassiren. Darieus had drawn the same map for the Jabberwock that he'd drawn for Tjaden.

Darieus had planned for the Jabberwock to arrive on Capital Day, and he'd given the Jabberwock a reason to attack. The monster expected to find Darieus in the capital that day, not King Barash. That's why Tjaden had wasted days practicing with machines and dressed in dark blue—to allow just the right amount of time for the plan to be carried out before Darieus presented his champion to the people and sent him off.

Tjaden turned to Elora. His voice was gruff, though his anger wasn't directed at her. "Did the Jabberwock bring you here?"

"Yes," she answered. "Well, I was so heavy-eyed in camp. I fell asleep and woke up right here. I don't know why he didn't just take me all the way to the glade where he lives."

Because it wasn't the Jabberwock.

"Did they give you anything unusual to eat in camp?" he asked.

"No, just the stew and some berries and cream. Well, the berries were special for me because I was a girl."

They drugged her. And they dumped her here for the Jabberwock to find. There never was an attack on the camp.

He knew his sword would never get them past the Tumtum's vines. Darieus never expected him to make it back, or he would have warned him about the tree and told him how to escape it.

Betrayal. Darieus had risked Elora's life to manipulate Tjaden into accepting the quest to kill the Jabberwock. Even if he succeeded, he'd never escape. Less important to Tjaden, but much graver, he had set the king up to be murdered in front of thousands of witnesses so he could unite the people behind a new, strong military leader.

Darieus is a traitor.

It was hard to believe, impossible to believe, but there was no other explanation. Anger held him rooted to the ground next to the Tumtum tree. *The entire kingdom is nothing but a pawn for him to get what he wants.* He tore a chunk of bark from the tree and threw it across the clearing.

That's why he made Tjaden a Knight before the quest. One more martyr to parade before the citizens of Palassiren.

Elora moved to stand next to him, reminding him he was not alone. "Why so uffish, Tjaden?" She placed her hand on his shoulder. "What is it?"

He opened his mouth to explain, but he stopped when he heard the flapping of leathery wings. The Jabberwock sped over them, dipping and bobbing through the air. He struggled to stay in flight, but crashed into the woods, just past the clearing.

It was perfect timing. Tjaden was angry enough to fight an army. "Quick, climb into the tree," he told Elora.

"No, I'm staying here to help you."

"There's nothing you can do; this is my task. Now go! It's coming through the trees."

"Tjaden, you don't have to do everything yourself. Let the people who love you lend a hand once in a while."

There was no argument for that. He'd never succeeded on his own. "I don't like this," he said.

"The Jabberwock won't hurt me," she told him.

That was hard to believe, but there was no more time to argue. "Stay clear of my sword. I don't know how this will go."

Tjaden stepped away from the tree, craving the opportunity to use his sword. His entire world consisted of protecting Elora. There was plenty of anger, but no fear and no thought of revenge.

The girl he cared about more than the world and everything in it. If he failed this time, she would get more than a few scars.

There was no way he would let that happen. Loosening his arms with wide, criss-crossing swings, he waited for the burbling beast.

His wings trembled as he flew. The faster he tried to fly the more herky-jerky it happened.

I won't be alone again. Not again. Someone had taken her while he was hunting; the scent of a man polluted his home.

The Jabberwock passed the Tumtum tree and saw them in the clearing. He tried to circle around, but his torn wing gave out and he crashed thunderously into the thick forest. Anger brimmed over, and his eyes burned with rage as he pushed through the tulgey woods. The dense trees made it difficult even for him. He plunged forward, whiffling[1] slowly through them.

---

[1] **whiffle**: To trudge laboriously.

The exertion mixed with desperation made him burble throatily. He gasped again and again in a mixture of a bleat, a warble, and a murmur.

Burble, lunge. Burble, lunge. The clearing was just ahead.

He burst through the final rows of trees and stormed into the clearing. Blood from his recent kill frothed in the corners of his mouth. More blood from the crash into the trees ran down his face and arms, but it didn't matter. The man was standing in front of her. In front of his beloved.

They will not take her away from me again.

He felt his eyes burning with rage. Bellowing, he stepped forward and raised his head, prepared to crush the intruder.

I won't let them hurt you. Never again.

For the slightest moment he gazed at the tiny human. His smell did not ooze the horror or panic common to most humans. The man rushed at him with a paltry weapon. Slightly surprised, the Jabberwock opened his jaw. At the instant he started to lash it forward, his beloved screamed, causing them both to pull up short.

"Tjaden! Catch!"

Something brown and murky came toward him and the man. The Jabberwock waited, curious about the container of pearly liquid. The man did not catch it. He swung his sword.

The object shattered, sending glass flying through the air along with . . .

Her.

The Jabberwock froze where he stood.

Not a substitute or an imitation like the girl in the clearing.

Her scent.

The unity, joy, and clarity of his former life hit harder than a bolt of lightning.

Home.

The magnificent aroma washed over him, cleansing his anger and hate in less time than it took to blink. He saw his beloved lying in the glade, brilliant green skin outshining the thick grass. She was smiling and laughing at some awkward step he'd taken. It was the most wonderful sight ever, and it instantly turned his hate to wonder. Despair became hope.

Tears of joy brimmed in his eyes, and for the first time in decades, the Jabberwock smiled.

PART V

> One, two! One, two! and through and through
> The vorpal blade went snicker-snack!
> He left it dead, and with its head
> He went galumphing back.

Tjaden didn't hesitate. The Jabberwock stood motionless in front of him, and he charged. The floodgates were open, and he vented his anger at Darieus on the Jabberwock. Each blow became a combination. *One, two! One, two!* His vorpal blade sliced the Jabberwock's underbelly.

One, two! One, two!

Tjaden was an unstoppable waterfall. Even the mighty Jabberwock was powerless to stand against him. He had to protect Elora, had to take her back to Shey's Orchard alive and whole.

The Jabberwock's tough skin was difficult to pierce, though every blow was delivered with all of Tjaden's strength. His arching swings made only superficial wounds, so Tjaden switched to penetrating strikes. In and out, through and through. No pity and no hesitation. An obstacle that wanted to stand between him and Elora was at his mercy. As long as Tjaden breathed, he would take the battle to his enemy.

Through and through the tough skin went his vorpal

blade. The Jabberwock swayed, and Tjaden continued to pierce the beast as it fell thunderously to its side.

Snicker-snack. Snicker-snack. His flame-bladed sword flayed the creature open.

Tjaden advanced toward the creature's exposed neck. He raised his sword, prepared to sever the head, and heard a thunderous "**WAIT!**"

Stunned, Tjaden took a step back. Had he heard the voice or felt it? His sword was still at the ready. Too many of Ollie's feints over the years had tricked him, and he teetered undecided.

"**Wait**," the Jabberwock breathed with less force. The voice was as deep and potent as thunder. Penetrating much more than ears, it was old, but without a hint of frailty. "**I remember her. Clear I see now.**"

Elora must have seen Tjaden vacillating because she stepped forward and put a restraining hand on his arm. Lying on its side, bleeding, dying, the Jabberwock seemed somehow happy. Relieved. His eyes were focused on something very distant. One wing swayed lazily in the air. The acrid scent hanging thick in the air turned Tjaden's stomach, but the Jabberwock breathed deeply through nostrils flaring wide enough for a man to climb into.

"**I regret I kidnapped beloveds. If give them back I could, give them back I would.**"

"I'm taking this one back," said Tjaden, still expecting a ploy.

"**I only . . . If only . . .**" The Jabberwock's breathing sounded wet. "**Now I'm never to get revenge for him who killed my beloved.**"

"You mean revenge on the soldier who killed her?" Tjaden asked.

The Jabberwock's eyes flared red, but only until his next breath. The sour aroma brought a peaceable smile to his face. "**Yes, revenge on him.**"

Labored breathing—deep and resonant from the Jabberwock, but rapid from Tjaden—filled the clearing.

Tjaden spoke. "I owe him revenge also. He betrayed me and attempted to kill the one I love like he did to you."

"**My head**," grunted the Jabberwock. "**Gift it to him, and revenge will be mine.**"

"I don't understand," Tjaden said. His sword was still raised and ready to strike.

"**Take my head**," the peaceful monster replied. "**Set it front of him. Our revenge it will be.**"

From where she watched, Elora asked, "Do you have to kill him, Jay?"

Before he could answer, the Jabberwock spoke. "**To live more I do not want. Killing. Snatching. These are not like my life. My life,**" he closed his eyes and inhaled so deeply Tjaden had to brace himself to avoid being pulled closer. "**My life is this.**" With eyes closed he savored two more full breaths.

"I will take your head and place it in front of Darieus. We will both be avenged," Tjaden promised as he took one step forward.

After relishing one more breath, the Jabberwock's smile turned into a threatening grimace as he opened his mouth wide like a serpent preparing to strike.

Tjaden's sword flashed through the air.

Snack!

The final sound echoed through the clearing, and the gaping head rolled face down into the dirt.

The echo died, replaced by Elora's hushed sobs. Tjaden held her for some time, willing to comfort her as long as she needed. After all, Elora would be the only one to mourn the mighty Jabberwock.

As they suspected, the tunnel path was blocked only a few paces past the entrance. A wall of vines, roots, and branches intermingled where he'd ignorantly entered the day before.

With effort, Tjaden cut some, but for every length he cut, two more came from the forest to take its place. The wall grew thicker with each slice, and roots emerged from the ground, moiling toward him. Tjaden had to retreat to avoid being caught.

"I didn't come this far only to be trapped," said Tjaden.

Elora forced a smile onto her tearstained face and said, "That's right. I'm not letting you off the hook until I get a proper rescue. What's our next move?"

"There's no way out through the glade?"

"No. I spent days searching it."

"Can we follow the spring underground?"

She shook her head. "I tried, but the water comes out of a crack in solid rock that's not even big enough to fit my head through."

Back in the clearing, Tjaden looked around, hoping to find something he'd missed. He studied the wall of trees. Mere inches separated each trunk. He handed his sword to Elora and said, "I doubt it will work, but I'm going to try climbing over that wall of vines."

Choosing a thick tree with textured bark near the entrance of the path, Tjaden began to climb. An abundance of branches made it easy, but before he was halfway up the tree, the vines appeared. He had to scurry down to avoid being caught. Back on firm ground, he stood next to Elora, ready for whatever the Tumtum tree brought.

"So the Jabberwock had to fly here, right?" Tjaden asked. "Because he couldn't fit any other way?"

Elora nodded.

"Come with me. I have an idea." He led Elora around the Tumtum tree. Root-like tendrils had already emerged from the ground where the Jabberwock's blood flowed from the neck and belly. The tendrils slowly churned the earth, mixing blood and dirt into a thick paste.

As they skirted the gore, Elora said, "The Jabberwock told me the Tumtum feeds on prey only at night. But I guess it won't pass up an easy meal."

Something the Cheshire Cat said tugged at Tjaden's mind, made him wary. But the details wouldn't come and he needed to keep the head away from the hungry roots. Using his sword, Tjaden prodded the gaping head. It teetered, but didn't react to his sword.

He poked again but the head remained in the same gaping pose.

"What are you doing?" asked Elora, walking toward the head.

"Elora, don't!"

It was too late; she had already reached the head and was rolling it over.

The head just lay there, grimacing up at the sky.

"It's harmless," said Elora. "He's dead."

Tjaden could feel the blush on his face as he grabbed the head by two tentacle-like protrusions and dragged it closer to the trunk of the tree. It was his own stupid fault for putting any stock in what the Cheshire Cat said.

"Just jumpy, I guess," explained Tjaden.

The broken wall of the circle where the Jabberwock had whiffled into the clearing lay ahead of them. It wasn't a clean-cut path, but there was a break in the wall of vegetation more than wide enough for the two of them. At the far end of the makeshift corridor, he could see a gap in the trees where the Jabberwock had caught the corner of the tunnel.

"Look!" said Tjaden. "There's the path." He took Elora's hand, and they began to pick their way through the fallen trees.

Within a few steps, the vines appeared again, and branches

began to bend toward them. Not as dense as the narrow tunnel, but more than he could hope to fend off with his sword. The image of the horses, screaming and kicking and biting, reminded him how simple it would be for him or Elora to get caught.

He could see a way out, but the Tumtum tree was determined to keep them from it. It was no different than when he was traveling to Palassiren with Elora. He saw her all the time, but might as well have been a thousand miles away. He had found a way then, and he would find a way again.

"Maybe a fire?" wondered Tjaden aloud.

"I tried that twice," said Elora. "The vines pushed my torch away the first time. The second time I built up a pile of dry wood and lit it. They just scattered the burning branches and smothered them."

"There's gotta be something. It's too bad you only know about healing with plants, not killing them."

"That's it!" Elora slid a vial out of one of the loops of her sash. "Jugglers oil. It's from black walnut leaves, and it's supposed to be an herbicide."

"Supposed to?" asked Tjaden.

Elora nodded. "I bought a book in Palassiren. It says you can prevent plant growth by putting it on the soil or kill plants by applying it directly."

Tjaden looked at the vial. It was about the size of his thumb. He craned his neck toward the top of the Tumtum tree.

"Don't be silly," said Elora. "I'm not going to kill the whole tree. Try putting it on your sword."

"Turn the vorpal sword into an herbi-sword?"

She grinned. "You'll make a fine Knight yet with your fancy words."

Wasting no time, Tjaden and Elora returned to the clearing. Taking only what was necessary, Tjaden prepared his pack and situated it on Elora's back. Then he walked to where the Jabberwock lay.

Even though most of the blood had drained, the head still weighed as much as a small man. The stringy tendrils that hung from the Jabberwock's face made satisfactory straps, allowing Tjaden to carry the head like a huge backpack.

"Ready?" he asked.

"I was ready two weeks ago." She shone with excitement as she wiped a layer of greenish oil on his sword's blade, then on the dagger.

More slowly this time, they stepped into the breach. A thin, woody vine rose from the ground across their path, reaching for Tjaden's ankle. He sliced at it. The tip fell to the ground, but the tendril seemed to grow longer and reach for him again. Then, before Tjaden could swing again, it snapped up into the air as if it had been burned. The vine shook in the air like a cat shaking water from its paw.

A thicker green vine came from the other side, and Elora lashed out at it. She only grazed it, but almost immediately the vine pulled away and writhed at the edge of the corridor. More vines appeared. Dozens. In front of them, behind, and a few over their heads, but none came within reach of the blades. If they all came at once, it would be impossible for Tjaden and Elora to defend themselves.

Step by step, they pushed forward. A bubble of empty space moved with them, vines and tendrils hovering as if deciding whether attacking was worth it.

Apparently it wasn't. The vines didn't pull back, but when Tjaden and Elora had walked a dozen paces into the opening, the vines reached their limit. The bubble opened into clear space. As fast as their heavy packs would allow, Tjaden and Elora hurried into the dark tunnel. A hug would expose their backs, so Tjaden took Elora's hand.

"As if I wasn't already madly in love with you," he said.

She smiled and squeezed his hand.

They talked little as they walked along the dark path, somewhat nervous of attracting any attention. In the confined tunnel, carrying the Jabberwock's head, it was impossible to escape the rotten stench. Elora still chose to walk directly at Tjaden's side.

Even when the pinpricks of light faded from the canopy, they walked on. Tjaden, his sword sheathed, kept one hand on the wall of the trees and the other in Elora's hand. The metal of the ring felt much better around her finger than it had in his pocket. Neither of them wanted to stop in the carnivorous forest, but rest breaks became more and more frequent as the head on Tjaden's back seemed to grow heavier with every step. Eventually, their eyelids also became too heavy to hold open. Only when lights reappeared above did they dare to sleep in turns.

After each had slept a few hours, they resumed their trek. Plentiful rivulets crossed the path, and Tjaden was glad he'd brought so much food. But by the time they reached the end of tunnel on the evening of the third day, their food supply was gone.

They made a small camp not far from the exit of the path. With the Jabberwock's heavy head off his shoulders, and without the tunnel pressing in on them, they could finally talk freely. As they sat in front of a small fire, Tjaden told her about Ollie—his dedication to archery, the praise from Darieus, the broken leg, and how proud he was to be able to stick two arrows into the Jabberwock.

"Ollie did that?" Elora asked. "I saw the injury, but I never even considered it might have been Ollie."

"I'm sure he'll tell you all about it."

"Knowing Ollie, anyone who comes near him will hear all about it."

Tjaden hadn't thought about that. "Oh no. I hope he's safe."

"What do you mean? Lying in his bed in the barracks, flirting with the nurses? Compared to what we've been through, that isn't exactly dangerous."

"That's not what I mean. Darieus was very selective about what he told us, but he revealed a lot of secrets. Enough for me to figure out who was behind your kidnapping and the death of King Barash. Darieus doesn't expect us to make it back, remember? If I figured all that out, Ollie will for sure, even with less information."

"And he's the only one who could expose Darieus. Do you think Darieus will do anything to him?"

"Not yet. Ollie can't do much harm lying in bed. But I'll bet there's a guard nearby making sure he doesn't talk to anyone. Probably an Elite. I wonder how many of them know the truth about the Jabberwock."

The thought of more of his lifelong heroes turning out to be frauds made Tjaden wonder if he wanted anything to do with the Elites. He scooted closer until he and Elora were shoulder to shoulder. They leaned on each other and Tjaden started to think it would all eventually work out.

"Why would he tell more Elites?" asked Elora.

"When Darieus killed the first Jabberwock, he had two hundred soldiers with him. That's what he says, anyway. Half of them died, but that leaves a hundred that know the truth, and soldiers tend to confide in each other."

"So why didn't he send one of them? Why a new recruit?"

"That's a good question. He has so many different . . . schemes; I can't begin to understand him. Even the Vorpal Knight nonsense was just to make himself seem more powerful."

"Vorpal Knight," said Elora. "I love the sound of it."

It did sound good, coming from her, but Tjaden just said, "It's only a title."

"So, Darieus kidnaps me and leaves me there with the map. The Jabberwock kills King Barash and you kill the Jabberwock. Then you and Ollie get trapped, all three of us die, and Darieus is the hero who had the Jabberwock killed."

"Probably," said Tjaden. "He might even keep the death of the Jabberwock a secret. No one would be able to confirm it, so Darieus could keep those lies going as long as it kept him on the throne."

"But how did the soldiers that put me there escape the Tumtum tree?"

"They might have something like your oil. Or maybe they didn't, and Darieus sacrificed them. But I still have no idea how anyone ever lived to tell about the tree in the first place."

"With that many soldiers, maybe they overwhelmed it," said Elora.

"Maybe," said Tjaden. "And it's possible they took heavy losses learning its secrets. Darieus wanted the three of us to die there. He'll probably send men to find out if I succeeded and look for the head. He really wants it for his collection."

"Let's get some sleep so we can get to Palassiren before he gets to you." Elora snuggled close and rested her head on his shoulder. She dozed off quickly. Tjaden stayed awake as long as he could. The precious time they had together shouldn't be wasted on sleep.

A few miles traveling southeast on the Harbinger Spoke brought Tjaden and Elora to the road that led to Silhaven. While Tjaden went into the town, Elora waited in a thicket with the pack and the Jabberwock's head. The coins Darieus had given him easily bought food, some rope, a huge canvas sack, and two horses.

Elora was singing to herself and putting flower petals into a pouch on her herb belt when Tjaden returned. With all the noise of the horses, it was impossible to sneak up and listen. They loaded the severed head into the canvas, but the horses were still skittish. Tjaden couldn't blame them; he also wanted to be far away from it. Two days certainly hadn't lessened the stench. They left Silhaven as soon as their supplies and the head were secured.

They avoided towns, but couldn't dodge all of the merchants and travelers on the road. The huge bundle received many stares, but they gave no explanations.

When they made camp at dark, they placed the severed head apart from themselves and the animals. Under the canvas, it was still frozen in the same threatening pose. Tjaden built a fire and, after eating, the two sat close and stared into the flames. Tjaden would rather watch a river flow than watch the unpredictable flames, but with Elora by his side, he didn't complain.

"Are you sure we should go back?" asked Elora.

Tjaden wanted to say "yes", but it would be a lie. "Not entirely. But what options do we have?"

"We're certain Darieus wants us dead, right?"

"I have no doubt."

"We could give him what he wants—"

"No way."

"Hear me out," said Elora. "What if we let him think he accomplished his goal? What if we disappeared?"

That was tempting. It wasn't like he had any chance of becoming an Elite. "We'd never see our families again. But we'd be together. And we'd even be alive."

"We have two good horses," she said. "And enough money

to start fresh. I'm sure there's a small town out in the Provinces where we'd never be found."

"Right now nothing sounds better than to go away with you and never be found." It was the truth, even though it was impossible.

"You're hesitant," said Elora.

"I made a promise," said Tjaden, wishing he hadn't. "For whatever reason, the Jabberwock wanted me to deliver his head to Darieus. I'm sitting here trying to find a way out of it, even though my father always used to say, 'Trying to find a way out of your word is as bad as breaking it.'" He doubted that she wanted him to go back on his promise, but even if she didn't care, she deserved a man with integrity.

"I don't want you to break your word," said Elora. "I also don't want you to die."

"The more I think about it, I wonder if we really could disappear. If Darieus sends men to investigate, and they figure out what we've done, he'd turn the kingdom inside out looking for us. Let's do what I promised the Jabberwock." Tjaden was worried his next words would come out sounding different than what he planned, but he said them anyway. "If you ever died, my last wish would be for my bones to rest with yours."

Elora leaned up and kissed him softly on the lips.

It took Tjaden a minute to remember what they had been talking about and gather his thoughts. "Darieus won't kill us in front of everyone. There's a chance we can convince him we're loyal, at least long enough to attempt to sneak away."

Elora laid her head on his shoulder. "It'll work," she said with much more confidence than Tjaden felt. "We've been through too much to let a little thing like a tyrant stop us."

Before long, Elora drifted off. The weight of her head on his shoulder seemed to negate the rest of the weight he carried.

Darieus would never give them a chance to tell anyone what they knew. Even if Tjaden had a chance to talk to someone, what proof did he have? If anyone was powerful enough to challenge Darieus, they would have done so when he seized the throne.

No closer to a solution, Tjaden eventually drifted off.

An hour into their journey in the morning, they reached the fork in the road. Tjaden looked for the grinning Cheshire Cat and told Elora what he could remember about the creature. It was nowhere to be seen. They walked along the same path he'd taken the first time since neither of them had any desire to have their eyeballs eaten. Even after everything he'd seen, Tjaden still didn't think it was possible for anything to eat dreams, despite what Cheshire had said.

When they reached the point where the paths converged, they searched again, unsuccessfully. After fifty paces, Tjaden turned to take one last glance and thought he saw the outline of a wide grin above the branch where the cat had been. It faded as he stared until he couldn't make it out.

Palassiren came into view the next day. Before getting close enough to be recognized by the guards, Tjaden and Elora stopped to change riding arrangements and rest the horses. Instead of riding double, leaving the other horse to bear the severed head, Tjaden rode with the putrid trophy secured awkwardly behind him. Elora, on her own horse, rode at his side. A noticeable entrance might buy them some time.

Tjaden allowed the horses a slow pace until they had a clear view of the guards at the gate. As soon as he was close enough to be recognized, he cut the sack from the head and urged his horse to gallop. The horse became skittish again and could not carry a smooth gait. With its unwieldy passengers, it went galumphing[1] toward the gates.

---

[1] **galumph**: To gallop awkwardly, yet triumphantly.

PART VI

"And hast thou slain the Jabberwock?
Come to my arms, my beamish boy!
O frabjous day! Callooh! Callay!"
He chortled in his joy.

A cry went up before Tjaden and Elora had entered the city, and by the time they reached the market-lined streets, people were gathered to see the cause of the commotion. As Tjaden and Elora passed the crowds with the evidence of their victory prominently displayed, the people erupted in cheering and encouragement. Children hid in their mothers' skirts, terrified by the beast's gaping jaws. Grown men and women shed tears of joy as they waved the happy couple through the streets. Cries of "Vorpal Knight" were the biggest surprise, especially when it was soldiers shouting and pounding their swords and staffs. The applause got louder and the crowds grew bigger as they neared the city's center.

They didn't slow or waver but rode straight for the large plaza inside the inner walls of the city. Instead of stopping in the center of the square in front of the palaces, Tjaden galumphed in wide circles around the plaza, allowing the surging citizenry time to gather. Thousands swarmed into the common square—cheering, crying, rejoicing.

Darieus, his military garb replaced by a purple royal robe with white trim, soon arrived with the rest of First Squadron. He stood on the platform, surprise and suspicion showing on his face as Tjaden slowed and reined in his horse. Before Tjaden got within ten paces of the platform, the Elites cut him off.

They aren't even going to let me near him. Their reaction confirmed what Tjaden already knew. Luckily, he'd planned for it.

Leaving the trophy and his sword tied to the horse, Tjaden dismounted and immediately bent to one knee. Faint blood stains still showed on the cobbles, and he realized that he was kneeling where the Jabberwock had killed so many of his brothers-in-arms. More blood on Darieus's hands.

The cheers from the crowd started to die down, but Tjaden remained in the same position with his head bowed. A hush crept up. Neither Tjaden nor Darieus made a move. When curious murmurs spread through the crowd, Darieus finally gave in and pushed past his men to approach Tjaden.

Darieus paused, looming over Tjaden. When he spoke, it was loud enough for everyone to hear. "And hast thou slain the Jabberwock?" He motioned for Tjaden to stand.

Keeping his chin high and his chest out, Tjaden rose. Playing along as if he were swollen with pride was easy. He just thought of Rodín.

Darieus quickly scanned Tjaden, probably for weapons, then said, "Come to my arms, my beamish[1] boy!" As he opened his arms to embrace Tjaden, a glimmer of contempt flickered in Darieus's eyes.

Tjaden knew down to his bones that Darieus would not let them live. It was a mistake to walk right into his hands. Tjaden should have insisted that Elora wait somewhere outside

---

[1] **beamish**: Radiantly happy.

of Palassiren. She would never have agreed, but there was no sense in endangering them both.

Turning back to the audience, Darieus announced, "Behold! My Vorpal Knight has slain the Jabberwock!"

A new level of applause made Tjaden want to cover his ears, but he resisted. Darieus basked in it like a snake in the sun. Tjaden attempted to remain calm as nervous sweat collected under his tunic. As the cheering continued, Darieus clasped his hands behind his back and took a wide stance as if to catch more of the praise.

The noise of the crowd kept Darieus's words from all but Tjaden. He continued to revel. "O frabjous[1] day! Callooh! Callay!" Darieus snorted as he chuckled. He placed a hand on Tjaden's shoulder and gripped it hard. In a voice so low that Tjaden wondered if it was meant to be heard, Darieus chortled[2], "Oh you brave, foolish boy."

Manipulation wasn't in Tjaden's nature, but it was time to use what he had learned from a master.

As soon as the applause died down, Tjaden called out, "Lord Protector Darieus, allow me to offer a token of victory!" He pulled away from Darieus's grasp, returned to the horse, and untied the detached head. He placed it on the edge of the platform like a trophy and breathed a sigh of relief. The final piece of the puzzle was in place. He had followed the Jabberwock's instructions, but suddenly Tjaden was unsure of what to do next.

Beast and despot faced each other. Threatening grimace matched by haughty smile.

The Jabberwock's heavy eyelids were closed, its upper lip frozen in a menacing snarl, and its jaws opened wide. Tjaden's sword had made a clean enough cut under the jaw that it sat

---

[1] **frabjous**: Fair, fabulous, and joyous.
[2] **chortle**: A combination of a chuckle and a snort.

flush without leaning one way or the other. Its oversized, flat front teeth were level with Darieus's shoulders. The smell was horrible, even worse than when the creature was alive. The color had faded slightly. Instead of the intense green-black the Jabberwock exhibited when alive, the lifeless skin had become dull, like a rotting lime just before mold covers it.

Whatever the Jabberwock had intended did not happen. Nothing did.

Darieus looked at Tjaden. Tjaden looked at Darieus, at Elora, at the Jabberwock's head.

Play the part of loyal Knight for now, Tjaden told himself. *Stay alive as long as possible.*

Tjaden stepped up next to the head and shouted, "Lord Protector Darieus! I present to you—the Jabberwock!" With a sweep of his traveling cloak he made a theatrical bow.

Darieus turned to face Tjaden, leaving the gaping jaws to his right. Not to be outdone, Darieus declared, "On behalf of the people of Maravilla, I accept this trophy!"

In an elegant gesture, the king regent fanned his robes wide and returned the bow. His right shoulder passed inches from the upper jaw of the Jabberwock.

As the wind from the flourish reached the Jabberwock's flared nostrils, the eyes twitched under the closed lids. The jaws snapped shut like a bear trap. There was no time to dodge or retract. The Jabberwock's buck teeth snagged Darieus by the torso as they slammed shut. Darieus flailed and screamed against the unyielding grip of the jaws.

The surrounding soldiers, including Tjaden, rushed to free him. The words of Cheshire's message played in Tjaden's mind as he yanked on the teeth.

You probably think it's impossible for the dead to sniff and the tamed to bite. Then something like, *Have you ever been nipped by a dead snake?* A week after death, the Jabberwock had sniffed his enemy's scent and reacted instinctively, like a snake.

Darieus's cries grew shrill and desperate as Tjaden pried along with other soldiers. Darieus's fingers clawed at the stones of the courtyard, reaching toward Tjaden's legs.

Tjaden looked down at Darieus's face and found him glaring back, his face distorted in rage. His screams had stopped, and he opened his mouth to speak. Without thinking, Tjaden took a step back. Surely Darieus would blame him. One word and Tjaden and Elora would lose everything they'd so nearly gained.

But words did not come out of Darieus's mouth, just a spray of blood. Darieus choked and tried again, but more blood gurgled out. A rattled breath escaped next and Darieus's head fell slowly to the side, eyes glaring accusingly up at Tjaden even in death.

Axes and sledges arrived to batter the skull, but it was obviously too late. A soft hand touched Tjaden's arm and Elora stepped in front of him. She wrapped him with her arms and laid her head on his chest.

Tjaden did not have to force or fake the tears that rolled down his face and into Elora's hair. For Tjaden, the hero had died a week before, but there had been no chance to mourn. His hero, the First Knight, the noble Elite Captain, died in Tjaden's mind much more tragically than the man trapped in the Jabberwock's jaws.

Tjaden had expected to feel the joy of vengeance, but instead, only a delayed pain of loss came. The death today had been justice. It was necessary, but not enjoyable.

As Elora held and comforted Tjaden, soldiers extricated the corpse. The Jabberwock's skull was smashed beyond recognition. It would never join the skeleton of his mate, but that was the price of vengeance.

The festive atmosphere had turned mournful, and the citizens cried as the crushed corpse of another beloved leader was shrouded.

Tjaden took a half step back and looked down into Elora's face. She smiled her beautiful smile. As usual, he saw everything good in her eyes. Their future was finally open and free, with no obstacles and no doubts.

Ten days later, Elora neared the end of her journey. Fourteen months until Tjaden made the same journey.

No, she thought. *Thirteen and a half.*

She'd been given an escort of a hundred soldiers this time. Word had reached every corner of the kingdom and her procession was greeted enthusiastically at every leg of the journey. In the dayroom of one inn, a bard played a song about the Vorpal Knight and his lady love.

The soldiers came to a halt at the Shey's Orchard Road and allowed her to take the lead. The setting sun was blinding, but she didn't raise her hood. If she did, no one would be able to see her scars.

The huge wabe was packed with people. Thousands of them. It had to be every resident of Shey's Orchard and all the surrounding villages—except the one she'd left in the capital. The person she wanted more than anything.

The thought of Tjaden brought a smile to her face. Not far away and not long ago she had girded his vorpal sword, thinking she had strong feelings for him. It took painful doubts and near deaths, but the love that had resulted overshadowed that infatuation like the Tumtum tree next to a sapling.

A blonde-haired girl broke away from the crowd, sprinting toward Elora. A man on crutches and a woman stepped away from the crowd. Her parents. They waited on the wabe at the front of the crowd as Lily ran ahead. Elora spurred her horse.

She didn't even let it reach a full stop before she jumped down and into her sister's arms.

Through tears, Lily said, "I'll kill you if you *ever* do that to me again!"

"I promise," said Elora. Hundreds of yards from their house, Elora was already home.

Lily looked into her face and said, "You look beautiful."

"That's because I am beautiful," answered Elora. She took Lily's hand and started walking.

"No, no," said Lily. "You have to do it the right way." She caught the horse's reins and helped Elora up, then climbed up behind her, sidesaddle. The soldiers followed when she urged the horse forward.

"So good to see you," said Elora.

"Better to see you, Sissy."

Elora didn't want to ruin the moment, but it was better to get it over with. "Sometimes the best news is the hardest to hear."

"What? What?" Lily held Elora's shoulders and leaned forward to hear.

"Maybe I should wait—"

"Don't you dare!" Lily slapped Elora's arm.

"Fine. The king's herbalist has agreed to take me on as apprentice."

"No!"

Elora nodded. "It's more of a tutelage. Six months only."

"The king's herbalist!" said Lily. "You'll be able to come home and teach Doc Methos a thing or two. Bring me a Knight to marry when you come home."

"Maybe if you were old enough," said Elora.

"I will be eventually." With mock offense, Lily said, "And if you don't bring me a Knight, I'll just go get my own."

"It's going to be hard to be away from you again, Lily."

"But not hard to be away from the Academy."

"That's just as bad," said Elora. "As close as we'll be, Tjaden's not allowed to see anyone. So close, but a thousand miles away."

"But he's *Sir* Tjaden. Don't Knights get any special privileges?"

"No. He's still a recruit." Elora sighed. "We can write letters."

"There's already one waiting for you at home," said Lily. "You have no idea how *bad* I wanted to read it. Unless becoming a Knight has suddenly made him eloquent, you'll be entertained if nothing else."

Elora laughed. "I don't see that happening." Tjaden could face any monster in the kingdom easier than trying to spell out his feelings.

They were nearing the last buildings before the wabe.

"Stop here for a moment," said Lily.

Elora reigned the horse softly and it came to a stop, as did the soldiers behind them. Their parents were smiling and waving from the front of the crowd. Elora waved and smiled back. She had sent a letter, but still hadn't talked to them. Other people in the crowd craned their necks to see why she had stopped. Many of the faces were unfamiliar.

"Ready?" Elora asked.

"Not yet," said Lily, looking down the alley next to Cooper Thom's shop. "A minute or two longer."

Elora followed Lily's eyes. The alley was empty except for a wagon with a tarpaulin over its bed. Something was dripping from the corners, but in the dark alley she couldn't see what it was.

A figure detached itself from the shadows and climbed onto the seat at the front of the wagon. He turned sideways and Elora recognized the profile. Brune.

"Precisely the first person I hoped to see when I got home," Elora said.

"Just watch," said Lily. Her voice held an eager edge.

Without even checking to see who was around, Brune looked under the seat of the wagon. He pulled out a bundle. Licking his lips he unwrapped it and shoved something into his mouth.

Lily's voice sizzled as she said, "I knew tarts would get him."

"What did you do?" Knowing Lily, nothing would surprise Elora even if Brune's head suddenly exploded.

Before Lily could answer, Brune sat on the wagon seat. The springs under the seat collapsed and he started falling backward. The tarpaulin must have been rigged to the seat somehow because as Brune fell backward the tarpaulin slid to the ground. A half dozen tarts flew into the air as Brune tried to stop his fall.

Brune landed on his back with a wet *splat*. Letting out a string of curses, he squirmed to his feet and tried to get his balance. Whatever he was standing in looked as slick as ice because his arms windmilled and he went down face first. Brune swam to the back of the wagon and dove over the edge and into the street.

Still swearing, Brune stood up and glowered at the girls, the soldiers, and the crowd. In daylight it was immediately obvious what was in the back of the wagon—manure. Fresh and wet and stinky as the Jabberwock. He shook his arms and bits of it flew in every direction.

Brune scraped a handful of manure from his chest and hurled it toward the closest target—Elora and Lily. It fell short, barely spattering the horse's hooves. The crowd laughed and he stormed away, leaving a manure trail wider than a parade. The filth Brune wore matched the foulness of his mouth and mind, but Elora did not enjoy seeing him humiliated in front of the entire town.

With eyes wide enough to fall out of her head, Elora turned slowly to look over her shoulder.

There was no guilt on Lily's face. Only a closed-mouth grin of satisfaction.

"What? I told you I'd wait til you came home."

PART VII

'Twas brillig, and the slithy toves
Did gyre and gimble in the wabe;
All mimsy were the borogoves,
And the mome raths outgrabe.

'Twas brillig.

The residents of Shey's Orchard had gathered on the wabe. Tjaden stood waiting in full military attire—dark blue uniform emblazoned with the Circle and the Sword, Grimblade Squadron patch on one shoulder. Though only fourteen months had passed, he had aged by years since they had last seen him.

Ollie rested on his heels at Tjaden's side, also wearing the dark blue. Tjaden glanced at the three bars on the left side of Ollie's chest. The first had a blue background with a gold arrow. The sharpshooter medal was difficult to earn, even for soldiers who specialized in archery. Ollie had earned it before completing training, despite being bedridden for a month. The second was a red drop of blood on a white background for his critical injury.

The third medal was much less common; only awarded thrice in the history of the Elites. It was plain white with a gold letter "J" in the form of a claw. Tjaden wore its twin. He had

insisted that Ollie be given the award since it was his arrow that had injured the Jabberwock's wing. Tjaden explained to Captain Markin, the new leader of the Elites, that the wound had saved him three times. First, it had prevented the Jabberwock from reaching the clearing and landing directly on top of Tjaden. Second, whiffling through the forest had slowed it down and given Tjaden time to prepare for the Jabberwock. Third, the coarse trail left behind the Jabberwock had allowed Elora and him to escape.

Next to the Jabberwock emblem on his uniform, Tjaden wore the Vorpal Knight pin: a flamberge sword, white against a dark blue background. But he could only stare at his uniform and Ollie and the townspeople for so long.

Why did time pass so slowly whenever he wanted it to go fast? He looked off into the wabe beyond the pavilion.

The toves, having been evicted from their nests under the sundial, wandered around the wabe gyring[1] and gimbling[2], then picking at the uprooted grubs and worms. Borogoves, looking miserable and flimsy in contrast to the festive atmosphere,

---

[1] **gyre**: To go round and round like a top.
[2] **gimble**: To make holes as with a gimlet.

honked lazily overhead. A pair of raths wallowed in the shade of a tree at the edge of the wabe.

Leaning to Ollie, Tjaden asked, "What could be taking so long?"

Ollie chuckled. "You still have a lot to learn about women if you expected her to be on time."

"I thought that's why the ceremony was scheduled at brillig—so she could have all day to prepare."

"I know you're as excited as an adolescent Jubjub bird, but give her a few minutes."

Tjaden blushed. He was about to defend himself when a murmur passed through the crowd. The sight when he looked up made his breath catch in his throat. It was impossible that anything could be as beautiful as what he saw. Realizing it was his bride, a warm shiver passed through his body. Ten feet tall didn't *begin* to describe it.

Elora wore white from head to heel, with a veil thin enough to show her radiant face and wide smile. The only exception was the tattered red ribbon around her wrist and her own red ribbon, no longer in her hair, but in her hand. Her dark hair was a stunning contrast to the brilliant white gown.

Around her neck she wore an oval medallion on a thin gold chain—white, with a claw-like "J" in the center. It was the only Elite medal ever awarded to a citizen. When young King Antion presented her with the medallion, she'd had to kneel and bow in order for him to reach high enough to place it around her neck. His mother, Lady Palida, had offered to call for a stool, but Elora claimed it an honor to kneel before the young king.

She took her place at Tjaden's side, with Lily not far off, then offered her hand and the ribbon. In contrast to his thick, calloused hand, Elora's was dainty and even silkier than the ribbon they both clutched. The gold ring, which still seemed plain compared to Elora, glinted in the sunlight.

In unison they turned toward each other. The world around them faded, as it had when he faced the bandersnatch and the Jabberwock.

Once again, Elora was all that mattered.

Tjaden said, "You look—"

A rath outgrabe[1] loudly. Its sneezing whistle completely covered what Tjaden had planned to say.

"Thank you," said Elora with a grin. "I think."

Mayor Tellef started talking, but his voice came from somewhere else. Tjaden didn't know or care if the audience still watched or if they were even still there. The mayor said their names as he got to the end of the ceremony.

"Tjaden and Elora, do you accept one another as husband and wife?"

The onlookers were silent as they opened their mouths to answer. The same noisy rath outgrabe again. Tjaden wasn't sure if Elora had answered. He wasn't even sure if *he* had actually said anything.

Elora said quietly, "You didn't let the bandersnatch, Rodín, the Jabberwock, the Tumtum tree, or even Darieus come between us. Is some mome[2] rath going to do it?"

Tjaden didn't resort to words. He pulled Elora close and kissed her. As she kissed him back the audience cheered and tapped and snapped.

"Ladies and gentleman," announced Mayor Tellef. "Sir Tjaden and Lady Elora."

The End

---

[1] **outgribe**: Something between bellowing and whistling with a sneeze in the middle.

[2] **mome**: Short for 'from home', as in someone who has lost their way.

Available Winter 2014 by Daniel Coleman—*Hatter*
The tale of Chism the Elite and of a young man named Hatta, an unlikely hero trying to decide between sanity and happiness.

GLOSSARY

Bandersnatch—A swift-moving creature with snapping jaws.

Barbantula—An oversized spider that hunts with barbs instead of webs.

Beamish—Radiantly happy.

Borogove—A thin, shabby-looking bird with its feather sticking out all around. Looks something like a live mop.

Brillig—Four o'clock in the afternoon. The time when you begin broiling things for dinner.

Burble—A mixture of a bleat, murmur, and warble.

Chortle—Combination of chuckle and snort.

Cuppy—Common name for a copper piece.

Duodec—A small gold coin worth 20 silver pennies. One twelfth of a gold pound (which equals 240 pennies, or a pound of pennies).

Eleventeen—Between the ages of ten and thirteen.

Frabjous—Fair, fabulous, and joyous.

Frumious—Combination of fuming and furious. Frequently used to describe a bandersnatch that has lost its temper.

Galumph—Gallop awkwardly and triumphantly.

Gimble—To make holes as with a gimlet

Gyre—To go round and round like a gyroscope.

Jubjub Bird—A desperate bird that lives in perpetual passion.

Manxome—More than fearsome.

Mimsy—Miserable and flimsy.

Mome—Short for "from home," as someone who has lost their way.

Outgribe—Something between bellowing and whistling, with a kind of sneeze in the middle.

Rath—A sort of green pig.

Saccharox—A large, shaggy animal with exceedingly sweet breath.

Slithy—Slimy and lithe.

Sprythe—Spry and sharp like a scythe.

Targus—A short creature that looks like a cross between a monkey and a crow. They are reported to eat dreams.

Thirteen—A worthless person or animal. Refers to the thirteenth of a litter. A runt, not worth keeping alive.

Thrip—The common name for a thripenny.

Thripenny—A large silver coin equal to three pennies.

Tove—An animal resembling a badger, a lizard, and a corkscrew. They prefer to make their nests under sundials.

Tulgey—Thick, dark, and entwined.

Tweedle—A simpleton; imbecile.

Uffish—A state of mind when the voice is gruffish, the manner roughish, and the temper huffish.

Wabe—The grass plot around a sundial. It is called a "wabe" because it goes on a long way before it, a long way behind it, and a long way beyond it on each side.

ACKNOWLEDGEMENTS

I've done over 30 rewrites of Jabberwocky and could spend pages here.

In short, thank you:

To the Cache Valley Chapter of the League of Utah Writers for not saying, "This sucks and you're a horrible writer."

To the Writing Excuses Podcast, my first writing instructors.

To EA Younker for the critique that first made my manuscript approach publishable.

To my beta readers, who suffered through the early drafts: Veronica, April, Heather, Jaycie, the Hoyts, and Truman.

To Ben Jensen, a writer waiting to happen.

To my editors: Daniel Friend and Sam Butler.

To everyone who read the 1st edition (novella) and gave feedback and left positive reviews. It meant more than you know to a first-time novelist.

To E.K. Stewart-Cook who created art that I'm proud to put alongside my words.

A mi artista de cubierta, Antonio José Manzanedo Luis, quién cogió la visión.

To KristiRae of Computers & More Design Services for beautiful formatting across formats.

To Timothy Barrett for your tireless audiobook work and unending encouragement.

To Mr. Carroll, without whom Wonderland would have remained undiscovered.

To my kids, the three main reasons I haven't become a writing hermit. Yet.

To Jodie for so much more than editing and design.

And to you, the reader, for trusting me enough to spend your time with my words.

ABOUT THE AUTHOR

Daniel Coleman memorized Lewis Carroll's Jabberwocky in 1998 and puzzled over the hows and whys for over a decade before attempting to tell the story behind the story. When he's not writing or firefighting, you can find him spending time with his wife and kids. He enjoys small-town living and is a huge fan of PEZ dispensers and ice cream.

Daniel Coleman also writes award-winning Contemporary Fiction (GIFTS AND CONSEQUENCES).

Win a Free Book!

Follow Daniel Coleman to be automatically entered in a monthly drawing for a free book of your choice. (Any book, any format—eBook, paperback, or audio!) With every Follow/Like/Subscription on Facebook, Twitter, Pinterest, or his mailing list you get one automatic entry into the drawing every month.

www.dcolemanbooks.com
www.dcolemanbooks.com/blog
Facebook.com/AuthorDanielColeman
Pinterest.com/DanielColeman
Twitter: @dnlcoleman

Look for the *Jabberwocky* audiobook and other audiobooks by Daniel Coleman on Audible.com and iTunes.

Sign up for email updates at www.dcolemanbooks.com

Made in the USA
San Bernardino, CA
22 April 2018